Escape the Doubt

Book one of the Shifting Series

ANDREA MICHELLE

Published by:

Andrea Michelle

Escape the Doubt

Cover Design: Artistry in Design

Cover Photographer/License: Coka and Veer

Interior Design: Andrea Michelle

Editor: Monique O'Connor James

❤️ Acknowledgments

TO MY HUSBAND *You are my best friend and the most wonderful Daddy in the entire world. Our daughters are so very lucky to have you. Without your support, I could not have made this happen. You picked up the slack, and urged me to continue when I escaped into a fictional world inside of my head. You knew what I needed, and even though it meant neglecting you, I was given that escape. YOU ROCK!

TO MY DAUGHTERS (Princess, Sassy and Trouble) *Y'all are my ultimate inspiration—three beautiful blessings that I thank God for everyday. You are the very reason I eat, sleep and breathe on a daily basis. Without the most important hat I wear, which is that of your mom, I would be half a person—incomplete.

TO MANY AMAZING LADIES *My Beta Team: I heart you ladies so much. Erica, Heather, Jess, Trista, Jen, Meg, Chelle, Alicia, Jamie, Myra and Angel - I love you soooo much. That is not enough O's for how much your support on this journey means to me. I adore you dearly for all of your kind words and encouragement throughout this crazy adventure. You get me. *My street team (The Working Girl's): y'all are the best and you make our street corner an exciting place to be. Thankfully, you all love Josh and Riley as much as I do, and make this process of bringing this story to life an easy one. *My Texas Dance Momma's: Clarissa, Stacy, Michelle, Maria and Jane—I miss you tons. Rachel Galloway, you became my first fan. We talked books before I became an author, and then I became the author you talked about—AWESOME! All of you have supported me, encouraged me to pursue my passion and I've loved every minute. Y'all were the first to realize I am crazy, and the first to fall in love with the characters that live in my head. Alicia Lyons Boudreaux, we met in college and here we are now as adults. Who would've thought that Cowgirl Kicker friend of yours would have wrote a romance novel? I'm so thankful to have a friend that loves reading as much as I do, even more grateful to have a friend support me while I do this crazy thing. – ALL OF Y'ALL ARE AMAZING AND I LOVE YOU LIKE CRAZY!

TO THE READER *I used to write for fun—as a hobby—a way to release things I wanted to say but never did (usually poetry or songs). It started in high school when I had one of those moments where I said and did something that I knew I would regret later. So, I wrote it down. The things I wished I had said. The emotion behind why I couldn't. In my writing, I released my regret, escaped the fear of failure and spoke the truth.

When some things started spiraling out of control in my life, that same fear came—that same dark feeling that this could and might go really, really wrong. I needed that same escape again in my life. So, I wrote it down, this time it was a story. Not a real story, but a story to help me not focus on the real one I was feeling lost in at the time. In the middle of that story, another one came. That is the one that helped me the most. That is the one that let me tap into the girl I was when it all began—back in high school. That story is the one you just read, and I thank you from the bottom of my heart for doing so.

I wrote, *Escape the Doubt* (yes, that title is special) for me originally. I pulled out my old poetry/songs and I gave it to my characters. I let it be hers, even his. The day I hit publish; I also let it be yours. I hope you enjoyed it.

This story was fictional, but growing up and falling in love are very real things young people face on a daily basis, and maintaining that love is something everyone in a relationship struggles with. Sometimes life interferes and gives us doubts in ourselves, and we make mistakes, or choose the wrong path, but in the end we are all given the chance to find peace in the storm—a chance to believe in something—create our own kind of beautiful. Again, thank you for reading, *Escape the Doubt*. I hope you continue the journey with Josh and Riley in, *Embrace the Moment*. I kindly ask that you leave a review behind for future readers. I read each and every one. Your thoughts mean the world to me.

TO FELLOW AUTHORS *Lord, so many of you have paved the way for other Indie authors like myself, and I thank you. The process to get here was full of uncertainty and many questions. I have a great deal of respect and huge book love to all of you. Some of you have been extra supportive during this new journey by answering my crazy questions, giving advice and embracing a newbie with open arms. I find it an honor to write amongst y'all. I look forward to future friendships being formed.

TO ALL THE LOVELY BLOGGERS *YOU ARE AMAZING! I love you all. None of this would be possible without you. Special thanks to: Kylie with Give Me Books for putting together my release day blitz, Debbie with I Heart YA Books for my cover reveal, Lyndsey with Booker Hooker for my lovely trailer and Ena with Journey's into Pure Imagination for my Blog Tour – YOU LADIES ROCK! I can't possibly list all of the blogs that helped make my debut a success without leaving someone out. Words really can't express how much I appreciate you. THANK YOU for the reviews, the posts—ALL OF IT!

 About the author

Once upon a time in the boot of Louisiana, a young girl made a mess of things and began writing dark poetry to cope. She often found herself daydreaming and creating stories in a far away land that didn't exist and was always out of her reach. Her mission was to move on, find love and a reason to believe in the beautiful things in life. She didn't expect to be counting her blessings daily for all that she has found since then. Her once dark poetry became colorful and bright—it became music. She found purpose and her make believe stories slowly vanished away. Her poetry also sat in the backseat, as more important things took priority. However, life can catapult you in the blink of an eye. A long forgotten coping mechanism of writing would once again become her escape. This time, though, she realized that this escape where she created stories was not a curse, but a gift. Embracing her voice, she breathes life into her characters and poetically weaves together stories for readers to enjoy. She is no longer the young girl who feared the unknown, but is stronger and has faith that beautiful things will always be in reach. She is married to her best friend, and is a mom to three beautiful daughters who are her favorite cheerleaders. She is excited to have the opportunity to share her love of writing with readers. The stories are fictional, but they are real to her. She has always felt things passionately and this new journey as an author is no different. She is no longer looking back, but looking ahead to this amazing adventure with all of you. She invites you to connect with her if you desire to do so.

Social links:
Blog:
http://authoramichelle.blogspot.com/
Twitter:
www.twitter.com/AuthorAMichelle
Amazon Author page:
http://www.amazon.com/author/andreamichelle
Wattpad:
http://www.wattpad.com/user/AndreaMichelle_8
FB Friend:
 https://www.facebook.com/andrea.michelle.79025
FB Author Page:

https://www.facebook.com/booksbyandreamichelle/info
Goodreads:
https://www.goodreads.com/author/show/2665501.Andrea_Michelle
Join my Support Group:
 https://www.facebook.com/groups/AndreaMichelle.fan/

Dear Reader,

I truly believe music is the perfect healer for a bad day or the inspiration to a beautiful story. I love to listen to music while I write; actually I find it necessary. This is the playlist that I felt moved me while I climbed inside Josh & Riley's heads. Enjoy :)

𝄢 PLAYLIST FOR THIS NOVEL:

*TO LISTEN AND FOLLOW: http://t.co/YiwCm97eSq

Let Me Go - 3 Door Down
Closer - Kings of Leon
Wish You Were Here - Incubus
Sweater Weather - The Neighbourhood
You Belong With Me - Taylor Swift
Broken - Seether (featuring Amy Lee)
Afterglow - Phaleh
Crash my Party - Luke Bryan
Wasting All These Tears - Cassadee Pope
In my Veins - Andrew Belle
You Don't Know Her Like I Do - Brantley Gilbert
Somewhere With You - Kenney Chesney
Through Glass - Stone Sour
Taking Over Me - Evanescence-
Pushing Me Away - Linkin Park
All Around Me - Flyleaf
Not Meant To Be - Theory of a Deadman-
There's A Wall - Miranda Lambert
The Way You Are - Bruno Mars
Beneath Your Beautiful - Labrinth
Counting Stars - One Republic

Demons - Imagine Dragons
Everything Has Changed - Taylor Swift
Sunny and 75 - Joe Nichols
Alleyway - The Neighbourhood
Angels - The XX
Love Song - The Cure
Holocene - Bon Iver
Realize - Colbie Caillat
Lips of an Angel - Hinder
Fall For You - Secondhand Serenade
Together - The XX
You've got the Love - Florence and the Machine
Down - Jason Walker

Table of Contents

Is taking a chance with your heart worth the escape, or was it better to have never loved at all? Can forgiveness really set you free?

After the unexpected death of her Dad, and the haunting manner in which he died, Riley Shaw built invisible walls around her heart. Barriers she created to protect her from splintering into broken pieces that couldn't be repaired. She was unable to move forward from her past, letting the guilt of her parent's mistakes dictate her own choices.

Dean Warren was safe. Being with him was innocent and peaceful because she didn't truly love him. His words held her captive in a false sense of security. His eyes were deceptive, and his promises of never pushing her beyond what she was willing to give were broken, leaving Riley in a state of regret and doubt.

Joshua Parker had the power to take what was left of Riley's splintered pieces and ruin her completely, or make her whole again. He was her best friend, her next-door neighbor—everything she wanted and settled on never having. Loving him was as easy as breathing air. The fear of losing him forever was more real to her than the feelings she couldn't escape.

When faced with the very thing she feared the most, and in the arms she thought were safe, Riley finds herself questioning every decision she has made over the past two years. When she finally escapes the doubt in her head, and accepts the truth in her heart, is it too late?

"I'm so close to the edge of the cliff that I know one more breath, one more inch, I could fall." –Riley Shaw

Recommended for 17+ due to underage drinking, sexual content and adult language.

 *Riley*

PROLOGUE

"**W**hat do you want from me?" my dad shouted at my mom.

"For you to listen. Just listen. You never listen. You just..." my mom yelled back not able to finish her sentence.

"I just what? I work my ass off, put a house over you girls' heads, you want for nothing, yet it's never enough for you, Claudia!" His voice raised a decibel louder.

"It's not about the money, Evan. You are never home. Look at the table for God's sake. You didn't even come home last night...AGAIN!" She gestured to the full plate still sitting untouched on the table from the night before.

"What were you doing this time, Evan? Or dare I say, *who* were you doing?" she asked with malice dripping from every word.

He recoiled from her accusation and looked at the table somewhat sheepishly—but not full on guiltily—before narrowing his eyes at her. Like a rubber band had stung him, he retaliated with angry words.

"You know what, Claudia? I made a goddamn mistake years ago—one you still throw in my face every chance you get. I was twenty-three years old and scared as fuck. I've reaped what I sowed a thousand times over. I've apologized a million times over, but you won't let the shit die. I don't even know why I try anymore. I CHOSE YOU!" He was basically in her face, cornering her into the kitchen counters. He bowed his head to hers, gripped her by her quivering chin and forced her to look at him. "When are you going to choose me?" he asked with such sincerity it ripped my heart into shreds.

Once a cheater. Always a cheater. That's what my mom's mother had told her. Lectured her, in fact, on how foolish it was to stay with him after finding out he had cheated. My grandpa, who I had never met, had run off when my mom was just a baby.

"I baked his bread, but he got it buttered by someone else," Grandma would say.

Needless to say, it'd been drilled into my mom's head that all men cheat. It'd been cemented into mine that love was just a joke.

All more reasons why I would never commit with my *whole* heart. Love was just temporary. Nothing lasted forever.

THE AIR I BREATHE IS FILLED WITH HIS SCENT
THE MUSIC SPEAKS EVERYTHING I MEANT
MEANT TO SAY, BUT NEVER DID TELL YOU
YOU HAUNT ME WHERE I LIE ALONE WITHOUT YOU
FEELING YOUR TOUCH AS IT VANISHES AWAY
MY OWN HEART IS THE ONE I BETRAYED

For those that have loved and lost.

 *Riley*

CHAPTER 1

Sometimes to escape the noise of haunting memories, you need your best friend's hand in your own, to help erase the sound and fill you with a sense of peace, even if it's temporary.

"I thought I would find you here," Josh says as he sits down next to me. He interlaces his fingers with my left hand as I trace over my dad's name on the tombstone.

"You okay? You look far away." He always worries about me, especially on this day.

I nod, swiping a few lost tears. "I was just remembering that day. Their angry words thunder so loudly in my head. It's been three years today, and it still hurts." I rub the throb in my chest that never dulls.

He pulls me to his side and kisses my forehead the way he always does.

"I don't think the hurt of losing someone goes away, Riley. Some days are better than others. But missing them—that feeling—I think it's always lying dormant. Something as simple as a song on the radio, or the smell of their perfume on someone else, triggers all those memories. And in one moment, you're trapped in the past." He sighs forlornly, getting lost in his past. I'm stuck in mine always.

I look at him, my best friend, his own pain from loss etched all over his face. The guilt kills me every day. He understands more than anyone how I feel, except for the guilt.

"I'm sorry, Josh," I whisper.

He cups my chin, tilting my face to his, "Riley, we do this every year, and every year you apologize to me. It's not your fault that your dad got in the car that night, or that my mom was a victim of his drunk driving."

"It's my dad's fault, and my mom's fault. Therefore, I am guilty by association. He should never have been on the road. I'm sorry we came into your lives. Because of that, you don't have your mom. It's not fair." I choke on every word as they burn out of my throat.

He abruptly stands, pulls me to my feet and places his hands on my shoulders. "Riley, stop blaming yourself, because I sure as hell don't. Yes, it hurts. God, it hurts some days to not have her here, but never, and *I mean never*, have I wished for even a second that you were not in my life. You mean the world to me, Riley Shaw."

His eyes are pleading with me to believe him. I don't reply with words. I nod my head and try to keep the tears from falling.

He grabs my hand and places a soft kiss on my palm.

God, I love him. Why is life so cruel?

As we walk back to his truck I stop suddenly, which causes him to bump into me.

I turn around and find his eyebrow lifted in question. I didn't want him to think I didn't have a response. I had one. The words were just caught in my throat before.

"You mean the world to me too, Joshua Parker. I lov…I mean…I care about you so much." I bite the inside of my cheek painfully as I realize my almost slip.

He stares at me for the longest moment with the strangest of expressions. I wonder if he caught that.

Shit!

He eventually smiles and interlaces our fingers. "C'mon, your mom is worried sick about you. If I don't get you home soon, she is going to send out a search party." He laughs trying to lighten the mood.

I hold onto his hand like he is my lifeline as I walk with him to his truck. If only everything was different, we could be together, like we were meant to be. I wish everything were different.

Once we're in the truck, Josh asks the question that I've been asking myself all day. "Why is Dean not here with you, Riley?"

I look out the window as the world passes by in a blur. Dean isn't with me today, because he isn't *with me* anymore. When I turn my face to look at Josh, I want to tell him everything—that we broke up two days ago—that it hurt like hell, but I didn't care like I should, because Dean wasn't the one I loved anyway. Every decision for the past two years has become one giant mountain of doubt I can't seem to escape.

I don't say any of that, though. Instead, I lie.

"He had to work, but I'm sure he will stop by later." *He won't.*

Josh studies my face, and I'm sure he's sensing the half lie or the withheld truth.

"M'kay…so wanna tell me what happened this morning to have your mom in such a state of panic that she thought you might catch a bus and disappear for good?" He grins, knowing my mom always thinks I'm on the verge of running away.

I'm too broken and weak to run away physically, however, emotionally I've been on the run since that day three years ago—maybe even before.

I sigh and laugh, although it's not a laugh of humor.

"I ran off this morning after yelling at her for the longest time. I told her that I remembered every word, every fight and every reason why I hate them both." I see that my words disappoint him, so I turn back to the window looking away. I hate disappointing him.

Today is one of those days where I do feel that hate for them. I hate that they had loved so little and fought so hard. I hate that my dad chose to drown his pain in a bottle, took his anger to the road, killing an innocent woman on her way home from her son's sports banquet for football. A son that is my best friend and the very person I love with every fiber inside of me, changing our futures forever.

Josh takes a deep breath, and I know he is about to spill his words of wisdom. The same thing I have heard from him more than once. *Forgive and forget. Let it go, Riley. Move on.* All words that are easier said than done.

"Riley, you need to forgive them. I have. My family has. We can't go back and change the decisions of that day. But if you keep living in the past, you can never move forward."

I know he's right. Deep down I do. They've ruined everything, though. His dad is without the love of his life. Josh and his sister are without their mom. They've stole happiness from them and because of that, I can never allow myself to have any happiness with him.

A bottle of booze, a car accident, and six feet of Earth on two important people had cemented my decision to never let myself have Josh. I didn't deserve him. Maybe, I was punishing myself for my dad's decision, but it's what I had to do. Every time Josh looked at me, he would see what my dad had taken from him. It was too much.

I used to wear my heart on my sleeve. I used to dream of a time when Josh and I could be together. Some of my sweetest memories are shared with him, yet looking back, even within those sweet memories there are bitter memories too, of a boy that was already plotting his invasion of my life.

4 YEARS PREVIOUS

According to the dictionary freshman means: fresh meat, a beginner, a novice, someone who is naïve, a first-try effort, or my own definition—the first time you'll screw up because you are too foolish to know better.

"Earth to Riley. Did you hear me? I think I want to kiss Laiken." Josh informed me.

I'd heard him fine. I'd just hated what I'd heard. Laiken was the first girl to look at Josh with hungry, curious eyes.

Since Josh and I had been best friends since kindergarten, he'd never seen me as a *real* girl. Besides, I was too scared to cross the line and lose my friend.

Josh was the quarterback on the JV football team, and Laiken was the head cheerleader on her JV squad. They were a match made in social heaven. I was a wallflower in the background looking in—but he saw me. He saw her too, though.

Josh and I were babysitting the brats, otherwise known as our little sisters. It was date night for our parents, which hardly ever happened, seeing as only one of those couples actually liked the other.

We were alone, which was not unusual. Even our parents saw us as innocent friends. If they only knew what I saw when I looked at him. How I craved him, then they might not have been as trusting.

I was busy making brownies. Baking was something I did when I was nervous and needed to keep my hands busy. Usually, I'd write in my journal, but Josh was there so...baking it was.

I was mixing like a mad woman. I felt like that. What was I supposed to say to his statement? My best friend—the boy I wanted to be mine—wanted to kiss another girl. Not just any kiss, it would be his first kiss. That's a big deal, right?

I could say…"Good luck, hope you do it well," or better yet I could say, "Hope it sucks, and she slobbers on you—maybe even bites you accidentally and scares you into never doing it again." Who was I kidding? Biting his lip would only make her the best damn kisser ever in the freshman class. Ugh!

I felt his grin, but for the life of me, I couldn't understand why he was grinning. None of what he said made me happy.

Stir, stir, stir.

Bastard.

I finally said, "I heard, Josh. I mean...I don't know what you want me to say, or why you're telling me this."

"I'm telling you because what you think matters to me," he threw out there.

Mix, mix, mix.

So, I told him the truth about what I thought about her...and him.

"Well, I think I don't like Laiken. I think she flirts with all the boys in school. I think the fact that she has already kissed three other boys while y'all have been hanging out say's something. I mean...she is so fake. She laughs at everything you say, and seriously, you're not that funny. Well, I mean...you are funny, but not like *all* the time." I rambled and realized I had said way too much.

He threw his head back and laughed.

God, I loved his laugh. It was the best sound.

"You're adorable when you are like this." He said grinning.

What was he even grinning about?

I poured the brownie mix into the pan, and bent over to place it in the oven. When I stood up, I noticed he was looking at my butt. I set the timer and ignored why he was doing that. I placed my hands on my hips and tilted my head.

"Like what exactly, Josh?"

He smirked like he knew something I didn't and locked eyes with mine.

"Like that. Like you're jealous." He gestured at my posture.

I grabbed the spoon covered in brownie mix and held it up in front of me like a gooey weapon.

"I'm not jealous, Josh." *I soooo was.* "Why would I be?"

I licked the chocolate goodness from the spoon. Brownie mix was the best. He cleared his throat and swallowed hard.

His eyes narrowed and he asked, "I don't know, Riley. Why would you be?" His eyes watched my mouth nervously lick the chocolate like he wanted a taste.

I rolled my eyes, "I'm not. If you want your first kiss to suck, then fine. It will, because Laiken isn't the right girl for you. Go for it. Have fun." *Please don't,* I thought.

His eyes flicked between the spoon and my mouth. A sexy smirk crossed his lips like he suddenly had an idea I wasn't privy to.

"Oh, I'm sorry, did you want some?" I asked, holding out the spoon for him.

His eyes were telling me something, giving me a clue. I dragged my tongue along my bottom lip, erasing any leftover batter. He nodded but didn't move. I went to pull the spoon back to my mouth, but he grabbed my wrist, holding the spoon hostage between us.

My mouth formed an O as he slowly licked a trail up the spoon…*damn lucky spoon*, I thought. I couldn't help but watch his mouth the entire time.

"Hmm," he moaned like he thought it was delicious. I thought his lips probably tasted delicious, too. Chocolate and Josh would be the best mixture of sweet. All these thoughts about Josh like that took me by surprise, but I couldn't help it. Something in me was changing. *Shifting.*

The air changed. He didn't let go of my wrist. He watched my eyes watch his mouth, and damn if he didn't wickedly grin at me. He pushed up close to me—so close, in fact, that his chest meshed with mine, and I suddenly forgot how to breathe.

"Um, what are you doing, Josh?" I whispered breathlessly.

He smiled, "Shhh…it's okay. You just have a little chocolate right there."

"Where?" I asked, embarrassed, but then he lowered his head and…oh hell.

He moved the spoon back to the bowl as he leaned in, and his tongue softly licked a spot by the corner of my mouth. I couldn't help but shut my eyes and softly moan. My body fell limp against the counter. I braced my hands on the edge just to keep my balance.

It wasn't until I felt the loss of his warmth that I knew he had stepped back. When I slowly opened my eyes, I found him watching me. My lips were parted, wishing for his tongue to enter my mouth.

I puffed out the breath I wasn't completely aware that I had been holding. He was studying my face with a satisfied look.

"I got it." He smiled crookedly, "So, about that first kiss...I could think of a way to make it *not* suck." *Oh, I could too.* I so could picture lots of ways.

I looked away from him, feeling the blush creep up to my cheeks as the image in my mind blazed.

"How is that?"

He stepped back into my space and gently tugged my chin to him, forcing me to meet his gaze. I was so trapped in his beautiful hazel eyes that I didn't notice him reaching into the brownie bowl and dragging his fingers all through the chocolate.

He laughed, stepped back tapping my nose with a chocolate covered finger and said, "Gotcha."

I squealed, "Oh, my God. You are so dead, Joshua Parker."

I reached in and coated my own fingers in chocolate. I began to chase him around the island as my heart was fluttering wildly. I wiped my hand along his cheek when I caught him and laughed hysterically.

He grabbed my hand before I could run away. My heart was racing. My breathing was fast, and I knew he was up to no good by the sinful little twinkle that danced in his hazel eyes. No good at all. My laughter fizzled out as something else took its place. Something unfamiliar, yet wanted so badly.

He took my messy hand, placed my index finger into his mouth, and began sucking the chocolate clean. I felt dizzy. I could feel his tongue swirl around my finger, and something in my belly clenched tight.

I stumbled back, hitting something hard. He let my finger go with a pop, and we stared at each other for the longest time. Not moving, just breathing.

He tucked a curl behind my ear. "That was fun." He smirked, and my toes curled. Did he not see how he affected me? What the hell was that?

"I um…yeah…I should get a napkin." I knew it was such a stupid thing to say. I should get a napkin. No, I should attack your face and lick it clean, that's what I should do.

I moved around him to wet a paper towel in the sink. He didn't move. He just watched me with an unreadable expression. Amusement maybe? Curiosity?

I reached up on my tippy toes, and started dabbing away the chocolate mess I had coated his cheek with. He was motionless with the exception of the way his chest was rising and falling.

"All clean," I said as I softly smiled.

He grinned, took the napkin from my hand, and began to *gently* wipe the chocolate off of my nose. Once he was done, he placed his hands on both sides of me, caging me in between his hard chest and the kitchen counter.

"I want to kiss you," he blurted out. *Wait! What?*

"I thought you wanted to kiss, Laiken?" Stupid Riley. Stupid, stupid Riley, I thought again. I just couldn't shut up.

He shook his head back and forth. "Nah, you were right. She isn't the right girl. There is only one solution to making my first kiss not suck, and that's if you let me kiss *you*."

His eyes never left mine. I wanted to kiss him. But the truth was that Josh seemed to not really know what he wanted lately. I wondered if I kissed him, would it mean Laiken no longer existed?

"Stop over thinking it, Riley. Can I kiss you?" He asked permission again—knowing me so well. I was over thinking it.

I nodded, "Okay."

"Okay?" His breath feathered across my lips as I nodded again.

I trembled in anticipation as he lowered his mouth to mine.

A gentle, soft, sweet peck at first was what he placed on my lips. As my hands reached up around his neck to pull him closer to me, I tangled his dirty blond hair in my fingers. He groaned deep in his throat, and I liked the sound. His tongue teased my lips, opening them and allowing him to deepen the kiss.

I was nervous. *What if I did it wrong? What if my kiss sucked and kissing Laiken would be better?* 'What if's' filled my head as my body hummed. I willed myself to shut up, parted my lips allowing him in, and it was like our mouths were made for each other. Fireworks were exploding in my head, and electricity shot through my veins. My tongue began to dance with his, and I never wanted it to stop. He tasted delicious.

It did stop though. Definitely not saved by the bell.

The doorbell rang, causing us to jump apart. We were panting heavily and staring at one another in shock. It had ended way too quickly for my liking. I felt on fire—tingling in a way I wasn't used to.

"Riley, Dean's at the front door." Tatum shouted loudly from the living room.

Josh raised his eyebrows at me, probably just as curious as I was about why he would be ringing my doorbell. Dean was a pain in my ass, but a friend nonetheless.

I struggled to slow my breaths. However, Josh had completely composed himself as though he was completely unaffected. Like nothing amazing just happened.

He left the kitchen and walked to the living room to open the front door. I followed in a cloud of confusion.

"Oh. Hey, Josh. What are you doing here? Is, um, Riley here?" Dean tripped over his words. He was always a little weird about Josh and me being so close, and he was more than tickled pink about Josh potentially dating Laiken.

"Yeah, man. She's right there. We're just babysitting the brats," he joked and pointed at me over his shoulder. I was still frozen in a state of *'what the hell?'*

I walked into the living room. My mind felt like it was on overdrive. Something life changing had just happened to me, and Josh seemed like he'd already forgotten it. I saw it briefly in his eyes when I looked at him. A feeling he wanted me to see, but it was gone in a blink of an eye—the softness turning cold.

I looked at Dean, and I knew he saw it too. Something unspoken had been shared between Josh and me. Dean's eyes darted between us both uneasily.

Josh said, "He's here for you," in a flat tone that I didn't understand. I nodded, words escaping me.

He did the guy nod to Dean, "She's all yours man," he told him. I was at a loss at what had just happened. Why had his mood suddenly crashed and burned? I wondered what he meant by that.

Josh seemed mad at me, and I didn't understand any of it at all. He pulled out his phone, and with all the power to hurt me with words he did just that. "I'll be in the kitchen. I forgot to call Laiken back."

Just a sliver of my heart fell apart that day. He had just kissed me senseless, and he was going to call *her*? What meant the world to me— had meant nothing to him? It hurt like a bitch.

I watched Josh walk to the kitchen. My mouth was wide open in shock.

Dean spoke to my back, completely dense to what he had just done. "I'm sorry to just stop by. I need to talk to you about something. Can you come outside?" He shifted uncomfortably with his eyes tracked to the path to the kitchen, as well.

I turned my eyes back to him and blinked a few times. I felt like I was going to cry. Josh had just kissed me, and it felt for me like the Earth moved. But then he was in the kitchen on the phone with Laiken, probably planning how he would kiss her next. Maybe that kiss would be—the thought died there. I nodded, and followed Dean outside wishing he would just go away and leave me alone.

We sat on the stairs of my porch. "What's up, Dean?" my voice cracked.

"Emily broke up with me."

"What? Why?" I asked.

He looked at my face and sighed, "Because she knows I like someone else, and she kinda likes Brad now anyway."

He shrugged like it was no big deal. I looked at him, but the right words were not there. Dean and I were friends but why would I care that he and Emily were calling it quits?

My mind was wandering. What's Josh saying on the phone in the kitchen? I should probably go check my brownies and interrupt him. I should go do that. "Brad, huh?" I said.

"Yeah, and I like someone else," he repeated. Again, I thought what did this have to do with me?

I mean...Josh had sucked on my finger. He had asked to kiss me, and he had put his tongue in my mouth. "You do?" I stated it like a question, but I didn't really care to know the answer.

He nodded, "Yeah, she has no idea how amazing she is. There has just always been something about her."

More wandering thoughts. What does Josh see in Laiken anyway? Doesn't he know that she flirts with everyone? Why would someone like her be any good for him? What did Dean just say? Oh yeah... "That's great, Dean. I'm happy for you. So who is she?"

I looked back at the front door. I really needed Dean to leave so I could go figure out what had just gone so epically wrong.

He whispered it so lowly I barely heard him, "She's you. I like you, Riley."

"What?" I said. Shocked, my eyes darted to his eyes. My mind was completely focused on what he was saying for the first time since we had come outside.

"You like me?" I pointed to myself like an idiot.

He reached up grabbing one of my curls like he always did and twined it around his fingers. All this time I thought it was a friendly gesture but now I think maybe it was just a way to touch me.

"I do. I tried not to. I mean...I tried to just stop it, but I always think about you," he whispered and tucked the curl behind my ear.

I swallowed hard and felt like I was having an out-of-body experience. Before I could rationalize anything in my mind, Dean turned my face to his. I didn't mean to, but I leaned into his hand as he cupped my cheek.

I was feeling sad. I wanted these words to be coming out of Josh's mouth, but his words were being spoken to Laiken as I sat there.

He moved his mouth slowly to mine, and I knew I should have pushed him away, but I couldn't move. I was frozen in shock. Josh had just blown me off.

Dean kissed me softly. It wasn't full of the fireworks that I had just felt, but it was—nice. Just a lingering peck, nothing more pushed, just a soft pause on my lips. When he pulled back, he was smiling like his Earth had shifted, but mine was spinning in circles making me nauseous.

I forced a grin back. The words were trapped somewhere inside of me. *I don't like you like that.* I should have said that. I wondered why I didn't say that. I just couldn't find my voice. He got up and walked backwards down my driveway.

"We will talk later, K?"

"K," I breathed.

I watched until he was no longer visible. And then I rested my head in my hands, letting a few tears escape.

After wiping my cheeks, I stood up, turned back around to walk into the house, and froze. Josh was standing in the doorway. He'd seen the entire thing. I could tell by how his jaw was set tightly, how his eyes were tracking Dean's departure. His arms were braced above him on the doorframe. His body stiff and beautiful, if he wasn't so angry looking that is.

I whispered, "Josh..." his cold eyes darted to mine interrupting me.

"Don't! You and Dean make a cute couple." He said it like he hated the idea of it, but he smiled at me like it was a brilliant idea.

I looked at him with all the confusion I was feeling. "We are not a couple. I think he's just confused."

"His mouth didn't seem confused, Riley" He took a few deep breaths and shook his head. "Look…Laiken and her mom are coming to pick me up. I already called my parents, so they know about it. I took the brownies out while you were… doing what you were doing out here," he said pointing in a circle at the steps I was just sitting on, and straightening his body in the doorway.

A tear fell from my eyes. I wiped it quickly before he saw it. He was being so mean to me, and I just didn't understand why he would be mad at me. I didn't set out to kiss Dean, but I guess I didn't stop it either.

"Okay. Josh, it's not what it looked like. I promise," I whispered as I went to move around him to get inside.

He seized me by my elbow, and when I didn't turn around to face him, he sighed heavily in his chest.

"A first kiss, a second kiss all in one night, Riley. That's what it looked like. Which one was better? Wait don't answer that. I will soon know the answer for myself, when I—,"

I jerked my arm back, and turned to him with all the venom I felt for how he was making me feel inside. "When you what, Josh? Kiss Laiken?"

He leaned into my ear, and his hot breath caused me to shiver as he whispered, "No kiss will taste as sweet as yours. Good luck with Dean."

And with that, he took off down the steps toward his yard.

I chased after him, "Josh, stop!" I begged.

He turned around, and I didn't know what I saw when I looked at him. Fear? Anger? Sadness? I just didn't know. All my life I had been able to read Josh. But recently, things were shifting, and I couldn't always read him. It *scared* me.

"What, Riley?" he yelled. He never yelled at me before. It caught me off guard. His hands were balled into fists, and he was obviously angry.

I walked right up to him, standing almost on my toes to meet his eyes. I placed my hand on his chest. His heart was pounding underneath my palm. I hated that he was so mad at me.

"I don't know what to say. I don't know what the hell happened tonight, but please don't be mad at me, Josh."

His eyes softened, his shoulders slumped, and he placed his head on my forehead in defeat.

"I'm not mad at you, Riley. I'm mad at myself. I shouldn't have said all of that. I'm not going to Laiken's tonight. I never even called her. I lied. I just—," he trailed off pulling back to look at me.

"You just what?" I said quietly.

He pulled me into a hug. I didn't know what to make of it, but I loved how perfect I felt with his arms around me. I hugged him back, like there would never be another time.

"You mean a lot to me, Riley. You're *my girl*, my best friend, ya know? All this stuff is confusing. You and Dean like that...well, it's just weird, and I don't like how it makes me feel." He released me, rubbed behind his neck, and looked up to the sky.

"Josh, you mean everything to me too. There is no Dean and me. I don't know what to say about what you saw, because I am just as confused as you are that it happened," I said.

His eyes darted to mine. "He likes you, Riley." He stated it like it all made perfect sense—like he already knew it. Did he know?

"I know," I said. I didn't before, but I did then. It's just that, I didn't like him like that.

"Do you like him?" His eyes studied mine with an intensity that I wasn't familiar with.

I shook my head back and forth. The answer came to me so quickly, although I questioned its truth. "No… not like that."

"Do you like me like that?" he asked, his voice barely above a whisper.

Yes, that I knew for a fact. *I did.* I looked at him. The truth was on my tongue, ready to fall freely into the wind. If I told him the truth, if I said—yes, it would crush me if he didn't feel the same. Worse, what if he did feel the same? And then I did something to screw it up, or he changed his mind later? My dad had loved my mom once, but he'd still cheated on her. He'd still hurt her beyond repair. I could lose my best friend if I let myself feel the truth—say the truth.

I betrayed my own heart that day.

What I said wasn't even scratching the surface of what I really felt for him. "You're my best friend, and I liked kissing you, and I don't like the way it feels seeing you with other girls. Shit, I don't even like talking about it or thinking about it but…but…" How could I explain? I was afraid he would hurt me. I was afraid that I loved him so deeply that he had the power to ruin me.

He gripped my chin, and the look in his eyes was killing me slowly. He whispered quietly, "But what?"

Tears began to trickle down my cheeks, I didn't know why exactly, maybe for the loss of the possibility. I just felt so emotionally drained. My system had been shocked.

"But…it's probably not a good idea. I would be lost without you, and we're only fourteen. Besides, you seem curious about everything, where I am fine with everything staying the same." I lied. *I wasn't fine.*

In a perfect world, where love didn't scare me to death, and forever existed, he would say what I wanted. He would have said –,"

It's a perfect idea, Riley. You're my girl, my only girl, and I will love you, only you forever".

We didn't live in that perfect world. In reality, he said, "I guess I *am* a little curious. Things stay the same…for now, but one day Riley, we may have this conversation again, and when we do, I hope you say yes."

His eyes bore into mine, and then he placed a sweet kiss on my forehead. I wiped at my eyes as he stepped back, leaving me standing in the yard with a feeling like nothing would ever stay the same. I hoped that conversation would happen again one day. I hoped that when it did, I would have the strength and security to say yes.

That conversation could have happened the next year, but my Dad made a bad decision that made it impossible to ever embrace. Instead, it blew away in the wind, whispering little doubts of why Josh and I could never be more than best friends.

CHAPTER 2

Some things are easier said than done, like forgiveness for example. Josh wants me to forgive. Forgive my mom, for being so unforgiving of my dad that she couldn't let herself heal and be loved. Forgive my dad, for not loving enough to have never cheated in the first place, and for putting that insecurity in her. Forgive my dad, for being so reckless that he took not only his life but also another. Forgiving myself for the guilt I feel for the harbored feelings I have toward them. Forgive them for ruining me. I just don't know how.

The ride back to my house is quiet. Josh hums along with Jason Aldean on the radio, while my thoughts drift to two days ago.

"Riley, c'mon we have been together two years. What are you waiting for?" Dean asked for the trillionth time it seemed. I'd stopped him from going any further with me, and he was frustrated as always.

I'd pushed on his bare chest, and he rolled off of me on a huff. "I'm just not ready. You promised to not push me, Dean, and yet every time we make out we end up in this same position." I said, annoyed with my pushy boyfriend.

He started kissing my neck and nibbling on my ear. "I could think of some other positions we could try," he tried to convince me with his lips. It wasn't *his* lips I yearned for. He would never be able to convince me.

I sat up completely exasperated. "Dammit, Dean, back off. I'm not ready. Stop pushing me."

This time Dean listened. He growled as he put his shirt back on. Why I'd ever pulled it off of him while we were kissing was beyond me. He stood and looked down at me curled up on my bed.

"How about I do us both a favor and back off completely, Riley?" He asked.

I shrugged. What did I care? I wasn't ready. I said I wasn't, and he needed to respect that.

I threw my hands in the air, "Whatever." It wasn't the first time Dean had asked for a pause, but something in his eyes told me this pause would be a permanent one. For the life of me, I just couldn't find a reason to feel upset about it.

"I'm serious, Riley. I'm tired of going in this circle with you. You're hot then you're cold. You kiss me like you can't get enough, grab at my shirt like you can't wait to be undressed, and then you just pour the ice on it. I'm a guy, Riley. I have needs and you…well, you aren't meeting them," he barked at me and adjusted himself in his pants.

I pulled my feet underneath me. I narrowed my eyes on the boy that I never should have been with and asked, "So...what you're saying is, you are breaking up with me for good if I don't have sex with you?" I always knew he was a jerk.

He shrugged. "Not to sound like a dick or anything, but yeah— pretty much. Riley, we've been friends our entire life. I've been a patient guy for two years, but you just don't seem to know what you want," he said, holding his hands out.

My mouth fell open, "I know what I want. I want you to stop pushing me to do something I keep telling you I'm not ready for. If you care about me at all, you would understand my feelings, and stop making me feel guilty." *I want Josh. I want my dad to have never killed his mom. I want a do-over.*

He sat on my bed and placed his hands on top of my legs. "I do care about you, Riley. I'm not trying to make you feel anything, but I *am* ready. I have been ready for a very long time. I want my first to be with you, baby. It's only special when it's with you. But I don't want to wait anymore, so unless you are willing to move forward *with* me, I need to move on *without* you."

At least, he was honest. I thought—thinking I should be grateful for having him be so upfront about his intentions.

I weighed my options. I could have sex with Dean—even though I didn't want to—in order to keep my boyfriend, or let him go. I just felt like sex was a big deal. It should be shared with someone you love. I didn't love Dean. Half the time, I couldn't even decide if I liked him all that much. The decision was easy.

I leaned into kiss his cheek, "I'm sorry, Dean, but maybe we should just break up."

He frowned but nodded in agreement. "I'm sorry too." He pecked my cheek and left.

"Penny for your thoughts?" Josh asks pulling me out of my head.

I have no clue how long I have been staring off into space, lost in the memories of life altering moments. "Huh? What?"

He chuckles. "You went somewhere for a bit. Wanna talk about it?" He touches my temple.

I wish I could tell him. He is a guy, he would know if I were just being a sucky girlfriend. But to tell him, would also mean he would have to disclose his own virginity or lack thereof status with me.

I don't want to hear about, much less know any of that. I'm not naïve. Josh has frequent quick flings with girls. The girl he is currently associated with is known for being easy. Plus, I hear the things guys say around school. Not to mention, Dean has, in so many words, told me Josh isn't into commitment, but likes having a good time. Ugh!

In my mind, Josh is still *untouched* completely. I choose to think that.

"I was just thinking about how growing up is complicated. Can you believe in four months we're graduating high school? Everything is going to change." I sigh, fearing that very thing…*Change.*

He gives me a side-glance and begins to chomp on his bottom lip nervously. He is thrumming his thumbs on the steering wheel, looking to be contemplating his next words carefully.

"Yeah, about that. I've been thinking too. What are your plans after graduation?" he asks.

I look at him, really wondering what he's been thinking about in regards to plans after graduation, and if they include me?

"Actually, I don't know, really. Other than moving out and into the dorms at UTA—I have no plans. I only applied nearby because I wanted to be close to home for Tatum, and well, Joey too. Plus, that's where Emily is going, so I guess that's all the planning I have done. What about you?" I hold my breath fearing his answer.

I already knew Josh had been offered football scholarships to a few choice universities. It wasn't a surprise. He was a damn good quarterback. I would miss watching him play football next year. Hell, I miss watching him now on the off-season. He might not be here next year, but that's just a possibility I've tried not to dwell on. I had attempted to mentally prepare myself for that fact.

He sighs, "I've been weighing my options. My dad wants me to accept the scholarship in Louisiana—it's not too far away, but I'm not sure that is what I want." He looks at me again before looking back at the road.

"What do you want?"

"Would you be shocked if I said to not play football?" He shrugs.

Yeah, a little bit I think.

"A little bit, to be honest, but not completely. There is more to you than just football—although you *are* really good. What would you want to do?"

A few silent seconds go by. I watch his face cloud over before he finally speaks. "Not play, just be me. Go to school here, or somewhere. I don't know." He pulls into his driveway and opens the garage.

I hadn't even realized we were back by our houses. "You have company it seems." He points at Emily's beat up sedan parked in my driveway.

I haven't told Emily about my break up either. She never liked Dean and me together anyway. For the longest time, I thought it was because she had a killer crush on him freshman year, and they kinda dated for a few weeks. I never made anything official until we were sophomores, so I think she was over it by then. Truth was, she thought I was too good for Dean. She thought I was crazy for passing up a chance to be with Josh.

She might actually high five me.

Before I open the car door, Josh grabs my hand. I turn toward him, my eyes looking down at his hand holding mine, and then back up to his face that still looks very guarded. I wonder what he is thinking.

"Try to be happy, Riley. I know today sucks, but I think it's more than that. You seem sad. It's not just today. It's been for a little while." His eyes penetrate mine with compassion and concern.

I feel my eyes glaze over—I am sad. "Thank you, Josh, for everything. You have been my best friend since I was five years old, and I wouldn't know what to do without you. But…I'm okay. I promise. At least, I will be, but you are so sweet to worry about me." I lean in, kiss his cheek, and hurriedly get out of the truck before I start confessing my love for him.

My filter seems clogged.

 *Josh*

CHAPTER 3

Best friend status sucks, and not because it's a pain being her best friend, but because I want to be more than her best friend. So badly, in fact, I imagined today that she almost told me she loved me. So badly that I am willing to give up a football scholarship just so I can stay near her. Crazy or in love? I'm leaning toward crazy since she has a long-term boyfriend.

When I walk into my house, the smell of mom's homemade chili invades my nostrils, and it gives me the worst case of nostalgia ever. Shit, I miss my mom.

"Hey Jo, it smells like heaven in here." I joke, thinking forlornly that I should have chosen different words given what today is.

When she speaks, she is half smiling and half frowning. "That was the point. I just needed a little bit of her today. Chili was her favorite."

My dad clears his throat, walking into the kitchen. "Actually, chili was *my* favorite and your momma just liked to make this old man happy." He says playfully, pulling on Joey's ponytail and clapping me on the shoulder.

"I take it you found Riley?" my dad asks me with the biggest grin on his face. He knows how I feel about her."

He would always say, "It's not a matter of *if* son. It's a matter of *when* she finally sees the light."

I shake my head at his good nature on today of all days. "Yeah, same place as usual on this day, both cursing and missing her dad. I just wish she would stop blaming herself for what he did," I say frowning.

I head to the fridge and pull out a can of Dr. Pepper, pop the tab and take a sip. My dad sneaks a taste of Joey's chili and gives her a thumb up. She smiles proudly but swats his hand away giggling.

My dad sits at the table with me as I read a text that just came in.

Collin: PARTY TONIGHT MY PLACE. U IN?

I send a quick reply,

Me: NOT 2NITE CHILLIN WITH THE FAM

My dad folds his hands under his chin looking deep in thought. "I am sure it's rough for her, son. Evan and Claudia were always fighting, and people in this small town talk."

"I know that dad, but she didn't get in that car. She didn't make that decision, but she stills feels like she needs to punish herself for what he did. She apologizes to me every year. I just wish she knew that when I look at her, I don't even think about what I lost. I mean...it sucks, but she is still *my* Riley from when we were kids. You know? She's not just the daughter of a drunken man that accidentally veered mom off the side of the road. I wish she wouldn't let that day define her." I didn't mean to say all of that out loud. My phone vibrates in my hand.

Collin: NEED A DISTRACTION HEAD ON OVER

On second thought, a distraction sounds appealing. Riley did say Dean was stopping by later. Options: sit in bed and think about what they are doing next door, or go to a party and erase those thoughts. Option two sounds more appealing to me.

Me: MAYBE I'LL STOP BY

He replies right away.

Collin: HEADS UP...A CERTAIN FEMALE IS HERE AND ASKING ABOUT YOU

I'm pretty sure I am more fucked up than I realized, because reading that text makes me want to stay away. I don't know how much longer I can keep up the charade that I have been playing. I don't have girlfriends. I go out with a girl a few times and when things start to head into the direction of a relationship, I put on the brakes and step out. I have a rep of being a player, guys just assume, and people see what they want to see. I am sure as shit not going to tell anyone that I'm not who they think I am, and to announce myself as a virgin would be social suicide.

It's not that I'm saving myself for marriage, or that I am against the whole idea of it. It's just that, I've never been with a girl that makes me want to share that with them. Trust me, it's not that I don't want to have sex. I am a hormonal eighteen-year-old guy for fuck's sake. I most definitely want to, but the only girl that has ever stirred up those thoughts is with someone else.

So when Preslee cornered me a few weekends ago at one of Collin's parties, I entertained the idea a little, and she got the wrong idea. Of course, it didn't help that I took her to dinner and a movie either.

I have no intentions of ever giving it to her. There is a reason she gets invited to Collin's parties. Besides—horny or not—she isn't the girl I want, and God, how I want Riley in all kinds of dirty ways. It kills me knowing she has been with Dean for two fucking years. Who dates for two years and not cross that line? Even though I know it's not logical, in my mind she is still pure and innocent. Imagining it any other way makes me want to punch shit—mostly him.

Me: NAH DUDE I'M DONE WITH THAT

Collin: YOU'RE CRUEL LOL

Yep that's me…cruel. Use 'em and lose 'em, that's what they all think.

"Did you hear me, Josh?" Joey slaps the back of my head.

"What? Ow, no, what?"

"I said, you should just tell her how you feel."

"I agree with your sister. It's time you stop running circles and just shoot it straight." My dad pats my shoulder, kisses my sister's cheek and leaves the kitchen. Shoot it straight? I wonder if he would be so open to me shooting it straight when I tell him that I decided last week at the sports banquet that I really don't want to play anymore. That's another beast to battle later.

I sigh, thinking about what I would say, what I would do? She has a boyfriend.

"Jo, she has a boyfriend. Not that I care too much for Dean, but she does. I'm not trampling on something she's obviously comfortable with." The words sting coming out of my mouth because I know Dean doesn't deserve Riley. He manipulates her, and his eyes wander when she isn't looking.

Joey turns around, wringing her hands in front of her. "Look, I probably shouldn't say anything, but I'm going to anyway…only because you're my brother, and I love you, and because I think you are wasting time. And well, we know that time is precious and not promised to us, so just hear me out. Okay?"

I nod.

"You love her, and whether she admits it or not, she loves you too. I think she just doesn't let herself because of what happened, like she doesn't think she can or should. It makes sense to her. And as far as Dean goes…well, I might be spreading the gossip but…a little birdie with inside information had told me that he and Riley have been fighting a lot lately. Also, that he stormed out a few days ago, hasn't called or been by the house since."

She takes a deep breath. "There…I said it. Take what you want from it. I mean…what do I know? I'm only fourteen, but I am a girl, and I know what I see in Riley's eyes when she looks at you. I also know that she doesn't look at Dean like that."

Ok, well now I'm curious. Joey spends a lot of time next door with Riley's sister Tatum—best friends since birth—born exactly one month apart. She has seen Riley and Dean interact within that house. I stay away when he is over.

"How does she look at him?" I ask her, not entirely sure I want to know the answer.

She shakes her head. "Like she is confused, like he is this weird puzzle she can't figure out, like he doesn't make sense. It's odd really. Sometimes, she just has her head tilted when he walks away, like she can't decide something about him. She doesn't look at you like that. Never has."

Hmmm… Interesting. I've actually noticed the same thing a time or two at school. Every once in a while, Dean will say something, and I can tell Riley wants to comment, wants to argue it, but she doesn't for some reason. It's odd because she talks to me. She calls me on my shit all the time. Also, I've noticed her looking at him with the same peculiar expression Joey just explained. Strange!

"Oh, wise one, how does she look at me differently?" I joke.

Joey's whole face lights up. "Like you hung the moon, Josh. Her smile is genuine. Her eyes sparkle. She laughs. She watches you when you aren't looking. I mean...like really, she watches you. I've caught her looking out her window right at you before. She was daydreaming or something. She just looks at you with a look of longing. It's sad really." Her face falls.

Does she watch me through her window? I'd say that is creepy, except I can't. I am guilty of the same thing. Our bedroom windows are directly across from one another. I've watched her too—before asshole Dean came along, Riley and I used to flirt through those windows. I even snuck in through that window a couple times to listen to music and cut up. I'd love to sneak in now and feel her up. *Jesus, Josh. Get a grip.*

"Hmm...Well, thanks for the inside scoop. When can we eat? That smell is delicious." Yep, I'm ending the conversation.

"Anytime, and now…it's ready." She rubs her hands together, begins pulling down bowls and sets about making us dinner the way mom used to.

My heart breaks for Joey. Losing mom sucks for our whole family, but Joey is a girl. She needs her. I know that is why she adores Riley so much. She looks up to her like a big sister. It's the same way Riley adored my mom, because she apparently craved a more motherly figure in her life.

"This is just like your mom's, sweetheart. She would be so proud of you," my dad tells her once were seated at the table. He's right. The chili is scrumptious.

"Thanks, Daddy," she says. I notice her eyes have become glassy, and I think she is trying not to cry.

She is the strongest kid I know. She never complains. She helps around the house doing things our mom used to do. She is amazing, and it's all the more reason why I don't want to move away when I graduate. I want to be here, to watch her grow, to help her when she needs it. Of course staying here has the perks of being near Riley, but it's not just that. Families can change or disappear in a heartbeats time. I don't want to miss anything.

CHAPTER 4

When all else fails…go to a party—except that is the last thing I want to do. I'd rather stay in bed and mope.

"Stop worrying, Riley. It's not your job to stay home and be Mom. We don't have to stay long, okay?" Emily tells me as we walk the short distance to Collin's house.

I am so not in the mood for one of his parties, especially considering Dean and Josh will most likely be in attendance. Seeing Josh is always the highlight of my day, however, seeing Dean evokes some strange feelings within me. He casts a spell on me, makes me doubt myself, and I feel all confused and stuff.

I didn't tell Emily that Dean and I broke up. Instead, I skirted the truth saying that we were fighting right now and pausing to catch our breath—which is not unusual for us. I don't know why I'm not telling her. I just don't think she would understand. Em has been having sex since she was fifteen. She doesn't even have to be in a relationship. If she likes him, and he likes her, then it is fair game. I think she wouldn't get it. She just assumes Dean and I have had sex, and I have never corrected her. It's easier that way.

As expected, when we walk up to Collin's, I notice Josh's truck in the driveway, as well as…Dean's motorcycle—what a jerk. I sigh realizing Dean didn't even care that today was a struggle for me every year. Nah, he went to a party.

Outside on the front porch Collin is sitting with Laiken straddling his lap. He doesn't see us walk up right away, but when he does, his reaction throws me off balance a little.

"Oh, shit!" He shouts and practically throws Laiken off of him. "I mean…oh hey, Riley, Em. I…urm, I didn't expect y'all *both* to come tonight."

Emily and I exchange a confused look, and I have a sudden realization that I'm not invited. Now that Dean and I broke up, I am no longer welcome. Dean and Collin are childhood friends, once even step-siblings for a brief failed period. And well, I guess since Dean is here, I am not supposed to be. I guess news of our break up travels fast.

"Em, let's just go. I'm sure Brandt is having a party. We can go there." I offer, knowing, in truth, I would be more comfortable there anyway. I only come to Collin's parties because it's where Dean wants to go, and Josh is usually here. If it were my choice, I'd be at Brandt's parties, because that is more my scene with *my* friends. Normally, that would be Emily's too, except she has been avoiding going there since her ex-boyfriend Beau, Brandt's brother, started dating someone else and making it kind of seem serious.

She scrunches up her face, and I know how she feels, but c'mon? Isn't she asking me to do the same thing by coming here? Oh, that's right. She doesn't exactly know that Dean and I are split. We are catching our breath. Shit!

"Riley, don't go. It's fine. I didn't mean anything like that. I just didn't expect you since, ya know, Dean's already here. It just surprised me, that's all." He shifts uncomfortably, and I'm not buying that load of crap. Not at all.

I notice that Laiken has already grown bored with Collin's lack of attention, and he doesn't seem to care whatsoever. She has moved on to a boy I don't recognize—some girls have no shame—just the thought that she had a thing for Josh before sends a jolt of disgust through my system. Ick.

Collin pries his way into the middle of Emily and me, placing his arms around our shoulders, and guides us inside the house. I mean...literally guides us. Like he is moving us where he wants us to be, like pawns in a game. He is acting so strange.

Several people look at us as we walk in. Conversations stop mid-way through syllables. Girls from school—which I normally wouldn't associate with, anyway—start whispering, and guys raise their eyebrows. They nod their heads one way, while Collin leads us the opposite way. I really, *really* feel uncomfortable and like all of my peers know something I don't. I get a funny feeling, and I know Emily does to, because she looks around with the same expression I am wearing.

Collin tells us, "Josh is in the game room, let's go in there. I know he would want to know you are here."

"I feel like I am being valet parked, Collin. What the fuck?" Emily jokes, lacing it with sarcasm, even though I know she is feeling a tad pissy.

He laughs nervously as he pulls his tongue piercing between his teeth. "Naw, just doing my duty as host." He winks.

Now it's my turn to laugh. "Since when Collin? We've never been escorted before, and you lost your shit outside just now. Something's up."

He tugs us along into the game room. The moment I see Josh curse and drop his pool stick upon seeing me, I know something is up—I am not delusional. He is not happy to see me here.

He reaches us quickly, looking over my shoulder at the door we just entered through.

"What are you doing here?" he asks disapprovingly.

I carefully remove Collin's fingers from my shoulders and step away frowning.

"Emily got tired of seeing me pouting."

Collin says, "Shit" next to me. I give him a side-glance of confusion, but he just shrugs. I continue, turning my eyes back to Josh.

"She wanted me to get out, but I'm not sure what we are doing *here*," I say, and give my girl a questioning look.

Josh pulls me slightly away, and Emily and Collin begin to have words. I'm not listening, but she is waving her hands and wagging her finger dramatically at him. Her red hair looks extra fiery right now.

"What's up, Josh? I've been to plenty of these parties, and suddenly I'm being escorted through a sea of hushed company and shifty eyes, even you look uneasy seeing me here," I inquire.

He takes a deep breath and puffs it out. *What the hell is going on?*

"Oh! No, *no, no*. That shit won't fly, Collin. That's my bitch over there." Emily shouts and points in my direction.

I look at the three of my friends with questioning eyes. Josh curses again, and in this moment, I know whatever is going on, I am the *only one,* not in the know.

"Alright, somebody better fucking start talking." I snap. I wasn't in the mood to go to this damn party, and I'm definitely not in the mood to play games.

Josh reaches for my hand, but I pull it out of his reach.

"Riley, let's go outside and talk, please?" His voice is quiet.

"Riley, you need to know something." Emily says.

"No, she doesn't. Just drop it, Em." Collin interjects.

"Come with me, *please!*" Josh begs, but he's being a little more demanding this time and reaching for my hand again. This time, I let him grab mine, and only because something in his tone warns me that I don't want to know what she is trying to tell me. He has his protective voice.

I go with Josh toward the door, and Emily and Collin start arguing again. Once we're outside, Josh walks us to his truck and picks me up to sit on the tailgate. I don't say anything. I've figured it out, I think. Dean came to this party with someone else. Emily doesn't know we broke up, so she is pissed, Josh just wants to protect me from being hurt, and Collin is covering for his boy.

"Who is she?" I ask once the silence becomes deafening in my mind.

He sighs, "I don't know what you're talking about."

"Bullshit," I bark at him. I'm not stupid.

His eyes meet mine looking for something. "It doesn't matter who she is. Does it?" he asks, and I shake my head.

He's right, it doesn't. I don't want to know. But two days— fucking two days—and he's already moved on. That stings, just a little.

"Will you take me home, please?" I ask Josh.

He nods and kisses my forehead.

I text Emily to let her know I'm leaving, but she doesn't reply right away. I should never have come here. I don't know what I expected, but definitely not this, not so soon.

CHAPTER 5

I'm questioning my sanity at this point. I should have let her see Dean's true colors, but I wanted to protect her. I didn't want her to feel that pain.

The ride back to our house is short and quiet. We only live around the corner. My heart is splitting in two as I watch her emotions cloud her face. She isn't saying anything, not asking questions, other than the one I evaded. Dean is a fucking prick.

I knew he was shady, and I've seen with my own eyes his sketchy ways when Riley wasn't around. But tonight, he was so out in the open about his intentions, it made me sick—it's still echoing in my memory.

Preslee was tipsy and clung to me. I just wasn't interested. She eventually got the hint and moved on. It was to my unpleasant surprise when I saw who she moved onto. Dean and Preslee walked hand in hand upstairs as Collin and Laiken walked downstairs, trading places. It grossed me out how flippant people were about this stuff. And here I had that same reputation—just fantastic.

"What the fuck?" Collin muttered taking the last step of the staircase, tossing Laiken to the side. He was done with her.

"No shit. Riley's at home in tears because it's the anniversary of her dad's death, and he's fucking about. Explain to me again why you're friends with that asshole?" I asked.

How was I ever friends with him? Collin and Dean used to be stepsiblings until their parents divorced, so they have a bond. I got it, but man, I couldn't stand that guy. Half the time, Collin tolerated his smug attitude. Dean has an ego the size of a small planet.

"Dean said they broke up a few days ago. So asshole or not, he's in the all clear, buddy." Collin told me, not that it would matter to him if they weren't broken up. Broke up?

"Few days ago huh? We both know this isn't the first time, and he could be lying, dude. She never said they broke up," I admitted. She would tell me if they had. Wouldn't she?

I've suspected Dean cheats on Riley. What does that say about me exactly? I've convinced myself it's because I am protecting her from being hurt, even though I know he is the one hurting her. I don't know what the real reason is. The sound of my turn signal brings me back to the present. I chance a glance in Riley's direction.

"Are you okay, Riley?" I ask her as we pull into the driveway.

She wipes at her cheeks, and shit—I hate myself right now. I'm not even the one that has fucked her over, but I feel like I did. I want to protect her, to keep her from all the disappointment she keeps facing in the people she trusts, including from me.

"Yeah, I'm good. You should go back to the party. Apologize to Emily for me. I shouldn't have left her there like that. We walked over. Don't let her walk back alone, please."

She's worried about everyone but herself.

"I'll um…I'll go get her and bring her back here. Ok?"

She nods, and abruptly turns in her seat to look at me. I swallow when I notice the edge of decision in her eyes.

"Why do you think my dad cheated on my mom? I mean…he loved her. I know he loved her. Why then would he do something so unloving? Didn't he think it would hurt her?"

Well, that wasn't what I thought would come out of her mouth. I have no idea how to answer any of that. And now I'm wondering if she isn't as naïve about Dean as I thought. Maybe she knows he cheats, but if so, why stay with him.

"I don't know, Riley. From what you told me he was really young—still in college—right?" She nods.

"I think he just made a mistake in judgment. He moved y'all here away from it, and I think he tried to move past it," I explain best I can think of.

She sighs. "So…do you think my mom should have forgiven him of that?"

Why is she asking that?

"I think she *did* to an extent. She stayed with him. Whether she should have or shouldn't have done, I don't know," I tell her shrugging.

She mulls that over. "I think she shouldn't have. I think his decision to cheat meant he didn't love her enough, or at all. She might have spent years with the wrong guy. It happens, ya know? And I get it. They had me to think about, but she got knocked up her senior year of high school. It was an accident that brought them together. Sometimes accidents change everything, and take away what's really meant to be."

Whoa! I'm not sure what she is trying to say. Did she think she had spent years with the wrong guy? Did she share an accident? I don't really have a reply. I'm too confused on her real meanings.

I study her face, wishing I could jump inside her mind and read her every thought.

I go to open my mouth, but she stops me. "Ignore me. I don't know what I'm saying. My head is all kinds of fucked up right now. I think...I'm just going to go get some sleep. Thanks for bringing me home, Josh—*again*. You always take such good care of me." She whispers the last part, a slight frown marring her features.

"Anytime, Riley. I love...taking care of you. Get some sleep. I'll see you tomorrow. Call me if you need anything." I kiss her forehead, just needing to touch her as always. Her eyelids flutter shut for a moment.

She climbs out, and I watch her walk inside.

When I get back to Collin's, all hell has broken loose in his front yard. It looks as though most everyone left except some few key players.

Emily, being true to herself, is giving Dean the business. He actually looks a little scared of her.

I would be. That chick takes no crap. Her red hair is flying around as her temper flares. When I get out of the truck, their heads snap to me.

"Does she know that he was fucking someone else while she was at home a mess?" Emily yells the question at me, making me flinch a little.

"No, she assumes he was here with someone, but she doesn't know the details. She doesn't know who," I grate through my teeth and glare at him.

"I didn't know she would be here. She never comes here without me," Dean yells at anyone who cares. *We don't.*

"You *come* without her though, don't you?" Emily knowingly says to him, and I almost choke on her choice of words. The pun was intended.

"You're such a fucking asshole. Always manipulating her mind to make her think she is safe with you. She isn't. You and I know you're full of lies. I'm glad y'all are done. She deserves someone so much better than you." She points her finger at his chest, "YOU ARE NO GOOD FOR HER." She deliberately drawls every syllable.

Dean steps right up to Emily daringly, to where they are almost toe-to-toe. Collin and I both move in closer, ready to intervene. Dean's voice takes on a low edge. "You used to think otherwise, Em. In fact, if I remember correctly you said it was soooo good." He smirks.

What the fuck did he mean by that?

The two of them stare at each other with such anger. I'm not sure what to make of it. You would think Emily herself had been with him, had been hurt by him. Odd.

"C'mon, Em, let it go. He isn't worth it. I promised Riley I would get you back to her house," I tell her, trying to tug her away and toward my truck. Collin is tugging on Dean in the opposite direction.

"As usual, great party, Collin," I joke and he salutes.

A few more steps and we are all clear. "Oh, and Em? Riley's a big girl. She can think for herself. We have history. We are a thing whether *you* like it or not," Dean tosses out into the wind—so not broke up, I assume.

I had Emily almost in the car but now she is halted mid step. She turns and places her hands on her hips. "Y'all broke up, Dean. Isn't that what you told everyone? Or was that a lie?"

Shit. What if he did lie? If he did, then why the hell did Riley seem so chill about his being here with someone else? Why am I not kicking his ass myself?

Dean smirks, and I want to knock him out. "Don't worry that pretty little head with the semantics, Em. It's really not your business, so STAY THE FUCK OUT!" He yells, and goes back in the house, slamming the door.

Once we're in the car, Emily lets out a slew of curse words that shock the hell out of me. When she's done, I put the car in reverse. As I'm looking back, I chance a question. "Want to tell me what the hell that was about?"

She growls, "I just hate him, like *really*, really hate him. And Riley, Jesus...she's so sweet and loyal. She doesn't see what a pig he is, and *he is* a pig, Josh."

Once I'm back on the road, and I realize she isn't going to elaborate, I dig a little more. "It looks a little personal, Em. Why is that?"

She gasps and then covers her mouth, and now I know I'm not going to like this. "Emily?" I question again.

"Pull over, Josh. Pull over." She cries.

I do. I place the truck in park on the side of the road. She hops out, paces a few times, and pulls on her hair. She climbs back in and takes a deep breath.

"It's just, I...he...Ah, fuck! Look...never mind. Listen, I'm going to tell her about this. Not tonight because she is too fragile, but later. She needs to know what kind of piece of shit she spent the last two years with. I just want you to know that I'm not keeping this a secret from her," she admits.

I nod as a prickle of unease hits my system. One, because I think Emily is withholding something. And two, because I think Riley might already know the kind of piece of shit she spent the last two years with. I just can't figure out why she has, if she did know. I put the car back into drive.

"She cares about you, Josh. It's always been about you. I don't know why she stayed with him. But...well...I thought you should know," she sighs, answering my internal question.

When I pull up to Riley's house, I wish Emily good luck, and she gives me her thanks.

Something was off with Emily about Dean. She seemed to know exactly how he is from personal experience. I have a good mind to go kick his ass myself, but I don't.

Instead, I go to the place I hope I can get some insight on what to do to help my best friend and the girl I love with all of my heart.

I go to my mom's grave.

CHAPTER 6

Realizing I might have spent the past two years wasted on someone who never really cared about me at all—sucks ass. I chose him because he was safe—because he didn't have my heart and the power to cripple me, but the fact that he did what I feared the most out of men, well that fucking hurts and is messing with my head in the worst way.

When I walked into the house from the party, my mom was sitting at the table with a glass of wine in her hand. The bottle of merlot on the table in front of her, and a shoebox labeled 'Evan' that she kept touching.

"Mom, you know you're not supposed to drink with your meds," I tell her. My mom has been on anti-depressants for a few years now.

"I know, but today I just needed…"

"I understand." Actually I do.

"Where is Tatum?" I ask her.

"Next door. I might have said something to upset her." Not surprising, I thought.

"Said what?"

"It doesn't matter. I will fix it tomorrow," she says.

"What do you have there?" I ask pointing to the box.

"Memories. He loved me, you know? I think he just forgot it." She opens the box and pulls out a piece of paper. A note.

"Can you forget that you love someone?" I ask her.

She nods and hands me the letter to open. "Yes, I forgot too," she tells me.

I open the letter and read:

Dearest Claudia,

   Before I begin I just want you to know that I love you. You lit up my life from the moment I saw you sing your heart out in the school play. I didn't tell you, but I went out of my way just to be near you, even added theatre to my elective just to hear your sweet angelic voice again. All the guys called me a pussy, but I didn't care. You're my best friend and the girl I can't live without. My love for music was nothing more than an extension of my love for you, and now that extension of love is growing inside your tummy, probably humming her own little lullaby. It might not have been planned this way, but it's perfect. You and me, and our little peanut. We should pack our shit, run away, and live our life on the road. Your voice, my guitar, and our biggest fan. Imagine the tips we would earn with a cute little baby holding drumsticks. Ha! Reality, we might be broke off our asses and living on Mac-n-cheese or Ramen, but at least we would have each other. Let's do it.

                              Forever yours,
                              XoXo Evan

"So y'all wanted me?" I ask her, my glassy eyes darting to hers. I just didn't think they did, really. It was an accident. *Unplanned.*

She looks at me for a beat. "Why would you ask that, Riley? Of course, we wanted you. Getting pregnant wasn't planned obviously, but it happened. After getting over the initial shock of it, we were happy, excited even. I loved him, and he loved me. We knew with or without a baby, we would be together."

"Then what happened?"

She sighs and pours another glass of wine, which is not a good idea. "Life, doubts, not trying enough. Lots of things."

I don't know why I start to cry, but I do.

"Oh Riley, what's wrong? Did something happen tonight?" she asks.

I nod and wipe at my eyes. "Yes, Dean was with someone else tonight. We had a disagreement, and it's only been a few days, and I can't help but think that this someone else might have existed before then. It's just so soon," I admit it.

I've noticed the way Dean looks at other girls when he thinks I'm not looking. Then there are those times I call him, and he doesn't answer, but will text me right back and say he just can't talk, but texting is ok. I never questioned it even though it bothered me. It seemed off. Shady.

"Oh honey, I'm so sorry. But I can't say that I'm surprised. He isn't the right boy for you," she says sipping her wine. She is beginning to slur a little.

She has had way too many glasses of wine, I think. "What? You said you liked Dean."

"Yeah, I said I liked him, but I don't think he is the right boy for you. He's nice enough, but nice only goes so far."

"What are you saying, mom?" Do I even want to know?

"Did I ever tell you about a boy named, Billy?"

I shake my head back and forth. Honestly, my mom and I have never had conversations like this before at all. The wine has her talking more than usual.

"Well, Billy used to go out of his way to compliment me. He would tell me he liked my hair. He would notice little things about me, like the little freckle by my eye. I never saw him as anything other than a nice guy. I had a secret crush on the new boy in theatre, guess who? Yep, your dad. There was just something about him. Your dad didn't always say the right things or compliment me the same way Billy did. Where am I going with this?" she asks, and I shrug.

"Oh yes, you see the difference was Billy was trying too hard. What he was doing was fake. And your dad, well, he was being himself. I knew he was whom I belonged too. He took my breath away, where Billy made me hold my breath. Hold my breath and wait for something bad to happen. Billy was too nice, but I knew something was amiss," she explains.

"Okay, so Billy was my Dean. Is that what you are saying?" I ask her.

"Exactly. When it seems too good to be true, it probably is."

I get it. I'm still confused, though. "But dad cheated on you, Mom. Isn't that a something bad?"

She frowns and nods sadly. "Yes, but honey, there were some amazing years before that. I don't know why he did what he did, but I know now that he did choose me. He moved us here and away from where she was. He tried to make me happy, but I just couldn't forget it. I couldn't escape the doubts and the insecurities to forgive him completely. I didn't *choose him,* and it's my fault he isn't here with us. I realized it too late." She begins to cry.

Her fault?

"How is it your fault, Mom?"

She doesn't tell me right away. She holds a picture of my dad in her palm and touches it gently, lost somewhere in her head.

"I made a horrible mistake. I just wanted him to understand why I felt the way I did. I needed him to know the immense pain he'd caused me and why it wasn't easy to just forget it, that I couldn't just forget it."

My voice sounds small and foreign when I speak. "What did you do?"

She wipes at the tears falling from her eyes. "Your dad and I met for dinner that night. He wanted to make up to me the dinner he had missed the night before. He apologized. He said he was working late because he had a deadline, and he fell asleep in his office. I didn't believe him. We went to Pete's Bar & Grill, and I should have been happy. I should have seen it as him trying. I was just filled with such bitterness and doubt that even after all the years, I knew I no longer trusted him. I told him that night that I was leaving him that I had found someone else. I said a lot of terrible things…things I didn't mean. Starting with the 'someone else.' There was never anyone else. There never could be. He was it for me. I just—God, his face when I spoke. I hurt him. I succeeded in my plan even though I'd hoped I would fail. I left him there, lost and broken. I will never ever forgive myself. I hate what I did. I hate even more that he was so lost that he did what he did. He called me, and I didn't answer. I could have prevented that accident."

Oh, my God.

"The worst part, Riley. He was telling the truth. When I cleaned out his office after the funeral, his co-workers told me he had been pulling all-nighters at work trying for a new promotion. If he got that promotion, he was going to ask me to re-new our vows and take me on a honeymoon since we never had one. We had a baby, we got married, we never went on a honeymoon, and our relationship was done in the wrong order. But looking back, everything he did was to say he was sorry, was to prove to me that he'd made a mistake but that he loved me. That he chose *me*. I just threw it all away, like he never mattered to me. And God, he did matter…you mattered," she tells his picture.

She grabs my hand and squeezes it hard. "He was everything, and I didn't see it until it was too late. Don't make the same mistakes I did, Riley. Dean isn't your Evan. Dean is your Billy. I think you know who your Evan is. I'm sorry, I'm so very sorry. I know you love Josh, and you think you can't because of the accident, but you can, Riley, and you should. You belong with him. Don't let the past swallow you up to where you can't live in today or see a better future. Find the beauty behind the ugly, baby, even if you have to dig deep to get to it, and just let it be its own kind of beautiful."

She releases my hand and stands, kisses my cheek, and goes to her room with the box cradled to her chest.

My heart is broken. I thought I was filled with guilt. There is no comparison of the guilt my mom carries around. I think I understand her depression better. I think I understand her fear of me always running away, only if we were allowed a do-over.

CHAPTER 7

Best advice: Remind her that you remember everything before shit got real. Something only I share with her, a childhood memory that says—"I never forgot"— hope I don't fuck it up.

It's been a few weeks since Collin's party, a few weeks since Riley has finally admitted she is single. Does that mean she is with me now? Hell, no. Why do you ask? One simple answer...high-school-rumor-mill.

First off, Riley doesn't know Dean was with Preslee at Collin's, and I am too much of a pussy to tell her. Why? Shit, if I know. However, she is fucking convinced that Preslee is with me. Crazy right? Not really, not when before that party, Preslee *was* clinging to me. I even took her out, funny how things work out. So funny, in fact, I can't even laugh about it. That's because it's not fucking funny at all. It's my life.

Adding fuel to the fire of this rumor...a week of mishaps, wrong interpretations of situations, and another week of coal to the flickering flame—the misunderstanding is now a roaring flame of bullshit.

Well, let's see, last Monday...Preslee stopped me in the hall and told me in front of everyone that she had a great time at Collin's party. What the fuck? Yep, that's what I thought too. If I remember correctly, she got bored trying and failed to maintain my attention. I brushed her off, and she got off with the dickhead upstairs. She does know that she fucked Dean, right? That is what I asked her later when she was waiting at my truck after school. She said, "Oh that. That didn't mean anything really, just fun, now you that's a different story." It was beyond ridiculous. She just didn't get it.

Then this Wednesday, Collin told me that Riley and Emily overheard Preslee tell a few of the cheerleaders that I was taking her out on Valentine's, and she had pink lace picked out to surprise me. Collin had the nerve to congratulate me. So not only was Riley not in-the-know that her asshole boyfriend did-the-dirty with Preslee, she thought I was the one doing it. Could it get any worse you ask? Yes, yes it can.

Today, Friday, Valentine's Day...Preslee is waiting for me at the tree Riley and I always eat lunch under. It's our spot—Riley's and mine—and Preslee is tainting it with her temptation. She is wearing my varsity hoodie, resting her body against the tree trunk. She seriously thinks she is seductive. Most guys would find her just that, except I'm not like most guys. I see Collin and Dean off to the side watching this all unfold, and my stomach is in knots because I don't know how to stop any of it without giving away my secret.

I lean in real close to her face not wanting to embarrass her by the things I am going to say. "Where did you get my sweatshirt, Preslee?" I ask, touching my hoodie.

She smiles innocently and sniffs the sleeve. "Aww...don't be mad, Joshie. I just like your smell *all over me*," she purrs emphasizing her words.

Shit. "Preslee, this needs to stop. I'm not interested in you like that."

She looks to the door of the cafeteria and smirks. I don't take my eyes off of her. She places her hand on my chest, and I cringe on the inside. "Listen. Josh, I like you like that. I get what I want, and I want you. Tonight, when we go out, I promise you will want me to. Just ask Dean over there how good I am or Collin for that matter."

My stomach is in knots. My throat is tight, and I don't know how to get this girl to back off. She is screwing everything up, and at the same time her words are fucking with my head. "Yeah, well...I already have plans, Preslee." I lie.

"Those plans involve me naked, right?" she asks, biting her bottom lip. C'mon, I am a freaking guy, a guy who hasn't ever had sex—just the word naked stirs an emotion. Ah hell!

And to top off the worst week ever, Riley makes an appearance with the perfect fucking timing in the world.

I see it in Preslee's eyes...the challenge, and the recognition that Riley means something to me. I see it in Riley's eyes...the sadness, and the jealousy. And then I see the satisfaction in Dean's eyes, and the worry in Collin's eyes. All that's missing is Emily's disappointing eyes.

Perfect freaking day, I wanted to shoot myself right where I stood. I wondered what my eyes said. Probably fuck it all.

CHAPTER 8

The one time I am single and finally ready to open up to Josh, he isn't available. Preslee has been a constant sour taste in my mouth for a while now. I knew Josh took her to the movies. I knew they made out at one of Collin's wonderful parties a while back. I was there with Dean to witness it. However, this is just going on way too long to not affect me. Josh doesn't do a few weeks, never has. Therefore, I have worked it out in my mind that she is his girlfriend. And—in walks jealousy. She is an evil bitch.

I have the worst case of the green-eyed monster when I walk outside to the tree in front of the cafeteria where Josh and I have always met for lunch since we were freshman. Lo and behold, I find him with Preslee. Even when Dean and I were dating, I ate lunch with Josh and Emily by that tree. Dean stayed inside with his friends. That is just how it was. Where is Emily? Hmmm…

Preslee. *That bitch.*

Why is she his new flavor anyway? Besides the obvious fact that she is 5'6—very blonde, has legs for days—pouty lips—bigger boobs, and is a very *easy* piece of work that I hate. She is opposite of my 5'2 petite figure, my average olive skin, my average dark hair with unruly wavy curls, and my strange indecisive eye color of blue and green. Oh, and the fact that she opens her legs when she smells a man. And I—well…nope —I'm not that girl. I can't even go there with a boy I've dated for two years.

So that is what Josh likes? Ugh. That thought is a major downer.

Something is different about her and him, and it niggled at me in the worst way. I worried Josh would meet someone and replace me in his life next year when he went to college. But seeing him do that very thing now, while my life is spiraling out of control, yet leading me right to him, has me feeling sick.

Preslee is leaning against the tree, looking as cute as ever in her jeans and Josh's varsity hoodie. He is standing very close to her. His left hand on the tree trunk, her head tilted and rested on his arm, entranced by whatever he is telling her. I stand there a few feet away frozen and watching with envy. With his free hand, he touched the hoodie near her face. She looked like she would drop on her knees right there if he had asked her to, and he was equally caught in her spell. I hated the looks they shared with each other. Intense. Serious.

My stomach is making weird somersaults, and my heart is beating way too fast. Every time I see Josh with Preslee lately I feel this sudden urge of panic. It was happening more lately, especially since I've been overhearing things people are saying about them. When she bragged about her pink lace lingerie she was going to surprise him with tonight, I thought I was going to die. I never used to let my jealousy bother me so much, but things are changing. I am changing.

Even when I saw her and him together a few weekends ago at one Collin's many parties—one I was actually invited to because I was with Dean then—I didn't even react this way. I didn't like seeing it. I never have, but I couldn't claim him. He would hang out a time or two with girls and move on. I didn't let myself think further into what they were doing together. I just told myself they were time fillers. They didn't mean anything to him, and he changed his mind so quickly that it never seemed personal or mean to much to him. Even that gave me a trickle of fear of ever being with him myself, if I let myself go there that is. I worried he would be the same with me—get bored, move on.

At Collin's party, I saw Josh and Preslee kissing in the hall, and I hated it. I hated it even more when she pulled him into the bathroom with her.

"Why are you such a man whore, Josh? You know you can do better than Preslee? Didn't she hook up with Collin last week?" I asked him, after he came out of the bathroom with her, and she was out of earshot.

He laughed at me. "We didn't hook up, Shaw. She just did me a favor." I gagged, and he shrugged like it was no big thing. "What? She offered, and I accepted. Is that a crime?" He smirked. Granted, Josh was a little tipsy, but still it grossed me out.

"You're a pig, Josh. I don't want to hear that"

"You asked, I told you. Besides, I'm not a man whore as you called it. I'm just bored and having fun."

Some random guy heard him as he walked by, and fist bumped him.

Guys.are.pigs, I thought.

All of a sudden, Josh tilted his head to the side, and hummed like he had a sudden idea. He tapped my nose with his index finger. "We could have fun together, ya know? And then I wouldn't need these distractions anymore," he said, gesturing to the other girls at the party and nibbling on his lip.

I rolled my eyes. "Yeah, ok, you're drunk," I said sarcastically. "Distraction from what exactly?"

He leaned in close to my ear, tucking my hair behind my ear, that single touch had me covered in goosebumps. His breathe in my ear caused me to shiver as he whispered low and husky, "From my fantasies of you."

I think I may have, "Aahhh'ed," and when he leaned back to look into my eyes, I swore he was going to kiss me. His eyes flicked to my lips like he was thinking about it.

I began to panic, realizing I wanted him too, but knowing I was at a party full of people, one of which was my boyfriend. Realizing I hadn't seen him in a while, I also wondered where he was.

My thoughts of a MIA Dean dissipated when Josh grabbed my wrist and brought it to his lips, never breaking eye contact. He left his mouth there briefly, feeling my pulse thump wildly, I imagined.

He grinned wickedly, before softly placing a kiss on my wrist and letting my hand fall away. "I'm kidding, Riley. You can calm down now. We didn't do anything in there but kiss. I was joking with you, but I've said it before, you are absolutely adorable when you are jealous." He walked away laughing.

I shake my head to rid my thoughts of the night I knew his mouth was on hers but wishing it was on mine. Josh must have felt my gaze on him because he turns his head in my direction and smiles beautifully, that dimple on his right cheek making me melt. It lights up and then flickers out, being replaced by an uncomfortable, nervous tick that I have come to know. He rubs behind his neck and straightens his body.

I don't miss the rolling eyes and look of aggravation I am getting from Preslee. She doesn't like me, and the feeling is mutual. Her eyes flick away from me to a spot behind me where I notice Dean and

Collin staring in their direction too. She frowns for a moment but then focuses her attention back on Josh.

He crooks his finger at me to come to him, and his eyes warm as they meet mine. My heart that was beating so fast just moments earlier has suddenly stopped beating altogether. Could a person have a heart attack at seventeen? I feared this boy would be the death of me. Not wanting to act freaked out...he is my best friend after all—I willed my feet to move.

"Hey guys," I say cheerfully as I walk to *our* spot by the tree. *That's right...it's our spot bitch, now move the fuck on.* Preslee just looks at me with disgust. I am interrupting her moment, by his invitation.

"Until tonight, Joshie," she says to him.

I want to gag. Joshie? Gah, could she be more annoying?

Apparently, she can be downright spiteful. With mischief and demand in her eyes, she grabs his face and shoves her tongue in his mouth. He stiffens but slowly relaxes into their kiss. Kissing her back.

I die a thousand times in that moment.

I turn over my shoulder to see if Dean and Collin are still watching, which they are. Collin with a knowing smirk, Dean looks pissed, before he walks away and goes back inside. Strange. What reason would he have to be pissed?

She releases his lips with a pop and glares at me knowingly. Josh looks shocked. He darts his eyes between Preslee and me a few times, as though he is pondering over a thought. Comparing us? Fuck!

He looks over my shoulder at someone, and then he leans into her ear, saying something that causes her to blush. He presses a kiss to her cheek as she smiles, and I have to force my breathing to slow—force the bile from rising. It is torture.

He sits down on the grass and pats the spot next to him. I watch Preslee walk away for a brief second before sitting next to him criss-cross and pulling my grapes out of my backpack. He kisses my forehead like he always does and stretches his legs out in front of him. All normal.

He looks so hot today, wearing dark jeans, a green polo that makes the emerald flecks in his hazel eyes pop. He runs his hand through his hair and grins at me checking him out.

He looks at me with a raised brow, "You okay? You looked like you were ready to claw her eyes out. What was that?" He asks, gesturing between Preslee walking away and I.

"No clue, Preslee just marked her territory, I guess. She practically peed on your leg." I laugh, but I was not amused. "But yeah—I'm good. Why wouldn't I be?" I lifted my shoulders and tried to act unaffected.

He studies my face for a moment, looking for something, and I let him. Looking at him through my lashes, wishing he could read the things I couldn't say.

He sighs. "To clarify, I'm *not* her territory. Something is bothering you. Your beautiful eyes seem lost. Anything you want to talk about? Maybe about Dean?" He asked me like he already knew something, and he wanted me to tell him about it.

I don't want to talk about Dean. It's been a few weeks, a long week in the present. Dean has called, has texted, and has done everything to say he is sorry and inform me that he just went on a date—nothing more—begging me to try again, I just don't have the energy to fight with him—so I ignore him.

Both Emily and Josh confirmed that Dean was at Collin's with another girl, no clue who, no clue if he was just hanging out with her and telling me the truth or if it were more than that.

Beautiful eyes? Did he call my eyes beautiful just now? I held his gaze, but had to look away before my brain to mouth filter malfunctioned. I couldn't help the small grin that crept to my face thinking he thought my eyes were beautiful, though.

"I'm good, Josh. Really. Dean and I aren't together, and I don't want to talk about it just yet. Okay?" I look back at him and smile softly. He smiles back and nods.

He pats his leg and pulls me back to lay my head on his lap. "Do you remember when we were little, how you used to always wear that Tinker Bell costume?" he asks me out of the blue.

My eyes dart to his, a little shocked that *he* remembers that, or why he is bringing it up now. "Yes, I do. My dad used to call me his little Tinker Bell, and you even nicknamed me..."

"Tink," he finishes. "I miss those kids. We were so funny together. You playing hot wheels with me in that costume."

"I still have one of those hot wheels," I tell him, hoping he doesn't think it's creepy. "You gave me a lime green one on my fifth birthday because you thought it was my favorite color since I always wore that green costume."

His eyes lock with mine as he begins running his fingers through my hair with one of his hands. My black shirt has risen up exposing a sliver of skin on my stomach. I'm wearing a frayed blue jean mini skirt with leggings and combat boots.

I don't even think he realizes he is doing it, but his finger is brushing across the exposed skin leaving a tingling sensation in its wake. He's tracing the heart tattoo on my hip, and I am inwardly coming undone. I have to cross my ankles and squeeze my thighs. I don't think he will ever realize what his touch, even so small, does to me.

I couldn't help but shut my eyes, and consume the comfort only he could give me. A soft moan escapes me on accident.

I felt his breathing pick up just slightly and his motions still. When I open my eyes, I find him staring at my face. I can't look away, and neither can he it seems. I'm curious when he swallows hard. My eyes are drawn to his Adams apple, and I notice his jaw twitches—it's so hot. I'm holding my breath when he glances briefly at my lips before he looks away, continuing his tender touch and twirling of my hair.

Looking up at my best friend, I wonder if maybe he feels the same way I do secretly, and if I should just throw caution to the wind and tell him that I want to try something with him.

I am so confused as to what to do. We have always had moments—many moments—where things went unsaid but our eyes told a different story. We both stood on the edge of friendship—and something more—but never crossing over.

He looks down at me, his once smoldering eyes now composed. "You never told me what made you decide to get that tattoo over the Tink one," he says out of the blue.

Josh's eighteenth birthday was last month, and he decided he wanted to get a tattoo. A black guitar for the passion he has in music. A passion stemmed from his mom. The guitar is wrapped in roses and thorns, three to be exact. The roses are gorgeous and all different shades of colors. On one, the tips of the pedals are reddish, and they fade to black. I asked him why he chose different shades for each, and he said, 'roses are deep rooted in symbolism.' He explained how each rose color holds a different meaning, red meaning love, beauty, courage and respect. That specific rose represents his mom. It faded to black because she passed. The second rose was soft pink. It represented youthfulness, grace and gentleness, for his sister. The third rose he never explained, he just smiled and said that was 'a secret.' It was yellow, coral, and the tips were the darkest red. Honestly, it was my favorite. The colors blended in a way that stole my breath at its beauty. I need to remind myself to Google its meaning one day.

I remember the cute little Tink one I was looking at, but I didn't realize he noticed me looking at it—that he'd paid that close of attention.

I lost a bet and promised Josh I would get one too. I almost got the cute little fairy. It would have been special for me. A childhood reminder of my dad as well as a sweet memory I held with Josh. I opted for a different one, though. I wanted something that meant something to me, even if it was deep rooted in sadness. I chose a black heart surrounding a treble clef, connected together by a bass clef. I loved it. It was dainty, small, and delicate—just like my own black heart. It represented the music between Josh and me—a song that could never be played and died before it could.

I smile sadly at Josh. "It's simple. I love music. I love writing it, I love listening to you sing it, and I love—," OH, MY GOD! I almost told him I loved him—*again*. Seriously, I need to work on my brain to mouth filter. "I love the tattoo, I mean."

He was smiling so wide, missing the sadness in my eyes that didn't match the happy words I spoke. "You like my singing?" he asks.

I twiddled with my hair and bit my bottom lip, "M'hmm, I like when you play too," I admit. Why couldn't I shut up? Good grief.

He grins a crooked grin and nods, "Good to know," he says touching his own tattoo on his upper arm.

"You should come out with me tonight. We can do whatever you want. Something that will make those beautiful eyes I love so much, not so sad. Forget all the shit you've faced for a little while, yeah?" He says, perhaps throwing his own caution to the wind.

Eyes he loved so much? I felt my throat tighten up as I looked at my best friend. I loved him even more knowing that he was willing to blow off his Valentine's date with pink lace in attempts to make me feel better, knowing the reward was not going to be any favors in the bathroom. Yeah, I didn't buy that he was joking with me that night. Preslee is known to give boys what they want.

I pushed the thought away. "You like my eyes? You've said that twice in like twenty minutes?" I ask, genuinely curious and rising to my knees to look at him. He seems caught off guard by my sudden movement and closeness to him.

He tenses for just a second before relaxing and shrugging his shoulders. "Yeah, I do. No one has eyes like yours. Some days they are blue, some days they are green, or days like today, they are a little bit of both. It's cool. They remind me of the beach, and I *love* the beach." He says it nonchalantly, but I think he emphasized the word love. I don't question it, or try to make it more than a simple compliment. He takes a sip of his Dr Pepper out of the can distracting me anyway. The way his throat moves is hypnotic.

"M'hm" I say, no other words are necessary. He likes my eyes. He thinks they are beautiful. Just like I notice how his hazel eyes change colors, he too notices the same about mine. It makes me smile.

"So, tonight?" He raises his brow.

"Sounds fun, and you're sweet to ask, but I *heard* you have plans," I say with a wink, air quoting around *heard*. I ruffle his hair making him laugh. I love his laugh.

"Anyway, I was kind of a bitch to Tatum all week, I feel kinda bad about it. I might see if she wants to do something." I really did feel bad about snapping at her all week. It wasn't her fault my week was one from hell.

"No dice, baby girl, my dad is taking the brats out for Valentine's. It's there, 'who needs boys' date, and my dad thought it was this brilliant idea. Truthfully, I think he just doesn't want to be alone," he says as the sadness of why he would be alone seep in.

There it is…that reminder that she's gone. Those little reminders always slap me when I least expect them.

"Come to think of it, I should probably stay with my mom then. She told me a lot of stuff. She's been…well, it's a long story. I will need to fill you in sometime," I say.

He nods.

"Sleepover with the brats, huh? Good luck with the giggling all night and listening to them talk about those boys 'they don't need.' Sounds fun." I laugh and push at his chest playfully. Our little sisters were totally boy crazy. Eighth graders…I remember it.

"Oh yeah, shitloads of fun. I should just have a sleepover with you at your house. That sounds like more fun in my book," he says wiggling his brows at me. His eyes are gorgeous, the golden brown and green dance together in the sunlight.

Seriously? Was he kidding? I mean he has snuck in my window a time or two, but that was just silly. By the wiggling brows he just did, I have a different idea of a sleepover all of the sudden. I just stare at him, and I feel my face heat.

"Um," was all I could manage to say. I turn my head away from his playful eyes before he sees me blush. I hoped, anyway.

He starts laughing at my reaction. Evidently, not fast enough. He grabs my chin and turns my face back to his.

"Ah! Ms. Shaw, where did that pretty little head of yours just go? I do believe you are blushing?"

Shit! I shove at his chest, "OMG shut up, you are so stupid, Josh, I am not blushing."

"Mmm hmm." He says as he takes a bite of his sandwich and relaxes his back into the tree. "You are a shit liar, Ms. Shaw."

"And you are delusional, Mr. Parker."

I watch his mouth move as he chews and then pop one of my grapes into my own mouth. His own eyes watch my mouth move. I seriously don't think I am crazy anymore. Josh and I have always been flirtatious with each other to an extent, but we have kept it friendly while I dated Dean. However, the way he is looking at me right now...well, it doesn't seem friendly. It seems like something else entirely. Something *more*.

And what was that comment? I had no clue what to do with that. Maybe he was joking and didn't mean it to be suggestive. I think he did though or maybe I'm the one that wants it to be. Damn.

Josh and I have last period together. We don't sit next to each other, due to assigned seating. Today we have a sub, and it is pretty much free time, so we all have our cell phones out, which is actually against school policy—but who cares. Josh is chatting it up with Collin, and I am doodling a poem about his eyes in my notebook when my phone vibrates on my lap with a text from Josh.

Josh: SO...ABOUT THAT SLEEPOVER THING? WHAT WERE WE DOING? CURIOUS

I look up at Josh, and he grins, I of course blush again as the image of us together flicks into my mind. He chuckles and looks down at his phone, typing again.

Josh: SEE YOU'RE BLUSHING AGAIN. I THINK THAT IS MY NEW FAV. SHADE ON YOU ;) DO TELL PLS.

Shit! I am at a loss. He is so flirting with me. I look at him, and he arches his brow and waves his phone at me gesturing for my reply. I cross my legs and tug on my skirt, his eyes track my movements. I am positive he is checking out my legs. Josh is a total boy, and it's not the first time I have noticed him look at me, but he is being obvious about it, which is unusual for him. Even Collin looks at him puzzled.

Me: YA KNOW CURIOSITY KILLED THE CAT

Josh: YOU'RE KILLING ME - DRIVING ME CRAZY

What? Why?

Me: WHAT? WHY? AND STOP LOOKING AT MY LEGS! YOUR GF IS GIVING ME THE EVIL EYE

I forgot Preslee was in this class until I felt her shooting daggers at me from across the room. I wish my own daggers would detonate her into nonexistence. She is looking back and forth between Josh and me with disapproval. He looks at her and smiles mischievously. She gives him a look that says she isn't happy with him. He just looks back at me and shrugs before looking down at his phone and typing out another message. He doesn't even care that she is annoyed?

Josh: SORRY BUT YOUR LEGS LOOK GREAT IN THAT SKIRT AND DAMN THEM BOOTS ARE SEXY AS HELL – CAN'T HELP IT

Another vibration...

Josh: THINK THE EVIL EYE IS ON ME BUT NOT MY GF SO DON'T CARE. NOW STOP STALLING. WHAT MADE YOU BLUSH?

I look over at her and sure enough she is shooting major daggers at him. Death to Josh looks.

Not his girlfriend?

Me: UM, OK. I THOUGHT ABOUT SOMETHING...IT FELT WIERD. BUT MY MIND JUST WENT THERE

Josh: THINK I AM FOLLOWING YOU. THOUGHT ABOUT WHAT EXACTLY AND WHY WEIRD?

Seriously, he wants me to say it. I can't.

Me: YOU AND ME

Josh: WHAT ABOUT YOU AND ME?

Me: UGH...PLS STOP. IT DOESN'T MATTER

That was getting to personal for me. I couldn't tell him what I thought about. Could I? Should I?

A 'sleepover' with Josh frightens and excites the hell out of me. He is sex-on-wheels, and I am still holding my "V" card.

Josh: STOP WHAT EXACTLY? IT MATTERS TO ME AND BASED ON YOUR REACTION I THINK IT MATTERS TO YOU 2

The bell rings and I literally run out of the door. Josh called my name and tried to catch up to me in the halls. But Preslee grabbed his hand and steered him in her direction giving me my escape. For the first time ever, I wanted to thank her instead of slapping her.

Josh called me twice and left a voicemail asking me what was wrong and to please call him. I just couldn't.

Later that night he text me...

Josh: HAPPY VALENTINE'S DAY PRETTY GIRL. TONIGHT I SHOULD HAVE BEEN WITH YOU

I didn't reply. I feared Josh didn't mean it the way I wanted him too. In my mind, he felt because he was my best friend that he should have been with me to cheer me up. Dean and I were broken up. I was spending Valentine's with my sad mom who ended up bailing on me to go play Bingo. So, actually I was spending it alone. I didn't want Josh's pity. I wanted him.

I wonder how his date with Preslee is going? Obviously he isn't enjoying her pink lace yet, or he wouldn't be texting me. Right? Then another text came through.

Josh: COME OUTSIDE I HAVE A SURPRISE FOR YOU

Okay? Confused. He's here?

Me: OK ???

I walk outside and sitting on the steps holding the most adorable white snowball looking kitten with a lime green bow is Josh. In his other hand is a gift box like a Chinese takeout container except it's lime green.

"Oh, my God. What is that? Well, I mean...I know what it is. But like...you know what I mean?" I give up. Why do I stutter like an idiot when he surprises me like this?

He holds the kitten out to me and smiles a megawatt smile, the kitten meows. I take it and hold it to my chest. It kneads into my skin and begins to purr.

"She's your Valentine's present. Your mom said it's ok. I named her for you. I hope you don't mind."

I look at him briefly and then back to my new kitten. He bought me a fucking kitten. My heart is in awe. "Named her what?" I can't stop smiling.

"Tinker Bell but I call her Tink. She's *beautiful*. Don't ya think?" He can't stop smiling either. His eyes twinkle like he is complimenting me, not the kitten.

I'm speechless. He named her Tink, after his childhood nickname for me. It's perfect. He's perfect. "I love it, Josh. Thank you." I look at the little takeout lime green box. "And what's that?"

He smiles a nervous smile and opens it for me. "It's a brownie," he says simply. It's a brownie? He buys me a kitten and names her Tink after his nickname for me. He gives me a brownie, which forever reminds me of first kisses with him. WOW!

"A brownie, huh? I um…I love brownies." I smile shyly and bite my bottom lip from saying the rest. I love him.

I love you.

I don't even think about it when I throw my free arm around his neck and hug him, careful not to crush my Tink, and then I place a peck onto his lips. I stumble back and cover my mouth, "I'm sorry, I shouldn't have done that."

He laughs and goes to say something but is interrupted.

"No, you shouldn't have," Dean's voice filters into my ears from behind Josh. He is walking up my driveway from his house down the road. He looks dark and dangerous, swaggering in the dark, but it doesn't affect me like it used to.

"What are you doing here?" Josh asks him, his voice full of anger that I don't understand. "I thought you had plans," he continues. *Plans?*

Dean steps up to the stairs. He eyes the kitten like he wants to boil her in a pot. I snuggle her closer to me, then he turns cold eyes onto Josh. This whole altercation has thrown me. "Don't go there, Parker," he growls. *Go where?* What is going on?

I look at Dean with all the confusion in my face. "Why are you here, Dean?" Josh's eyes are daring Dean to say something, declare some reason he is here.

He looks at Josh then back to me. "You won't return my calls or my text, and you ignore me at school. It's Valentine's Day, and you're my girl. I needed to see you." He says it like it makes perfect sense. *It so doesn't.*

My mouth falls open before the sass I feel builds up. "I am not your girl anymore, Dean."

"But you should be. I think we should get back together, Riley. I love you." He loves me? Since when?

"You love her?" Josh shouts and then begins laughing. "You have got to be fucking kidding me, right?" he snarls at Dean.

"Fuck off, Parker. This isn't your business," Dean snaps at Josh.

"Hell it isn't. You don't get to shit all over her and then tell her you love her, and think everything is just gonna be peachy again," Josh says.

"Isn't that up to her. Pretty sure she can tell me what she wants. Right, baby?" He asks me in a sweet voice that is no longer sweet to me.

I am baffled. "Right." I take a deep breath. "I want you to leave, Dean. I'm not your baby, and I don't buy for a second that you love me. I smiled for the first time in a while just now, before you came up and took the smile from me. So...please, leave me alone. I just need some space, Dean," I explain.

He looks off put. "You smiled because of him?"

I nod.

His warmness turns to anger. "Ya know Riley? It seems like he makes you smile a lot, don't ya think?"

"He's my best friend, so yes," I answer.

He looks between Josh and me, then tilts his head to the side like a light bulb has just gone off, and he just realized something. "No, it's more than that. Are you fucking him?"

How many times is this boy going to shock me? I don't even get to reply before Josh has pummeled Dean to the ground.

"Stop, stop. Oh, my God! Just stop," I yell, trying to pull them apart and keep my little Tink safe. My brownie falls to the ground, making my sweet memory dirty.

They eventually listen to me and both stand wiping blood from their lips and nose. I'm shocked.

I look Dean right in the eye. We are at eye level with me standing on my porch. "I think you should leave, Dean. Now!"

"Fine by me," he shouts and leaves the way he came.

Josh pulls me into a hug as I begin to cry. I don't even know why I am crying. I just can't believe I spent two years with someone that would talk to me like that.

When I pull away from Josh, I find our faces are a breath apart. Our mouths almost touching, he rubs his thumb under my eyes. I just want to lean in and feel his tenderness on me. I don't.

"I'm sorry," I whisper.

He looks at me as though my pain is his own. "Don't ever be sorry for needing me, Riley. If it's a hug, if it's to talk, if you just need someone to hold your hand I am here, never be sorry. Okay?"

I nod. "Okay."

He looks down at my brownie that is mixed with dirt and grass now. He frowns and then smirks a little. "Sorry, 'bout that. Looks like I owe you another brownie."

I smile thinking about another brownie, which in my mind is another kiss from Josh. "Yeah...you do," I laugh.

Later that night, after going to Target to get kitty stuff for my new baby, I text Emily and told her all about tonight. She told me she was on a date. When I asked with who, she told me she didn't want to tell me just yet. I told her I wanted the details tomorrow, so we made plans to do a girls' thing.

I'm snuggling with Tink and listening to Josh sing, *In My Veins* by Andrew Belle through my bedroom window, acoustic with his guitar. I don't know if he knows I can hear him, but what I do know, is that Josh is most definitely in my veins, and I can't get him out. I don't want too.

I must have fallen asleep to his soothing voice. I woke with a chill from the window being cracked. Tink is so cutely snuggled up in my blankets. I smile and kiss her fur. I can't believe he bought me a kitten. I grab my phone to check the time and notice I have a text from him.

Josh: YOU LEFT YOUR NOTEBOOK IN LAST PERIOD WHEN YOU RAN OFF. I FOUND YOUR POEM, AND I DISAGREE. JUST THOUGHT YOU SHOULD KNOW.

Oh no! He had my notebook where I wrote the poem about his eyes. I didn't know how to explain that without explaining everything. What did he disagree about?

GOLDEN BROWN WITH FLECKS OF GREEN
PENETRATE THROUGH WHAT'S MOSTLY UNSEEN
TEASE ME, ENTICE ME
FORGET ME, HAUNT ME
SEEING WAY TOO MUCH, BUT NEVER ENOUGH
HIS HAZEL EYES, WHICH I LOVE
THOUGH BEAUTIFUL, ARE NOT PERFECT
THEY SEE EVERYTHING, BUT MY SECRET

 Josh

CHAPTER 9

I can't get the scent of Riley out of my mind—almond and coconut mixed with vanilla. She smelled delicious when she was hugging me earlier tonight. The fact that I put that smile on her face was the best ego boost. And when she kissed me like she had too, but then backtracked like she shouldn't have...well, it took everything to not push her against the door to her house and ravish her mouth further, make sure she understood I felt the same way. That the brownie I gave her was a reminder that one moment with her was never forgotten, never enough. Fucking Dean—ruining her moment of joy.

I had the sweetest dream I have ever had. Riley and I were sitting at the lake, the one with the playground that we used to play at when we were kids. She was wearing this lime green sundress and a pretty flower clipped in her hair as soft, curly tendrils delicately fell around her face. She was walking toward me slowly, her blue/green colored eyes were sparkling in the sunlight. When she stepped up to me, her smile took my breath away. I ran my index finger down her arm, and she shivered, and goosebumps immediately covering her skin. She stood on her tippy toes and reached her hands around my neck, tangling her fingers in my hair like the first time we kissed. When I finally tasted her lips, she moaned, and I just wanted more of her. She pulled away, stepped back and rubbed her fingers across her lips feeling where my lips had just been. She stepped back and crooked her finger to follow her. I do "C'mon, Josh. I need you. Now!" she said over her shoulder in a sultry voice. I follow her. I can't wait to get wherever it is she wants me to be. Then I wake up. Damn sweet dream was over before we even got there.

I take a long, cold shower that morning. Holy shit. It was so real. I wanted it to be real.

When I go to my room, I find a text from Riley waiting for me on my phone. I can't stop smiling.

Riley: I LOVE MY NEW BED BUDDY. SHE IS SOOOO SWEET. TY AGAIN

I read her text a few times and smile. I decide to open the notebook she left behind in class, the one with the poem she wrote about my eyes. I rip it out for safekeeping. She thinks I could ever forget her. She thinks I don't see her secret. I know she has feelings for me. She just refuses to act on them. I take out my pen and leave her a message of my own. My plan is to give it back to her and let her find it all on her own. Sit and wait.

I send Riley a quick text.

Me: YW I'M GLAD YOU LOVE HER BUT...I'M JEALOUS

Take the bait. Take the bait.

Riley: WHY IS THAT?

She took the bait.

Me: BC SHE SHARED YOUR BED WITH YOU

A few minutes go by with no response, and I fear I crossed the line but then my phone pings.

Riley: *BLUSH

There it is. She is thinking about it.

Josh: MY FAV SHADE ;)

Riley: I KNOW ;)

I head outside to get some air. I need to come up with a plan to move things forward with Riley besides flirting. Now that she is free there is nothing holding me back.

CHAPTER 10

There is nothing worse than your heart and your mind fighting against each other. Mine were in constant battle lately. My heart wanted Josh. I knew I could have him. He was making it clear that he had feelings for me, but my mind believed he wasn't available for the taking. I never wanted to be the other girl.

Every memory, every reason why I loved him, why I still love him, every moment that I let pass me by was haunting my thoughts. All the times that I could have made a different decision and been with Josh, not with Dean.

I just knew the little broken pieces that were already a part of me would become shattered and unfixable if I opened up and lost his friendship. And here I was, never having done so and broken into slivered pieces anyway.

When I wake up this morning to sweet purring next to my pillow, I feel a complete sense of joy, a joy that Josh gave me. I send him a text, and the series of text that follow only make my mind more confused, yet intrigued.

He keeps throwing these hints out there, leaving little suggestions in my head.

I head to the kitchen finding a note on the fridge telling me my mom and Tatum went to town for groceries. I sit on the couch twiddling my thumbs, petting Tink and flipping through the channels, aimlessly searching for something and nothing. All of my thoughts go back to my Josh situation. Being in love was the pits.

My mom walks through the front door with groceries overflowing her hands, Tatum as well, "Is there more?" I ask.

"In the trunk." My mom nods to the door.

"I'll get the rest," I tell her.

I am still in my PJ's, turquoise plaid shorts, a black cami without a bra and bare feet. I leave Tink sitting on the couch, head down the steps of our front porch, and to the concrete driveway to grab the bags left in the trunk. My mom has an issue with parking in the garage, something about my dad's tools and where his truck used to be. I get it.

There is just one bag left, a bag full of canned goods. I grab it and shut the trunk.

I am walking back toward the steps when I see Josh sitting on the front steps of his porch. He doesn't see me, his head buried in his phone. Distracted seeing him there without a shirt, I lose my footing and stub my big toe on the concrete.

"FUCK!" I yell. Oh damn, it hurts like a mother. Ouch, Ouch, Ouch!

"Nice mouth." Josh says, locking eyes with me.

I am hopping around like an idiot holding my toe. Not thinking, I drop the bag of canned goods in my other hand and—with all the amazing luck in the world—it falls on my uninjured foot.

"Shit, shit, shit," I mutter bending over humiliated and in pain.

"Problems, princess?" he laughs at my clumsiness.

I can hear the rustle of the grass as Josh walks over to where I am hunched over in pain. I see his bare feet first. Sexy. My eyes leisurely move up his body as I slowly begin to stand straight. Ah hell! He has on running shorts low on his hips, no shirt. All I see is his chiseled chest, sweetly sculpted with perfection, the guitar tattoo across his arm wrapped in roses and thorns, his large biceps are begging for my hands to hold them, to strum those guitar strings. My breath catches and my eyes trail back down where his shorts are hanging low on his hips, and I see that "V" that leads to his— Oh my!

"Enjoying the view, pretty girl? I know I am," Josh says, breaking me from my trance of sightseeing.

My eyes snap to his, my back straightens. "Huh? What?" I breathe and find his eyes on my chest where my headlights are on display. Typical.

He blinks dazedly a few times then he laughs, and kneels down before me. "Let me see?" he says gently tapping on my ankle for me to lift.

It hurts like a bitch. He is kneeling down on one knee, and I inwardly gasp at the image of him like this before me. It makes my heart flutter and dance a little. I lift my hurt foot although I am not sure which toe is hurting the worst at the moment. Suddenly, I'm feeling numb and a little tingly. His eyes meet mine briefly before he becomes Dr. Parker and analyzes my embarrassment.

"It's bleeding a little. What got you so frazzled, Riley?" He looks up at me knowingly with those beautiful pools of honey and emerald. The sun is dancing in them, making them glitter and possess me. My heart begins to race and skip.

"I, uh, I don't know. I just lost my balance." I stutter and lie through my teeth.

He picks up the grocery bag and starts to carry it inside for me. "Let me help you out with that," he tells me and taps my nose.

Josh and I make our way to the kitchen where my mom is unloading the groceries with Tatum.

"Well, hello, Joshua." She greets him with a curious smile.

"Hi, Mrs. Shaw. How are you?" He asks placing the canned goods into the pantry, ever the helper.

"I'm good, honey. What brings you by this lovely morning?" She asks him, but her eyes are on me encouragingly.

"Well, actually...I was just sitting outside getting some air, when your daughter here forgot how to her feet." He chuckles at my clumsiness. My mom and Tatum both look confused.

"I stubbed my toe," I say. "It's all good."

"And then the can of green beans attacked her other foot. Can you believe that?" He smirks.

I shove at him and begin helping my mom put the groceries away. "Would you shut up?" I tell him in my most 'I mean business' voice, but I know my face is telling him I'm playing. "You are soooo funny, Josh."

Tatum giggles. "Sounds sarcastic, Josh."

He just grins at me, and I grin at him. Playful Josh is my favorite Josh of all.

My mom shoo's us away with a flick of her wrist and a knowing grin. "I got this. You kids run along," she says smiling a contented smile.

"Can I go next door?" Tatum asks my mom, followed by an always 'yes.'

"I swear if I let her, she would move next door," my mom tells us before we walk away.

Josh laughs. "Well, if that is the case then I am moving in with y'all. No way could I survive two fourteen-year-old females. That is just too much estrogen and drama." Images of Josh and me sharing a room pop into my mind, and I fidget where I stand.

Josh went to my bedroom while I grabbed a Band-Aid from the bathroom cabinet. When I step back into my room, I find him standing by my dresser, reading the poem I had written on my mirror with a sharpie.

THE AIR I BREATHE IS FILLED WITH HIS SCENT
THE MUSIC SPEAKS EVERYTHING I MEANT
MEANT TO SAY, BUT NEVER DID TELL YOU
YOU HAUNT ME WHERE I LIE ALONE WITHOUT YOU
FEELING YOUR TOUCH AS IT VANISHES AWAY
MY OWN HEART IS THE ONE I BETRAYED

I just watch him for a moment. His tanned skin glistens from the sun filtering through my window. His lean muscles are gorgeous. He has his hand lifted and is tracing the lines along a heart I drew last night.

It is two broken halves. One is black, and the other is red. It felt like my own heart, broken with half of it dead and unwilling to love, the other half alive and wanting to grab onto it forever.

"You really do write lovely words," he says lifting his gaze to mine. "They are sad words, a little misguided but beautiful all the same," he continues.

"Thank you." I climb onto my bed noticing my notebook sitting there—the notebook—with my poem.

"When did this get here?" I ask him.

"I handed it back to Tatum this morning before they left. She must have brought it inside." He explains, and I nod.

He starts looking around my room. "Where is Tink?" He asks.

I jump up. "Oh crap! I left her on the couch when I was getting the groceries."

He goes to the door. "I'll go get her. Be right back," he says.

I smile and then my eyes are tracked to my notebook. I flip it open to my poem except the page is missing—ripped out. He must have kept it. I flip through the pages, and sure enough, it's gone, but then I notice something. He left me his own message, his own poem on one of the dividers of my five-subject notebook.

HER SMILE BRIGHTENS MY DAY LIKE SUNSHINE
ONE DAY I HOPE TO CALL HER MINE
I GET LOST ON THE BEACH IN HER EYES
SHE IS BEAUTIFUL AND NEVER EVEN TRIES
I SEE WHAT SHE KEEPS HIDDEN BENEATH
JUST A MOMENT IS ALL THAT WE NEED
A SONG TO EXPLAIN ALL SHE MEANS TO ME

Oh, my God! I'm out of breath—out of words. I don't know what to say. I don't want him to know I saw it—not yet.

Quickly, while I think he isn't looking, I close it and place it under my pillow. When I look up, he is leaning against my doorway with my new baby in his hand. His eyes are cast down to my hand on my pillow. I clear my throat, and his eyes snap to mine. Did he see that I read it? I hope not.

He really is distracting standing there without a shirt on. My mouth is suddenly dry, and my hands itch to glide along his skin. His abs are ridiculous for a guy so young, but with sports and drills, he works hard, and it shows. He kicks the door closed and walks to place Tink on my bed, she immediately crawls to me rubbing her body against my leg. I pet her and place her on my pillow, where she kneads away and curls into a ball.

Josh hasn't said anything since he walked back into my room. He moves across from me and is standing in front of my dresser, his hands gripping the edge and his feet are crossed at the ankle. He looks edible, and I don't hide the fact that I am visually tracing over his frame. His face is serious and unreadable, not a smirk, not a grin, just—watching me.

I turn my eyes away from him, and lean toward my window remembering all the memories we shared together.

Like the time I saw him napping with his window open, and decided it would be hilarious to shoot my water gun straight through it and soak him. It was seriously funny. Or during the winter, when it was too cold outside, how we would write messages to each other on our dry erase boards. That is before we had our phones to text.

"Where did you go just now?" he asks me softly, breaking me free from my trip down memory lane.

I swallow and realized that, without thinking, I had trailed a heart with my index finger along the dust and dew on my window and wrote, 'I love you.' I wiped my hand across the words erasing them before he could see. "Just thinking," I whisper.

"About? You were smiling, must have been a nice thought." His voice takes on a low tone that makes me want to look at him.

I turn to see his eyes on the glass window, where my hand just was. "Yeah, it was," I say looking at him. "A lot has happened between these two pieces of glass. I was just thinking about some of my favorite memories," I say without thinking. I shouldn't have said that, now he knows I think about him. *Shit.*

His eyes lock with mine, his mouth curls up. "Oh yeah?"

"Yeah, what are some of your favorite memories—and not in general of us—but involving these windows?" I ask him.

He runs his index finger along his bottom lip. "Do the ones where I watched you undress count?" he says watching my reaction closely.

My mouth falls open. "No, you didn't?" I ask. "Right? You didn't, right?" I stutter.

He giggles. "Hmmm sorry, but I'm guilty. I mean...if you leave the curtains open and you know my bedroom window is right there, I figured it was an invitation," he says, pointing at the window with a cute smirk on his face.

I feel my face heat, just the thought of Josh watching me should creep me out but it doesn't. It kind of makes me feel warm.

"Urm...well, now that we know you're a pervert, please continue. Favorite memories?" I goad him.

"Well, there are two. One with just you and the other with you and me," he says. "First one was when you were like thirteen I guess, anyway, you had a hair brush in your hand and your hair was in a ponytail. You were dancing around in your room and singing into the brush dramatically. I just remember thinking you looked so happy and carefree. Some pieces of your hair had fallen out of your ponytail and into your face. I had this strange impulse to want to touch it and place it behind your ear. M'hm, I realize I sound like a stalker-peeping-Tom, huh?"

I just look at him. At thirteen? He wanted to touch my hair, he watched me even then? I didn't find it stalkerish. I thought it was sweet. I shake my head back and forth feeling my eyes get a little glassy.

I swallow down the lump in my throat. "Okay. So, next one?"

He continues, "The second memory was last year, actually. It was pouring down rain outside. I had my window open because I love the sound of the rain. It's soothing. I watched from the window as Dean pulled up into your driveway and dropped you off. I remember thinking he was a douche because he didn't even get out to try and cradle you from the rain. Nope, he just dropped you off, even pulled away before seeing that you were inside. It was a shitty thing to do. I mean...there could have been a creeper watching you."

"Like you?" I joke. I can't stop the smile that has permanently graced my face.

He laughs. "Yeah, like me. Well, I heard you curse, and I realized you were locked out of your house. Your mom wasn't home, and Tatum was at my house. I went outside, and by the time I got there, you were already by your bedroom window trying to pull the screen off. You cursed again because you couldn't get it to come off, and you must have hurt your finger because you sucked on it. I just remember you looked so fucking sexy standing in the rain like that—dripping wet and angry—and your finger in your mouth. The way your t-shirt was clinging to your body was well—distracting. I offered to help you, and you jumped out of your skin because you didn't know I was out there. I popped the screen for you, and lo and behold that window of yours was unlocked. You thanked me and went to climb in but you—,"

"Slipped…fell right into your arms," I finish his memory. I remember it.

He nods and runs his hand through his hair. My fingers twitched to do the same.

I tell him, "I remember that night, too." I feel my breathing become shallow.

He moves forward to come sit next to me on my bed, his eyes mirroring my own. His voice is low and husky, "I just remember how much I wanted to taste the raindrops falling down your neck. I wanted to kiss you so damn bad that when I went to bed that night, I replayed it over and over in my head until I felt dizzy," he confesses. I don't miss the flick of his eyes to my mouth.

Ah hell.

"Josh," I breathe.

He brushes his knuckle along my cheek, and I shut my eyes loving the way it feels. He moves his hand to my mouth where he pads his thumb along my bottom lip, and cups my chin. I slowly open my eyes finding his smoldering with want for me. I can't take it. I need to kiss him.

Without a second thought, I move to where I am straddling his lap. I grab his face and his eyes study mine. I'm seeking permission and fighting with myself for doing this. He has a girlfriend. God, I know I'm making a mistake, but I can't stop it. Everything in my body is buzzing and telling me to kiss him. It's a need now, not just a want.

"I wanted to kiss you, too," I admit breathy and prepared to do just that.

His eyes dilate right in front of me, and he swallows hard. One of his arms snake around my waist, pulling me closer to him, while his other reaches around the nape of my neck to pull my mouth to his. "Kiss me now," he demands in a hushed whisper.

I do. God, I kiss him like my life depends on it. And in this moment, I believe it to be true. He ignites something in me that I don't understand. A feeling I can't control—it scares me to death yet makes me want more.

Somewhere in that kiss, my conscious wakes up and I pull away, stopping this mistake. "Oh, God. Stop! Crap, I'm so sorry. I don't know why I keep doing that. I um, I—," I falter.

I climb off of him and stumble backwards touching my lips, my words trailing off into the rest of the unspoken thoughts.

He looks confused, unsure. I feel the same.

"It's okay, Riley. I'm not complaining," he tells me, watching me cautiously under hooded eyes.

"You should, though. You have a girlfriend, and I'm just...your best friend," I say feeling my throat tighten.

"Friend," he mouths with distaste and shakes his head.

I place my hands over my face humiliated. He stands and removes my hands. "You're wrong, Riley. I *don't* have a girlfriend. I wish you could see that," he says.

I don't reply. I just stare at him, unsure. "But...Preslee?"

Suddenly he looks angry, and it throws me off guard. "I don't get you, Riley. Why does this bother you so much? Preslee and me? Which there is no me and her, by the way," he says. "I keep telling you she isn't anything to me," he adds.

"It doesn't bother me," I respond quickly with a lie.

"The hell it doesn't. You have been fucking bothered by it since day one. Why is that?" He practically shouts at me.

I stare open mouthed unable to speak.

He cups my cheek softly and raises his eyebrows expectedly. "Answer the question, Riley. Why is that?" He asks again more demanding this time, but softer.

I swallow and meet his eyes. "Because she is taking you from me." I tell him honestly.

His eyes are studying mine. "Taking me away how, Riley? I'm not yours." His voice is low now. "Unless you want me to be," he adds. "Is that it? Do you want me to be yours, Riley?"

Shut up. Please, shut up!

I stare at him, swallowing down the lump in my throat a thousand times. My body is shaking. "I'm scared."

"Scared of what, Riley?" He asks leaning his mouth down to my neck, molding his chest to mine. I know he can feel me trembling. He has to be aware of the affect he has on me.

"Of you, of what I feel for you," I say on a whimper. I can't breathe. God, he is kissing my neck, and I can't think straight.

"How does this feel? Does this scare you?" He whispers in my ear before nibbling it.

I whimper, "Yes. Shit, it feels...God, it feels..." I don't finish the statement. I grab his face and begin kissing him again. What the hell is wrong with me?

He lifts me up, and my legs wrap around his waist on their own accord. My hands are tangled into his hair, and he turns us around, walking back to my bed where he lays us back down. His body is pressed to mine in all the right places. His bare chest feels like heaven, and the way his mouth moves with mine—oh dear God. It's impossible to fight this. I'm so screwed. I want to be screwed. Fuck.

We are completely out of breath, when he pulls back looking down at my face, the seriousness etched in every feature when he speaks softly the words I have longed and feared to hear forever. "Riley, I don't want to be your best friend anymore." I have literally been kissed senseless.

His forehead is crinkled in concentration. I rub my finger along the line to smooth it. "You don't?" I ask.

He shakes his head back and forth. "No, I want to be more. I want to be with you."

I stare at him looking for the insincerity, but I don't see it. All I see is truth, and in this moment, I trust my gut. My gut tells me Josh is safe. Josh is the one I love. Josh is the one I am meant to be with. I have wanted to hear those words for years. So for the first time, I embrace them instead of running from them.

"Okay," I whisper.

"Okay?" He says, suddenly excited.

"Yes, I want to be with you too, Josh," I tell him and then he is on me again. His hand tickles up my ribcage and cups my breast gently as I moan. I have this burning sensation I'm not used to. We are a tangled web of desire.

He doesn't push any further though, and when he pulls back again I see the question there in his eye. To stop? To keep going? But sensing I am probably not ready to keep going, he slows...and in this moment, my heart becomes completely his. I just hope he protects it, cherishes it, because I can't take it back. It's all his now. I am his.

I have decided that his mouth is my new favorite taste in the world. I could kiss him forever. It's addicting, and I am goner.

CHAPTER 11

I can still taste her, feel her body trembling in my arms. I wanted to do more, to push her for more, but I had to wait. I needed this to be perfect, not rushed. I wanted to take my time with her, get there the right way.

"Hey, Josh. I need to go into work. I was supposed to take Joey and Tatum out today, though. Do you mind trading duties and being their escort?" my dad asks me as I walk back into the house with the biggest grin on my face.

"Sure, can I just drop them off somewhere and pick them up later?" I ask.

"Yeah, whatever. I put some money on the counter. Just keep me updated, and all's good boy." He pats my shoulder and leaves.

I haven't really come down from my 'Riley high', and I don't really want to. I'm thinking I have two options here: First option is to toss the brats off somewhere. Head home to my empty house where I can convince Riley to skip over all the—let's take this slow stuff and jump right into—I have been waiting years to get lost in you stage. The second option is to take her on a date so to speak, talk about what's really going on, and put the ball in her court.

Okay, so obviously…I want option one, but I know Riley. So, option two is the way to go. I send her a text.

Me: I'M ON BRAT DUTY TODAY. PROMISED EM I'D DRIVE SOMEWHERE. WANNA KEEP ME COMPANY?

Riley: SURE :) TIME?

Me: NOON - WE CAN DO LUNCH

Riley: K

Me: STILL THINKING OF YOU

Riley: :) ALWAYS

Jesus. *Always.* She has no idea.

CHAPTER 12

With new beginnings comes a whole new set of fear and doubts. I wish I were normal. I wish I wasn't so scared to let him love me. Today, I'm going to try because I can't stop loving him.

When Tatum and I get outside, Josh is leaning against his brand new-shiny-Toyota Tundra, an early graduation gift from his dad. It has a full cab, completely loaded, and I am in love with it. I also hate it because it is a reminder that Josh could leave me soon. That is, if he accepts his scholarship. I could very well lose my best friend and there is nothing I can do to change it.

That is my biggest fear by starting something with him. He has the power to ruin me. Giving him my heart is a huge risk. He could take it and stay with me forever, or he could use it for a little while, and then move onto the next. I'm trying not to let my mind jump to the worst possible scenario and just let the happiness be—for once I'm taking my mom's advice.

Taking in his appearance makes my stomach do funny flip-flops. He is a beautiful creature, an Adonis in his almost manhood. His head is down, his dirty blond hair falling into his face, a mess of layers. He is playing on his phone, not noticing us standing in our yard. He is wearing low riding, faded jeans, black boots crossed at the ankle, and a black t-shirt exposing his gorgeous tanned arms. The tattoo that wraps around his muscled bicep peeks through. This boy oozes sexy—even standing just like that.

Tatum tugged on my arm giggling at me, "I thought you said let's go," she says and shakes her head at me knowingly.

"Oh yeah, sorry. I just was—,"

"Ogling our neighbor," she finished my sentence and took off across the yard laughing.

Josh looks up as he hears her, his hazel eyes twinkling in the sunlight. "Hey, Tator Tot. Joey's inside. Go get her, and tell her I said to hurry it up. Will ya?" he directs my sister.

She gives him a look, crosses her arms at him, halting short of the front steps. "Seriously, Joshua. You're going to have to stop calling me, Tator Tot. I'm not a kid anymore if you haven't noticed," and she does a little twirl in her sundress.

It's February in Texas. We have very indecisive weather here. One day it's chilly and the next day it feels like Spring Break. Today it's Spring Break—beautifully warm.

He clears his throat to keep from laughing and grins at her. God, his grin is adorable. He has this one dimple on his cheek, and I just love it. "Whatever you say, Tator Tot. Go get Jo so we can go. Please?" He waves her off, and she sticks her tongue out at him before heading into his front door. I laugh from a few feet away. Real mature.

His eyes suddenly lock with mine, and everything inside of me does a somersault, my heart skips a beat inside my chest. His smile melts away all of my doubts and insecurities and leaves in its place this warm and fuzzy feeling. Everything about him makes me feel better.

Throwing caution to the wind, I run and jump on Josh, wrapping my legs around his waist and kiss his cheek.

"Someone is happy to see me. Miss me so soon?" He says laughing, "Not that I am complaining or anything. I kind of enjoy your legs around me like this," he pinches my side making me squeal.

"You're such a guy, Josh. And yes, I missed you." I say ruffling his hair, pushing off his chest and placing my feet back on the ground. "I was going to just hug you, but then I decided to—,"

"Throw yourself at me instead?" he laughs.

I laugh too, "Yeah, um...sorry about that."

Josh opens my door, ever the gentleman, and places me into the seat. It is sweet, and it makes me smile. Before he shut the door, he kisses the top of my head. He always does that. "Stop apologizing. Okay?" I nod. "And you are more than welcome to throw yourself at me anytime," he adds making me blush.

I lean into him and kiss his cheek. I keep doing that lately, even before things shifted. I wonder if he has noticed.

He stares at me searching my eyes and opens his mouth to say something, but doesn't. Instead, he pats my leg and shuts the door.

Josh climbs in, and not two seconds later, our sisters are climbing in the backseat with Joey already the back seat driver.

"Hey, Josh. Will you drop Tate and me off at the mall? Please, *please, please.*" she whines with puppy dog eyes at her big brother over the center console.

"Yeah, just stop whining." He looks over at me, "Where are we going, Riley? Please, tell me not the mall?" he asks with a pleading look that makes me laugh.

"Um, yeah, not the mall. I hate shopping, besides I'm hungry, and food court food is yuck." I tell him honestly, earning me 'boo's' from the back seat from our two sisters.

"What girl hates shopping, Riley? You're so weird." Tatum interjects.

"This girl." I point to myself, as Josh pulls out the driveway with a smile. I begin flipping through the radio stations, settling on the one I know will annoy Josh the most just for a laugh. He hates rap music, or anything he deems ridiculous music that makes no sense.

I blare Major Lazor, *Bubble Butt.* The girls and I start dancing and singing like fools. Josh watches me amused with a raised brow.

"Ok. Seriously, this song is so ridiculous," he groans and flips through his iPod to one of my favorite songs. He winks at me as the song filters through the speakers. Our sisters complain briefly before taking a snapshot of themselves together with duck faces. I'm sure to post on Instagram.

"Yep, you are right, but it's fun to dance too." I say and wiggle my hips a little. "But I soooo *love* this song." I start humming along with Kenny Chesney.

Josh starts singing the lyrics to, *Somewhere with you.* I am majorly swooning when he sings the chorus as if he is singing it directly to me.

I watch him sing, the deepness in his voice stirring something I have hidden deep inside. He steals glances at me as he sings the words, serenading me into submission. Something in his eyes makes me squirm uncomfortably, yet deliciously, as well.

I shut my eyes and let his voice, his words—envelope me. I pictured us on a deserted island, just him and me. His guitar is in his hand, and my toes in the sand as I listen to him serenade me, before he just can't stand it anymore, and he tosses the guitar aside and touches me in ways no one ever has. Just us, two mouths and one love...like my favorite song sings about. My moment of bliss in my mind is interrupted. I shift in my seat feeling something stir deep down.

Joey leans over the seat, "OMG, Riley. Did Tatum tell you that she punched Wesley in the face? He called her a bitch, and this chick here...punched him. Funniest shit I had seen all day."

"Watch your mouth, Jo!" Josh says with his mouth in a hard line.

"Whatev. I mean...yes sir, Daddy." Joey rolls her eyes and laughs at her brother.

Joey sits back, and I lean over my seat to look back at Tatum. She was giving Joey a 'WTF' look.

"Actually, no she hadn't said anything," I say annoyed and giving my own 'WTF' look at my sister.

"Wait, wasn't that the boy I saw you at the movie with a few weekends ago when I was with—?" he stops midsentence and looks at me nervously.

"With? Forget her name, Josh?" Joey chimes in sarcastically making me cringe.

"I remember her name. I just—," he clears his throat. "Sooo, what's the story with you, Tatum?" he conveniently changes the subject, glancing at me sideways, and then back at Tatum through the rear view mirror.

I sigh, relaxing back into my seat and looking out the window. I hated hearing about Josh with other girls. And that comment just reminded me that Josh had been going out with Preslee. I didn't know what to think of it.

He squeezes my knee gaining my attention. I mouth *‘Preslee?’* And he nods, yes. I sigh a second time.

Isn't that craptastic? I hate Preslee. At least, he is honest. I plaster my fake smile on.

"Yeah, that's him. He tried to kiss me, and I pushed his face away. When he grabbed my butt in the parking lot, I kicked him in the balls. I mean...why are boys going suddenly crazy lately?"

Joey laughs and claps her hands, "greatness" she says.

Josh and I share a look, knowing exactly why boys are suddenly going crazy. It is called puberty, and all them little boys are suddenly complete perverts.

Joey leans over the console again, "anyway...Wesley told some of his friends that Tatum French kissed him, and now they all want to hang out with her. As if."

Joey leans back in her seat again, and Tatum squeals an obscenity at her friend.

"What?" Josh and I say in unison looking at each other with wide eyes.

I notice Josh is gripping the steering wheel so tight his knuckles turn white. He cares about my little sister like she was his own.

"It's all good. I handled it. I told those said friends that he is a liar and that if his breath didn't smell like dog crap then maybe someone might kiss him, but it certainly would not be me." Tatum says dryly but with amusement in her voice.

"We nicknamed him smelly Wesley. He almost cried. It was so funny. But then he got mad and called her a bitch, and she punched him in the nose. Like I said, it was greatness." Joey says laughing hysterically.

I was shocked. My little sister handled her own with her first bad boy experience, although I was a little disappointed she hadn't come to me with this.

Joey and Tatum were only allowed to go on group dates so far. I worried a lot about Tatum. She was a lot of talk but little bite. She had a hard exterior and tried to act like shit didn't get to her, but I knew better. However, she had just proven to be stronger than I had given her credit for.

Joey says sardonically rubbing her palms together, "Earned her D-hall though," she adds as an afterthought.

"Totes worth it," Tatum says before changing the subject to something else.

 *Josh*

CHAPTER 13

I saw it flicker in her eyes. The doubt that I was telling her the truth about not being with Preslee. I know she wants to believe me, but between cheating dads and an asshole ex-boyfriend, she is on the fence. Two steps forward—one step back.

We drop 'the brats' off at the mall around noon, leaving Riley and me alone.

"Wanna grab lunch?" I ask.

"Yes, but are you going to keep trying to feed me sushi?" she questions back.

I've tried and failed many times before to get her to try it.

She always said, just thinking about it makes her feel queasy, "Raw fish—blech..." she mutters.

I laugh and grab her hand across the seat, "Yes. Don't you trust me?" I grin.

Her eyes twinkle with amusement. I love her eyes. They are so beautiful. I also love how she is in a good mood, which is actually unexpected to be honest. I figured I would have to try a little harder after that little comment from Joey. What the hell was she thinking saying that? She knows Riley's issues.

"I trust you with my life. I guess if I die from food poisoning then that will be my mistake, huh?" She tells me grinning back. I don't miss the dynamics of that statement.

"It's not all raw fish. You would love the ones with crab. Just try it. If you don't like it, I will take you to get anything you want, after I eat of course."

"Um...K,"

Preferably you in my bed and—Crap! Thinking with the wrong head again, Josh.

I laugh nervously and start tickling my fingers up her bare leg. "I promise you will enjoy it," I wiggle my eyebrows teasingly, but I am totally serious. I am also aware that I am no longer talking about sushi, whether she catches that or not she doesn't say. I can't seem to stop it, and the look in her eyes tells me she likes it. So I quit trying to.

She playfully swats my hand away, and I notice her rubbing her legs, which are now covered in goose bumps. I am affecting her. Perfect.

She clears her throat. "Let's make it fun, Josh. Since you *want me* to try new things, how bout I make you a deal?" She gives a mischievous look.

Holy shit. The way she said, 'want me.' Damn. Anything with wanting her and fun together, I will agree...where do I sign?

"I'm curious. What do you have in mind?" I say as I slide into the parking spot at the sushi buffet around the corner, and shift into park giving her my full attention.

She blushes, now I can't wait to hear her idea of fun. "I urm...I...will try the sushi, but you have to let me drive your truck on the way back to pick up the brats."

Okay? Not what I expected. Something tells me she just made that up on the fly. That is not what she was going to say.

I open my mouth to call her on it, but then think better of it. So, I shut my mouth and begin mulling it over. This is actually tough. This truck is my baby. No one drives it but my dad or me.

"I...uh, I think..." I pause for a minute, eyeing her over as I strum my fingers along the steering wheel. How to make this a win for me too? I've got it. I pull my bottom lip into my mouth. Ah hell she flicks her eyes to my lips. This is so fucking hard. I just want to throw her on top of the hood of this truck and drive into her. That's what I want.

I shift in my seat—again. "Yeah, ok...BUT, I have my own stipulation."

"Uh, okay. Why are you smirking at me?" she asks sounding annoyed, I hadn't even noticed I was smirking.

I shrug, "You eat the sushi, and I let you drive, but then you have to watch a horror film with me Friday night—scarier the better, and the whole thing, Riley."

Her mouth falls open, as I knew it would. "But, Josh? I hate scary movies. You know that." she whines in protest and pouts. It's fucking adorable. Last time I made her watch a scary movie she freaked out, put all the lights on in the house, and constantly told me her house was haunted. I laughed at her then, this time I plan on haunting her myself. I made a bet with her that she wouldn't make it to the end, and she didn't. She lost the bet, and black ink was the consequence.

I laugh again at her reaction, enjoying her fear. Riley, trembling. In my arms. In the dark. Perfect. "Yeah, but you will have me with you. It will be fun, and the next movie can be your choice." I bribe her.

"Oh, yeah? My choice huh? Like a hot vampire movie? Oh, or a romantic comedy? Or a—,"

"Point taken, Shaw. Deal or no deal?" I hold out my hand for her to shake.

"Deal." I shake her hand, and she softly gasps like it burned her. I raise my brow in question as I release her hand and open the door. I swear it felt like she shocked me too. "Don't move!"

I walk around and open her door for her. When she hops out, I make sure I stay in her space to where her body has to slide down mine, and then I kiss her nose when she inhales deeply.

I interlace our fingers as we walk into the sushi buffet. These moments with her are my favorite, and also are my undoing.

CHAPTER 14

Doubt- to be uncertain about; consider questionable or unlikely; hesitate to believe; to distrust; to fear; to be apprehensive about etc. OR as I call it...the bitch that fills my brain with demonic voices that make me crazy.

The sushi place is small. It has a buffet of different kinds of sushi. Josh was right the ones with crab are delicious. We couldn't stop laughing at each other trying to work the chopsticks.

"How do I put it in my mouth?" I ask trying and failing to pick up one of the bigger California rolls with my chopsticks.

Josh sputters his Dr. Pepper and says, "Um, you just put it in."

"It's so big though. I don't think it will fit." I continue eyeing the roll in between the two sticks. I was unaware of where Josh's dirty mind was when I was running my mouth.

"Yeah, it's big. Just put it in slowly, and then moan your pleasure from how good it taste." His voice took on a purr that got my attention.

I pick my head up and notice him staring at my mouth. He drags that damn bottom lip along his teeth and makes a seething sound. That was hot. And suddenly, I realize just how suggestive all I just said was. I felt embarrassed yet shy.

However, I decided to play along with his little dirty game. I put the sushi roll in my mouth, surprisingly working the chopsticks well enough. I chew slowly with my eyes closed and moan softly in appreciation of the delicious taste on my tongue. It really was mouthwatering. When I am done, I lick my bottom lip. He curses, and I laugh.

"Oh, my God, Josh. Does your dick always go to the dirtiest of places? Even food gets you riled up? Guys are so weird." I scold him rolling my eyes.

"Sorry, and not weird. I couldn't help it. That was hot. You are hot." He says staring into my eyes, popping his own sushi roll in his mouth, flipping roles on me as I now watch in awe.

In my mind, I'm picturing Josh on the buffet table not sushi. Yeah, I want to taste that.

My mouth is dry, so I sip my tea, "Whatever. I was talking about the sushi roll, you pig." I laugh at him thinking I'm just as bad.

"Damn lucky piece of sushi," he winks.

I just laugh at him. I love playful Josh. The waitress brings us our fortune cookies a little later, and Josh grins at me full of mischief as he opens his fortune and reads it.

"What are you grinning at over there?" I am thinking I probably don't want to hear his answer. His mind is stuck in the gutter today as well as mine.

He laughs a throaty laugh and tilts his head adorably as he tents his hands under his chin. "Do you know what you're supposed to say after you read your fortune, right? Ya know, to make it dirty?" As I thought. *In the gutter.*

I raise a brow, "Um, no. What do you say to make your fortune dirty, Josh?"

He laughs again, "*In bed.* You read your fortune and say in bed. And then your fortune will come true, in bed that is." He sucks his bottom lip into his mouth and grins at my reaction.

I am blushing, and my mouth has dropped open. Wow! "Uh, um, yeah, I hadn't heard that actually." I point to his fortune, "soooo...what did yours say?"

He picks it up and threads it through his fingers. "Hmmm, yes, *mine.*" He drawled giving me a heated look. "Well, it says, 'your natural charm will attract someone special' *in bed,*" he winks at me, and I about melt in my chair. He points to my unopened cookie, "Open it, let's see if we're on to something," he smiles a megawatt smile at me.

On to something? What? I crack open my fortune and scan the words with my eyes before swallowing. Knowing that if I read this out loud he is definitely going to feast on this one. "Sooo..." he encourages me with a roll of his big hand to continue.

I raise my eyes slowly to his. He is curious. His thrumming on the table is matching that of my bouncing heartbeat. "Um, ok. Well, mine says, 'your wildest dreams will come true soon' my voice drops to a whisper *in bed.*"

He laughs and leans forward really close to my face. "I'm sorry? I didn't hear that. You were whispering. Say it again, please." He smirks and cups his ear, I sigh.

"You're cruel and twisted, Joshua Parker."

"And you're avoiding giving me your fortune, Riley Shaw. Repeat, please." He gestures toward my fortune with a nod of his head.

"Ugh, it says, 'your wildest dreams will come true soon' *in bed.*" I say my voice just above a whisper but louder than before. His face is full of triumph. *Bastard!*

"So, Ms. Shaw...what would those wildest dreams be, per say? I do hope they include me?" he asks with a wiggle of his brows.

And the feasting begins. I wag my finger at him "Oh no, Parker. I'm not sharing any fantasies of us with you." I declare and then realize my mistake. Shit. I walked right into that one.

His face melts into shock, and then a flicker of curiosity and mischief cross his eyes. "Fantasies, wildest dreams, me, you? Hmmm…Is there no chance my *natural charm* will attract you pretty girl? You are special to me, just a little taste…in bed." he bites his lip again.

I really wish he would quit doing that. I can't help that my eyes watch his teeth sink into that lip and that something quivers in my belly, or that I want to sink my own teeth into his lip. He knows I am looking at his mouth, and he seems happy about it. His words. Damn his words.

I mock exasperated and disinterest. I look away and start looking at my fingernails and fiddling with my hair. "Your natural charm attracts a lot of girls, Joshua. No fortune cookie needed to tell you that." I regret saying it as soon as I do. Why did I say that? Stupid, stupid girl.

He recoils slightly, "Whoa! Way to buzz kill it, Riley. I wasn't talking about other girls. The only girl that comes close to special for me—is you. You're my girl." He sets his mouth into a straight line. My playful Josh is gone.

Fuck!

I stare at him for a beat before speaking, a little unsure of how to back pedal. "I'm sorry, Josh, I didn't mean to insult you. You know you're special to me too. Right? You're my best friend, and I shouldn't have said that. It's just...well, I don't want to be just another girl to you. You change your mind often. I guess I'm just a little...cautious." I explain.

He frowns, "I'm more than your best friend, Riley. Remember? And you will never be just another girl to me. You.are.mine. My girl. I will never change my mind about that. Please, believe it." He says gripping my chin.

I want too. God, I want to believe it. I just don't know yet if I do.

"So, girlfriend. I think I owe you a ride." He rubs behind his neck nervously but holds out his hand for me to grab.

A ride? Seriously, is he proposing we just jump right into that? And then it hits me. Whoa, Riley. Slow the hormones chick. I'm about to drive Josh's baby, his pride and joy, his beast of a truck. "Oh, my God, Josh." I let out a squeal of excitement and bounce in my seat. "I'm soooo ready."

He grabs my hand and jerks me up to stand right in front of him a little roughly. I gasp at his sudden movement as it surprises me. Damn, he smells amazing. Like body wash and a scent that is just *him*. It's delectable. He towers over me, and I have to look up at him. His face is unreadable as he looks down at me.

He leans down to whisper in my ear, and my breath catches, "That's what she said...in bed," he breathes, and I shiver. He straightens and looks down at me, his face completely composed. He doesn't smile, he doesn't say anything further, he just turns and tugs at the hand he is holding for me to follow. I release the breath I wasn't even aware I was holding.

CHAPTER 15

Who knew sushi could be so fucking sexy?

I was having such a good time with Riley. I hated that she stopped herself from enjoying it. I understood where she was coming from though. I guess I have given off the impression that I have been with lots of girls and that I change my mind all the time.

I'm going to have to explain, to tell her the truth. I need to work it out, how to say it, what to admit.

When we get in the truck, I am nervous as hell that she is going to drive. I mean she is so tiny. My heart is beating all kinds of crazy. One, because of her in general and two, she is driving my fucking truck.

I'm distracted when I get a text from my buddy, Brandt. Letting me know he is throwing an impromptu engagement party tonight for Beau, his little brother, and he wanted me to come.

Beau used to be one of my really good friends until he graduated and went to college. We drifted a little, but he is still a good friend of mine. We used to all hang out together, he and Emily actually had a thing for a while last year but it fizzled.

And Brandt...well, he did my tattoo and Riley's for that matter. That was a sight in itself. She has it on her lower hip, in order to do that she had her jeans opened and low down there. She was trembling in fear, and I pictured her trembling from my touch, my mouth.

Anyway, Beau and Brandt are probably the coolest guys I know. Their parties are badass and typically equate to trouble, but it's been awhile and I'm sure Riley will want to go as that is usually where she prefers to hang anyway.

Where Collin's parties are open for random hook ups, shooting pool and watching ESPN on the big screen in the game room with all your high school friends, Brandt's are a whole other type of beast. Free alcohol, older crowd—college age, poker games that sometimes include loss of money or loss of clothes, and it usually ends with someone getting in a fight.

Riley is usually hanging out with Rebel and Emily, writing shit in notebooks for Rebel's band, all innocent and cute and oblivious to the crowd. Rebel is Beau's twin sister and used to be the girls third wheel, although I tend to think she may be hiding a dark secret from those two.

Rebel sings in a garage band to Riley's writing. It's all for fun. They don't even have a name, but truthfully I think they wish to be a bigger thing. Riley's words are dark and beautiful, she doesn't think so, but she sings those words hauntingly beautiful herself. She doesn't like to sing though. Something about her mom singing and a bunch of bullshit.

CHAPTER 16

Leather smells amazing. Leather mixed with Josh's scent and the power I feel about to drive this truck… OH MY! It's a heady concoction

I send a quick text to Emily after Josh takes my picture in the driver's seat.

Me: OMG DRIVING JOSH'S TRUCK :)

Emily: WTF? HE LET YOU? WHAT DID YOU HAVE TO DO FOR THAT TO HAPPEN?

Me: LOL I ATE SUSHI

Emily: HUH? THAT'S NOT INTERESTING. SUSHI? *YAWN! AT LEAST SAY YOU LET HIM GRAB YOUR BOOB

Me: YOU'RE RIDICULOUS

Emily: FIRST A KITTEN, NOW HE LETS YOU DRIVE HIS TRUCK? HMMM…

Me: YOU HAVE NO IDEA! TELL YOU L8TR GTG

I laugh at my stupid friend. "What's so funny?" Josh asks.

"Emily thinks she's funny, that's all." I put my phone back in my purse.

"How's that?" he ask, not looking up from his phone, typing a text, as well. To who I wonder?

"She just wanted to know what I had to do for you to let me drive your truck. Evidently, eating sushi was a boring story to her."

I have my cheek placed right to the vent, letting the cool air blow on my face. I feel hot all of the sudden.

"Oh yeah? And what would have been a better story?" he ask putting his phone away and turning his eyes to mine.

Even with my cheek in the cool air, I feel the heat warm my face from just the image of Josh's hands on my breast, remembering how good it felt from earlier. I laugh nervously, which causes him to raise his eyebrows.

I whisper, "Um, she said I should at least let you grab my boob." I chance a look at him and find his mouth gaped open.

He begins tapping his finger to his lip and puckers. I want to suck his lip into my mouth. "Hmm...Now why didn't I think of that?" he winks and my stomach coils deliciously. My pulse begins to race.

"Relax, Riley. I was just joking." He adds when I say nothing further. He knows me so well.

I watch him settle back in the passenger seat, looking sexy as hell. He is trying to act cool, but I can tell he is nervous by the way he keeps rubbing the back of his neck. It makes me smile that he trusts me to drive his precious piece of artillery.

"So, you and Preslee?" I ask unsure if I should even go there.

He swallows hard and his jaw twitches. He answers my question with a question, something he did often, "Me and Preslee, what?" I hated when he did that.

"You sure she isn't your girlfriend? She seems to think she is, and you don't typically take girls to the movies."

"I take you to the movies." he answers quickly, his eyes darting to mine.

This boy is frustrating, "I don't count, and you know that."

He reaches over and places his hand on my bare thigh right beneath my cut off jean shorts and squeezes gently. I stifle a moan and the secret tingly feelings that are becoming more apparent every time he touches me. "I know no such thing, you count to me."

I look down at his hand placed on my leg and then back up to his face finding him watching me carefully with a serious face.

"Okay,"...I say slowly. "So...you're being evasive, Joshua Parker. Why is that?"

He removes his hand and sighs, "I'm not being evasive. I've already told you she's not, and I'm not lying to you about that. She wants us to be together. I don't. End of story. So...you and Dean? Wanna tell me about that?" he asks looking completely pissed off now and completely switching roles on me. Yep, I regret asking it. Stupid doubts.

"Nothing to tell. We aren't together anymore. I'm sorry again. This is all just so confusing."

"Tell me about it," he speaks to the window.

I'm doomed to ruin this before it begins aren't I? *Riley, just let it be beautiful.*

I fasten my seatbelt and begin to adjust the mirrors and the seat height before I pull off. I don't meet his eyes again and put the truck in reverse.

"Careful Shaw, take it nice and slow." Josh's voice takes on a low husky tone. I feel powerful as I began my journey in his seat. I am a short petite girl, and so being this tall in his truck feels unnaturally awesome to me.

"Seriously, Josh. I can handle it." I glance quickly at him, before putting my eyes back on the road. My nerves are all frazzled.

"Can you now? I'm not so sure you're ready."

What? I glance at him again. "Too late for ready, Josh. I am already in the driver's seat?" Why do I feel like he isn't talking about his truck?

"Damn straight. You definitely have *all* the control."

What does he mean by that?

I stop at a red light, my heart racing.

"Take a right at the light, change of plans." Josh says reading a text from his phone.

"But the mall is the other way. Wzup?"

"Brats are going to the movies. My dad is picking them up later," he informs me

"Oh. So, where are we going?" I ask taking our detour.

"To the lake for a bit," Josh eyes me nervously.

"O-Kay," I say slowly and full of nerves of my own.

Every time we go to the lake (our spot), I get a case of nostalgia about how I made a fatal mistake in our friendship freshman year, and how I let the moment pass.

4 YEARS PREVIOUS

Josh and I enjoyed the quiet away from home. We walked hand in hand the few blocks to the lake. We were at our spot under our tree, watching some kids play on the small playground that was set to the side. The tree had a swing hanging from it, and I was sitting in the swing, my feet crossed at the ankles. Josh was lying on his back with his hands behind his head. His eyes were closed, and I watched the serenity on his face, envious because I didn't feel serene. A few families were in the picnic area. A lot of laughter was in the air that day. I watched wistfully, wishing my family was like that.

I was already a little sad and not in the best moods that day. I had overheard Emily and Laiken at their lockers earlier at school discussing Josh. After Josh kissed me—after Dean kissed me, our little bubble of friendship most definitely changed. Josh was catching the eyes of boy crazy girls left and right, and I wasn't naïve enough to not know he saw them too. Dean—well, he only saw me. I told him earlier that I just wanted to be friends, but he wasn't giving up easy.

Laiken said that Josh asked her to the freshman dance, and she said yes. My heart ached. A pang of jealousy had been billowing inside of me the entire day. He knew that would hurt me. He had too. It was our first dance. Josh and I should be going together, but he didn't choose to share that first with me. It confused me.

Josh knew something was wrong, and he asked me, but I just brushed him off. How could I explain all I felt? I couldn't risk him not feeling the same. I tried to explain it before, but he admitted he was curious about other girls.

Evidently that day my mouth had a mind of its own.

"I heard you're taking Laiken to the freshman dance?" I didn't mean for it to come out like a question or harshly but it did.

Josh suddenly lifted up on his elbows and looked at me. "Where did you hear that?" he asked.

I looked down at him, "Straight from the source, she said you asked her, and she said yes."

"I did, she did." He said simply and sat straight up to look at me face to face.

I looked away from his hazel eyes that always saw too much but also never enough.

"Oh." I just stared at the lake, at the families enjoying their day. Why didn't my parents spend their time like this, maybe then I could tell my best friend how much this hurt me. Maybe then I wouldn't be afraid to let him in. Tell him that I wanted it to be me. Take what I could, even if it didn't last.

I felt like the girl in the Taylor Swift video, *You belong with me.* Except, Josh wasn't going to kiss me in the end. He would kiss Laiken. Kissing Josh haunted my every thought. I wanted to kiss him again. I hated that he immediately went right back to her.

We were silent, sitting there for a while. I didn't have the words to say next, but Josh did.

"Riley, it's just a dance. Besides, I heard Dean asked you. Didn't he?"

I hadn't thought for a second about how me being asked to the freshman dance would affect him. It never occurred to me that it would bother him. Dean was our third wheel, not a big deal. I told Josh already that I didn't like Dean like that. I just figured he would get that.

I looked over at him, his face guarded and unreadable.

"Um, yeah, he did. Yesterday."

"What did you say?"

"I said, I would think about it."

"Oh," he paused studying my eyes, "Have you?"

"Have I what?"

"Thought about it?"

"Not really, but I guess I will say yes. No one else has asked me."

Josh tilted his head to the side searching my face for something.

"I see. Did you want someone else to ask you, Riley?"

I stared at his beautiful hazel eyes, déjà vu attacking me. The words were on the tip of my tongue—again. But instead I jumped up and said, "It's getting late Josh. We should probably go home now."

The look of confusion and something else haunted his face. We walked home in complete silence. He held my hand the entire walk, a friendly gesture on his behalf of course.

Josh didn't speak much to me that week. I think he needed a time out, and truthfully, so did I.

The day of the dance had my stomach in knots. Not happy butterflies, no those were knots of nausea, and I wanted to call the whole thing off. I wanted to cancel on Dean, bake some brownies, eat every last bit on my own and dream about soft lips on mine—not Laiken's.

"Knock, knock. Can I come in?" The voice I loved to hear was standing in my doorway, looking ever so handsome in his dress shirt and tie. I felt breathless.

"Hey. You um, look…um, yeah…you look really nice, Josh." I stuttered. Nice? Apparently, I'd lost the ability to be articulate.

He grinned and stepped into my room, shutting the door behind him. "Thanks. You look beautiful, Riley. Dean is a lucky guy." His smile didn't quite reach his eyes.

I frowned, "I guess. So, what are you doing here?" I said, trying to not think about dances with Dean, dances with Laiken. Stupid dances, I thought.

He pulled out his phone and turned on, *Just the way you are* by Bruno Mars. "We may not be going to our first dance together, Riley. But I want you to be the first girl I dance with. So, what do you say, pretty girl? Can I have this dance?"

I thought I was breathless before, speechless before, no right then, in that very moment, I was suffering a heart attack. Surely I was. My heart was pounding in my chest. He reached out his hand to me, and I took it, wrapping my hands around his neck as he placed his arms around my waist and the small of my back.

He hummed the melody and kissed my forehead. That moment was sweeter than that one with the chocolate. I was in a bubble of bliss, and I wanted to beg him to stay with me just like that…who needed the dance anyway?

When the song ended, he placed a soft kiss to my cheek.

My bubble didn't last forever. He told me thank you, and gave me his best wishes for my first dance—also first date with Dean. I wanted to take it all back. That first should've been with Josh, but it wasn't.

I went to the dance with Dean, and Josh went with Laiken. One of my firsts was spent with the wrong guy.

CHAPTER 17

Enough is enough... I'm so fucking pissed that she doubts me. It's time to shoot it straight, like my dad said. Going to our spot by the lake, I'm going to tell her the truth.

We arrive at the lake and sit in the truck uncomfortably. The air felt thick of things unsaid. She kills the engine and looks at me. I remember every moment with her that I should have fought harder, said something different, made her realize just how perfect we are together.

I don't say anything to her just yet. I just climb out of the truck. She seems frozen in her seat, unable to move. I open her door, and she turns her body toward me.

I look into her eyes, thinking they will haunt my dreams for the rest of my life. It's now or never, Parker. No more wasting time.

"Come with me," I speak in a low demanding voice and hold out my hand for her to grab, which she does.

We walk to the pier on the edge of the lake where I sit down in silence before lying back to look up at the clouds. I pat the spot next to me, and she joins me placing her head on my arm. She curls into me. It just feels natural to have her like this, like she belongs right here in my arms.

I attempt to lighten the mood by joking about the shapes I can find in the clouds. She finds a cloud that looks like an elephant. I find one that looks like a two-headed turtle.

I clear my throat and think *here goes nothing.*

"Riley, do you believe me when I tell you that you are special to me?" I ask barely above a whisper still looking up at the clouds.

In a small voice, she answers, "Yes." She squeezes closer to my chest. I look over at her, but she won't meet my eyes. It is warm today and yet she is shivering. I wonder about it. She told me she was scared before. Does being with me frighten her this much?

I silently will her to turn her head to mine, but she refuses. She stays as still as she can.

My breath feathers along her cheek when I say, "We have a lot of memories here at this lake and under that tree over there. Don't we?"

"M'hm," she finally turns her head toward my voice, and her breath catches when she looks at me.

I place a soft kiss to her nose. "Let's go." I tell her sitting up and holding out my hand for her to hold. If I am going to do this, I'm going back to the beginning, to the moment I should have changed something. There were so many times I could have said it. I could have done it differently. The moment by that tree freshman year was one of those.

She looks at my hand reluctantly. I can tell she is nervous. When she finally places her delicate hand in mine I almost lose my shit then. "Where are we going?" she asks in a tiny voice.

I nod my head toward the tree, "Our tree," I smile.

When we get to the tree, I sit on the swing and pat my lap for her to sit on me. She does, placing her arm around my neck and cradling her head on my shoulder. "Did you have fun today...with me?" I ask softly as we watch the ripples in the lake.

"Yes, I always have fun with you, Josh."

"It's easy, huh? The way we are together, like it's meant to be." I am threading her hair in between my fingers when she lifts her head to look at my eyes. I cup her cheek.

She leans into my touch and squeezes her eyes closed. I can feel her body shake. She is starting to panic. I don't know why she does this. But she does. Every time I try to cross the line, she pulls away. All I want to do is take away her pain, and she wants to push me away. This time she nods, and I feel wetness on my hand as silent tears fall from her eyes.

I sigh and tuck a strand of her hair behind her ear. "Please. Don't cry, Riley." My heart is in fucking shreds at the pain she carries. She can't trust any of this to be real, and it kills me. I kiss her cheeks and wipe away the tears. I kiss her eyes where they fall. I kiss her forehead the way I always have, and then I stand us up. I grab her face and make her look at me.

"I know you don't trust this. Us. Any of it. I know you felt betrayed by Dean, and I know your Dad cheated on your Mom and broke his promises. But please Riley. Please believe me when I say…every day since we were five years old, you have been a crucial part of my life, a piece that I had to have to be complete. I have spent years loving you. Yes, that's right. I fucking love you, Riley. I always have and I probably always will. I'm not the guy you think I am. I don't change my mind often about girls. I don't fucking care enough about them to even use my mind, because every waking thought, every fucking dream is filled with you. It's always been you for me. Always. I just had to wait for you to realize you felt the same. That you knew, you deserved to be loved. Dean never loved you, Riley. He lied to you all the time. I will never lie to you. I promise." I put it out there, put my heart on my sleeve and held my breath for her to embrace it and never let it go.

Her eyes are still closed tightly, and when she finally opens them, I'm scared as fuck for what she is going to say.

But then she smiles and steals the breath right out of my lungs. "I love you too, Josh. I've only ever loved you." She says in a soft voice that I almost can't hear.

I feel the tension, the fear fall away. She loves me. I love her. We can be happy. Finally.

I kiss her, loving the taste of her salty tears being melted away and everything that is Riley becoming mine. I am not lying. I truly believe I will love this girl forever.

I sit back on the swing, and I pull her onto my lap where she is straddling me. She wraps her legs around me, and I love the feel of her like this. She rests her head on my chest. Her hands are around my neck, and my chin rests on her head, and I'm inhaling the scent of her hair. I swing us gently embracing this perfect moment.

"Wanna know a secret?" I ask her.

"M'hm," she mumbles into my chest.

"My tattoo, the third rose, it's for you." I say and her head snaps up.

"What? What do you mean?" she asks studying my eyes.

I lift my sleeve and rub my fingers along the rose that is hers. "It represents friendship, falling in love, unconscious beauty and desire. I blended the colors because you are all of that for me." Her tiny fingers touch the rose delicately.

She bites her lip and turns her gorgeous eyes back to mine. "Wow!" she breathes. "Mine is for you too, although in a different way."

"How so?" I ask interlacing her hand with my own.

CHAPTER 18

Trusting someone with your heart is so damn hard. But I do love, Josh. I have wasted so much time. I don't want to waste another minute without him.

I am about to reveal my secret too. Josh just admitted his tattoo and the rose I love so much is mine. For me. He never knew my own was for him, until now.

"Well, I always felt like my heart was dead or half beating, so I made the heart black, but it surrounded the treble clef for you. The music is yours. The heart and the treble clef are connected. I guess...I kinda hoped one day that your music would breathe life into that black heart and teach it to love, create music together." I've never admitted how deep my reasoning was, not even to myself I think. It was more than his music. It was the music he and I shared, the music that I thought we could never have.

His eyes study mine, and he is quite for the longest time before he places his hand on my heart. "Your heart is beautiful, Riley. I feel that. The beating. Not half alive but thumping wildly. That's our music, Riley. It's not dead. It's just beginning, our song together will never end."

I place my hand on his chest feeling his own heart, alive, beating wildly and for me. I drag my hand up his chest and along his face where I trace his jaw, his mouth, and his ear. Tracing to memory his features. I run it through his hair and he groans. I wrap both hands around his neck and lean into his face. I lick along his lips and tug a little on his bottom lip with my teeth like I have wanted to do all damn day. He has one hand on the rope holding the swing and the other cupping my ass.

Our kiss is slow, meaningful, full of love and absolutely necessary.

I pull him as close to me as he can get and yet it isn't close enough.

After Josh and I went home, we decided to go separate ways. I think he needed a cold shower, and I needed...well, I needed him, but that wasn't a possibility right now.

"Hello" I answer my phone plopping on my stomach on my mattress.

"How's my favorite short friend?" Emily asks me glumly.

"She is awesome."

"Great, cuz I'm on my way to your house." She honks her horn "Hey asshole, learn to drive." She shouts at someone.

"Ok, so you're heading over now. Why?" I ask just playing.

"As if I need a reason. I miss you bitch." She laughs.

Urm...K, "Miss you too. Why do you sound annoyed?"

"One, people don't know how to freakin drive, and two, boys are confusing. I gotta talk to you about something, K? Oh hey, who drives a white beetle bop?" Emily asks, and I think she is speaking to herself, so I don't reply. She tends to ramble her thoughts off, not realizing she is talking out loud.

"It's parked out front your house, maybe they're at Josh's?" she mutters, and the phone goes dead.

"Um, K." I say to the deadline and head to the front door to let my crazy friend in, because apparently she is already here.

I open the door, and she attacks me. "Miss me much, Ginger?" I joke with her.

"I did, until you called me Ginger. You know I hate my hair?" she gripes and crosses her arms like a toddler.

I laugh and peek my head out the door to see that, sure enough, a white Volkswagen bug is parked out front.

"No clue who that is," I mutter and we head off to my room.

Once there, I lay on my bed and Emily jumps into full story mode about how she had a major freak out moment with self-tanner. "I totes forgot to wash my hands, Riley, they were fucking orange like a pumpkin."

Poor girl hates her skin and her hair. She has strawberry blonde hair, which I think is gorgeous, and also why I call her 'Ginger'. She can't stand her hair, though. Her skin, although beautiful in its pale form, doesn't tan but burn, hence her self-tanning 'oops'. She is always trying new ways to change herself. She is crazy. But—I love her.

"So, how did you get it off?" I ask noticing they are still a little orange, but I don't dare tell her I notice, she would freak out even more than now.

"A thousand showers, hot baths, alcohol swabs, the works."

I nod and bite my lip to stifle my laugh.

"So, wzup with Mr. ohmigod his hazel eyes-Em, those six pack abs make me thirsty-gives me wet dreams-hm… hm… hm…hottie next door?" she asks nodding her head toward my window, fanning herself dramatically and rolling her eyes at me.

I am exasperated, "Oh my God, Em. I don't even sound like that."

She puts her hands on her hips and tilts her head, "Oh my God, Riley. You so do"

I stick my tongue out at her and she laughs.

"Soooo?" she asks rolling her wrist and her eyes dramatically.

"So, I think I'm like his girlfriend now." I say sheepishly, and then cringe when she squeals and jumps up and down clapping her hands.

"Eeeekkk…I'm so happy for you. It's about damn time. I hate Dean. Josh is who you belong with."

"I know, I just didn't think I should belong with him, ya know?" I say, and she frowns knowingly.

"I found this in my notebook. I wrote a poem about him that he accidentally found and kept, and in its place he left this." I pull the notebook from under my pillow and show her.

She reads and widens her eyes, "Dude," she raises her eyebrows.

"I know."

"What did you say?" she asks me.

"Nothing, I said nothing." I pout and put the pillow over my head.

"Why the hell not?" she nudges my leg and yanks my pillow away.

"Because, he is Josh, and this scares the living shit out me, Em. This isn't like Dean. This is Josh we are talking about. Just since this morning, I've already inserted my friggin' foot in my mouth more than once. Of course, he doesn't hold it against me. He just says these things and then kisses me senseless, but still *oh my God*...I just feel like something bad is going to happen, and I am going to lose him." I explain.

She stares at me with wide green eyes, "Ok. Out of breath yet? Look, I get it. I do. Sometimes, you just gotta put yourself out there and pray for the best, Riley. Trust me. I know," she sighs and frowns.

"I just don't know"

"Riley, look at me." I do. "When Beau told me last year that he thought we should break up because long distance relationships never work, I thought it was the worst idea ever. I knew he would meet someone in college better than me. And when he came home over Christmas break with Kristen, I knew I was right, but I realized something else, Riley. Ya wanna know what?"

"What's that?" I pick at a piece of invisible lint on my comforter. I don't want to think about colleges or going away.

"I realized that, what he and I had wasn't real love, it was just fun, easy. The way he looks at Kristen...well, he never looked at me like that. She makes him happy. They laugh, they smile… it's just different. But it's beautiful to see, so beautiful, in fact, it hurts to see it, and not because I love him. No, it's because I want that, a love like that."

Emily grabs my hand, "Riley, Josh looks at you the same way Beau looks at Kristen. And you smile at Josh the way Kristen smiles at Beau. It's love, Riley. And it can be beautiful. Just let it be."

Didn't my mom say the same thing?

"I'm trying, ok?" I need to change the subject. "So, what did you need to talk to me about?" I ask.

She sighs, and I pick up Tink off my floor to snuggle. "Ya know, I've been loving the single life since my break-up with Beau, kissing a lot of frogs before I get to my prince has been my new favorite hobby. But I've found a frog with ocean blue eyes that I can drown in, and a lip ring. Also, a tongue that does this twirly thing in my mouth, and—you know—down there." She moans, pointing to her vagina. I slap her leg.

Actually, I don't know. Now the image of Josh going down on me is stuck on replay.

"Oh, sorry. Anyway, I'm a little confused by it, because I probably shouldn't be...um, entertaining this idea being who he is and all." she nibbles on her thumbnail nervously.

M'Kay. So, who is it?

"Who is it?" I ask.

"Brandt," she throws herself back on my bed dramatically.

"What the fudge? Brandt as in Beau's brother, Brandt?"

She nods her head looking ever bobble head like.

"Oh my God. Oh, wow! I mean...I just don't know what to say to that." I tell her.

"Yeah, I know. Me neither. At first I thought I was just drawn to his eyes because they remind me so much of Beau's, but then...well, I realized it's more than that. I like him. Like I think about him, and not about Beau, so that mean's something, right?"

She asks me like she wants me to convince her of it. I mean...I just don't know what to say. "I don't know. What would Beau think about it?"

"Actually, he's okay with it. Beau proposed to Kristen, and they are having an engagement party tonight. Well, Brandt is throwing a party, so probably not a typical kind of engagement party. Brandt invited you and me. You have to come with me, because even though I know Beau is okay with it, I'm not sure I completely am yet. Ya know?"

"Oh, wow. Um, okay. Yeah, I will go with you. I wonder if Josh is going too?"

She shrugs, "Text him," She suggests.

"M'Kay" I send a text to Josh.

Me: GOING TO A PARTY AT BRANDT'S *HAPPY DANCE* WANNA COME WITH ME?

Emily is in my closet picking out my outfit for me. Evidently, I can't dress myself. After about ten minutes of no response from Josh, I get a weird feeling in my stomach, and I don't know why. He always responds right away.

"He didn't answer," I tell Emily. Something feel's off.

"Don't worry, Riley. I can see the wheels turning in your head. Not every guy is a douche like Dean, and not every guy is a cheater like your dad. Stop comparing all their shitty behavior with Josh. He's probably doing something or doesn't have his phone. It could be any number of reasons." She tells me and hands me an outfit to put on. "Here put this on."

It's black knit (very short) shorts, a white top that sits right above my navel, with a black heart in the center. *Very suiting,* I thought, and that pit in my stomach grew wider.

I put on my black combat boots, the ones Josh loves. I strap on leather studded wrist bangles and put on my silver hoop earrings and diamond studs in my second hole. I comb through my dark brown wavy hair that is now streaked with dark blue, and decide it looks like a frizzy mess, so I put it into a messy bun on top of my head. I am naturally tanned and don't need much makeup, so I just add some blush for a touch of color, add soft black eyeliner, a little eye shadow, and mascara to complete my smoky look. I put on some nude lip-gloss that tasted like coconut, and stood back to stare at my reflection. The Riley in the mirror was shaking her head at me with disapproval.

I felt a little edgy about going to this party, but equally anxious to get out of my head for a little while. Best thing about going to Brandt's, free alcohol and no need for id. Brandt could care less, and since he was a bartender at a restaurant during the week—he made the best damn drinks. Plus, I get to chill with Rebel, and if there is anyone in this world that gets my dark poetry—it's that bitch. She even puts it in her songs for her garage band, often trying to convince me to sing with her. Nuh'uh. No way. No how.

After letting my mom know my plans and a speech of being responsible. Em and I head out the door, literally coming to a halt at the scene unfolding before us. What the fuck? I knew he was lying.

I open the front door. We are walking down the steps heading to Emily's car, when a giggle has my eyes darting straight to the white car parked in front of my house—a guest definitely of Josh's.

Preslee is sitting in the driver's side, giggling at whatever the hell he is saying to her. Josh is bent down with his back to us. He is leaning into the window of her car, talking to her. No crime in talking, right?

Neither, Emily nor I budge. Both of our eyes are trapped in this sight. Emily mumbles, 'Fucking bitch' under her breath, and I mumble, 'Fucking liar' under mine. She grabs my hand, squeezing it comfortingly. My breath is rapid, my heart is beating out of my chest, and I want to scream. I want to fight. I am pissed at what I am seeing.

He kisses her cheek and stands to watch her leave. Her eyes clock us standing in the distance. She smirks, waves goodbye, and drives off. I want to slap her, and rip her damn ponytail out.

When he turns around to head to his house. He freezes on the spot, his mouth gaping open, and his eyes widen before darting to the car driving away and back to mine. 'Fuck me' he mouths. *'Fuck you' is exactly my thought.*

Anger forms and my blood boils. My eyes narrow and become cold. I tug on Emily's hand, "Let's go," and we walk to her car ignoring Josh's presence.

"Wait, Riley. It's not what you think." He is there in a heartbeat and grabbing my arm as I open the door to get in.

I yank it away. "Let me go, Josh. You don't know what I'm thinking, and if you did, you wouldn't be standing so close to me right now." I warn him with a glare.

He swallows and steps back just a bit, "She just stopped by. I didn't invite her, just listen. Where are you going? We need to talk," he pleads.

I climb in the car, shut it and roll down the window. "I'm going to a party, which you would know about, if you weren't busy with your *not girlfriend.*" I air quote it.

"Now back the fuck up. I'm going to drink myself into oblivion, and forget all about the fucking liars in my life or *not* in my life anymore." I spit harshly and begin to roll the window up.

"Fucking liars?" he shouts, "I'm not lying to you. Riley, STOP! I've never lied to you. Fuck my life," he shouts louder, throwing his hands in the air.

We drive away, leaving him standing there in my driveway. I am now on a mission. My mission is to forget, Joshua Parker. Forget that every fucking guy is a cheater and liar, and forget why I feel so completely broken and lost. Forget that I gave him my heart against my better judgment, and he didn't cherish it, he didn't protect it. No, he took it, confused it and then tossed it aside—all in a matter of hours.

I tried playing it safe. I tried to protect my heart at every corner, and every fucking decision has led me to this exact spot anyway.

Alone and disappointed.

CHAPTER 19

What the hell is wrong with me? Why can't I not fuck this up?

I had the best day with Riley. I tell her I love her. We make this official. And as if the universe hates me, my doorbell rings. It's Preslee.

"What are you doing here?" I ask annoyed and honestly surprised.

"I didn't know where else to go," she sniffles, and it's only now that I realize she has been crying.

Fuck!

"Come in." I open the door to let her in. My dad and Joey are still not home, so having Preslee alone definitely doesn't feel right. If Riley sees her, this is going to look *really* bad.

"I made such a mess of my life, Josh. I can't believe this is happening to me. I just didn't know who to go to," she starts crying again and telling me things.

I look at her bewildered, "Okay. Start with what happened, I guess."

"I'm pregnant."

Holy shit! She's what?

"Pardon?"

She begins to sob, and I have to get her some tissue. "Yeah, I just found out. I've only been with one person for that to happen."

Now I'm even more confused, because I know she has been with more than one person. At least, that's what I've heard.

"What do you mean, for that to happen?" I ask her, needing to understand for some reason.

"You know? Without a condom. I can't believe I was so stupid. He promised to pull out, but he didn't." she explains.

"Who?"

She looks at me as though I should know, but I don't. So, I don't understand why she gives me that look.

"Dean, it was Dean. It has to be his baby. I've been careful every time, except for that one time with him."

Oh shit. Oh shit.

"But Preslee, that was only a few weeks ago?" I say.

She shakes her head back and forth. "No, it wasn't. That wasn't the first time Dean and I fucked, Josh. He used to call me all the time, but only once did we not use a condom. It has to be his."

Oh, hell no!

"Preslee, you do realize he had a girlfriend. Right?"

She looks at me with cold eyes. "Yeah, but she wouldn't fuck him. I mean...after two years—she still wouldn't give it up. I just helped him out. I didn't expect him to dump her or anything. It was working, what we were doing but now... shit, now it's all a mess."

Riley's a virgin?

"Why are you telling me this, Preslee?" I'm glad she did, but I just don't understand why.

She shrugs, "I don't know. Because my fucking life is a mess, and I just don't know what to do. I wrote this letter to my parents, and I wanted to see if you would give it to them."

She hands me an envelope labeled, 'I'm sorry.'

"Why can't you give it to them?"

"Because, I'm leaving. I'm going away, and I just need them to know I'm sorry for disappointing them." Something in her eyes scares me a little.

"What do you mean, going away?" I open the envelope and read the letter. She is saying she is sorry, and that she can't go on living like this...etc.

Oh my God.

"Preslee, this doesn't sound like you're just saying sorry and going on a trip for a while. This sounds like a suicide note." I tell her.

She begins to cry again. Shit! "It's just a letter, Josh. Will you give it to them or not?" she asks standing up and heading to the door.

I grab her arm by the elbow, "No. I won't, and I won't let you do this either. You need to tell Dean the truth. It will be okay, Preslee." I plead with her. No guy, no situation is worth killing yourself over.

She throws her arms around me, and I hate to do it, but I hug her back. When I pull away, she thanks me.

I tell her, "Look, just don't do anything stupid, okay? You need to talk to Dean and figure this out. There are other options besides the one you're thinking of."

She kisses my cheek, "you are such a sweet guy, Josh. I wish it were you."

Um? *I don't!*

"I will walk you out."

She nods and I walk her to her car.

When I turn around and see Riley standing there, wide eyes, shocked—pissed off. I know immediately she is thinking the worst. She thinks I lied and that I played her.

'Fuck me' I say under my breath.

I try to grab her arm and make her listen. But she refuses. She calls me a fucking liar and basically tells me she doesn't want me in her life anymore.

In a matter of a few hours, she has gone from loving me to hating me. Once again Preslee and Dean are to blame.

She won't stop. She won't tell me where she is going, and it's not until I'm back in my room punching the shit out of my wall that I notice her text asking me to go to Brandt's party.

My first reaction is, 'Good, now I can fix this because I had plans to be there already' my second reaction is, 'fucking hell, Brandt's parties are filled with booze and bad decisions.' She just told me she plans on drinking herself into oblivion to forget me.

This.Can't.Be.Happening

CHAPTER 20

I feel like my heart has been through the fucking shredder, and that I will never be the same. I want to feel numb, feel nothing and just be done with this shit. I will never put my guard down again.

Emily and I are in the car, my quick breaths filling the air. The Neighbourhood is on the radio playing *Sweater Weather*.

Emily lights up a cigarette and rolls the window down. She takes a drag offering it to me "it will calm your nerves," she says, and I accept choking as I inhale.

"Thanks," I cough.

"I can't believe what I just saw," I tell her. I attempt to take deep breaths to calm myself down.

Emily blows some smoke out her window and glances at me. "Maybe it's not what it looked like," she says full of optimism.

I glare at her, "Not what it looked like?"

"It sure looked like she spent an hour at his house, and he kissed her goodbye. It sure looked like guilt when he turned around." I snap.

She flicks the ash out the window. "Look, I'm not saying it didn't look suspicious. I'm just saying that it might not be what you think. They could have been just talking, it might have been innocent."

"Innocent? How so?" I ask.

She takes another drag before handing it to me. I don't even smoke but it makes me dizzy and...well, focusing on that feeling is better than the throb in my chest.

"I'm just saying, there might be truth to what he said. Preslee is a snake, and she could have come over uninvited. You should at least let him explain before you judge him and end this before it's even started."

"Can I tell you what else I think, Riley?" she asks even though she has already spelled it out completely. She clearly is on a roll.

"Yes, Oh, wise one. Please, continue?" I am aware I sound like a bitch.

So does she, she glowers at me "Don't do that, I'm just trying to help." I sigh and apologize.

"I think you are looking for a reason to make this not work. You were waiting for the bad before you even saw him out there."

"Yeah, I know. It's called a gut instinct. It's called protecting myself, but look where it got me?" I can't believe I was stupid enough to think anything could ever be different. Love never plays fair.

"No, Riley. It's called fear. You expect for him to fuck up. He might not have done anything wrong, Riley. Josh isn't Dean. Josh isn't your dad. And I'm just saying, keep an open mind that Preslee is just up to something."

I know she is right.

I grumble, "Whatever. We're here. All I want to do tonight is forget him for a while, forget my feelings and become numb." I open the door and get out, she sighs and shakes her head but joins me.

We walk inside Brandt's house and are immediately engulfed in cigarette smoke. I will smell like an ashtray when I leave here.

Their house is small but cozy. Right away we are in the living room. Filling the space is one recliner, a leather sofa, and a giant big screen with a surround sound stereo system that has *Red* by Chevelle filtering from the speakers.

To the left, are their bedrooms, and straight ahead is a bathroom. To the right, is the tiniest kitchen known to man. The kitchen and the living room are open to each other with a bar area where Rebel has parked her ass in a stool, as she picks up and puts down multiple alcohol bottles.

They don't own a dining room table. Nope, it's a card table that is housing two guys I don't recognize, surrounded by empty beer bottles.

At the card table, those two guys are...playing cards. How cliché. It makes me laugh. In the corner, is another couple groping each other and making out.

Brandt walks from down the hall and stops dead in his tracks as he eyes over Emily and she him. It's so bizarre to watch. Brandt is dressed in all black and looks like he just left the biker bar, where Emily is standing in a blue jean mini skirt, pastel pink cami, and pink flip flops. Her ginger hair twisted up in a hair clip. They are so opposite, like fire and ice. But in this moment, they look they want to devour each other.

I shift uncomfortably, "C'mon." I nudge her toward the barstools.

She hugs Rebel, and I don't miss the daggers Rebel shoots at her brother. She doesn't seem very thrilled with the lust filled looks Emily and he just shared. Rebel nods an acknowledgement to me and me to her.

"Nice shirt," she says.

"Yeah, well I have a black heart—a dead one." I say and she looks at me with confusion.

"Ignore her, she is in a shitty mood." Em tells Rebel.

Rebel runs her palms together, "Some of the best writing comes from shitty moods. Wanna head to the garage?" she asks me.

The garage has been transformed into a music room, where Rebel and I write and mesh brains. Her band practices there. Believe it or not, before the accident, I attempted to dabble with singing alongside Rebel. It was natural, being that I used to do the same with Josh for years, when he would play guitar.

Nope, not thinking about Josh. I don't sing because my mom sang and because I don't want to be like her. Singing made me feel something I didn't want to feel, so I stopped and settled on writing for Rebel. Besides, she fits the persona better than I.

I debate and decide nope. This time, I don't want to write it down, I want to drink it away. Maybe I am my Father's daughter after all.

"Nah, I wanna drink. Gimme that." I say, reaching for the tequila bottle and a shot glass.

I pour what will be one of many shots to come tonight. "To forgetting assholes," I cheer and tip it back.

Emily sighs, Rebel looks curious, and the card table guys laugh. Brandt just watches nervously typing on his phone.

Rebel pours herself a shot, "Fucking pricks. Who needs em?" She goes to take her shot, but one of the card table guys smacks her ass, making her spill tequila all over the floor.

"You do, sweet cheeks," he says smugly.

I laugh and swear Rebel is about to kick this guy's ass. But she just grabs a napkin, bends down on her knees to wipe the mess and whines, "Dammit, Jeremy you made me waste a good shot of tequila."

My mouth hits the floor when card table guy—that I now know is named Jeremy—turns in his chair toward Rebel and grabs his groin. "I've got a good shot you can take in your mouth right here, darlin'."

Oh my God! Now, I know she is going to kick his ass, except Brandt is on him first before she has a chance.

I *love* Brandt's parties.

Brandt grabs him up by his shirt. "That's my fucking sister man. GET OUT!" he shouts.

Jeremy grins arrogantly, "You gonna let him throw me out like that, baby?" he looks to Rebel.

Is that her boyfriend? I have never seen Rebel with a guy before. Hmm...this is interesting? She just shrugs and throws back a refilled tequila shot.

Jeremy huffs and storms out, I laugh again and grab another shot. "To free entertainment," the tequila burns a little going down, but I have a mission.

I am a tiny person, maybe 105 lbs. and it isn't taking much to get me feeling lightheaded. I love it.

"Hey, shortie. You might want to take it easy. You alright?" Brandt asks patting my head and making me feel like a child.

I turn and eye him up and down. He really is a handsome guy. His hair is spiked green today, his ocean blue eyes piercingly beautiful, that fucking lip ring is hot just like Emily said. Suddenly dark and dangerous looks appetizing.

Emily nudges my shoulder, "Don't even think about it, bitch." Brandt looks amused at my tipsy manner, yet a little concerned.

"I'm fucking perfect." I tell him, licking salt off my hand, taking another shot and sucking on a lime.

"Urm, Em? Wzup?" Brandt asks her.

"A misunderstanding, I *think*. But she is on a mission to forget it."

She tells him like I am not standing here at all.

"At this rate, she will be passed out before Beau and Kristen even get here," Brandt says.

I cheer, "Awww...Beau. I love Beau. Isn't it so sweet that he is getting married? Love, fucking love. It's a beautiful thing, huh?" I say in a singsong voice before I lower my speech to a snarl. "Except, when they fuck you over and it's not. They change the rules and don't tell you. They cheat, they lie, and they make you admit you love them, even say it back, and then just *shit* all over your heart." I ramble as I pour another shot.

"Oh damn," Emily says.

"Fucking hell, Emily." Brandt says taking the shot glass out of my hand.

"Baby girl? Look at me. What happened?" he asks me. I know he is worried. His brotherly side makes him want to protect me from myself. Too bad tonight, I don't want to protect myself. I want to lose myself.

His eyes really are gorgeous. "I don't want to think about it, Brandt. Please, just let me forget it for a while. I'll behave. I promise." I whine and lie.

He studies me but then nods.

I go back into the living room that is now crowded with a lot of people. Some I recognize from Brandt's tattoo parlor, the guitar guy and drummer from Rebel's band—I can't remember their names—my head is a little fuzzy. No Beau or Kristen yet. Yay, for no Dean. No Preslee, *No Josh* or any fucking high school people I fake even liking.

Card table guy #2 (who is kinda cute actually) is now leaning back on the couch with his hands propped behind his head watching me.

I'm feeling the effects of the tequila, and I love it. I feel numb, dizzy, and my body feels warm.

Kings of Leon *Closer* starts playing on the surround sound, and I can't help but let myself get hypnotized by the rhythm and words.

"Let's dance," I grab Emily's hand and don't give her a choice.

"Oh, okay. Shit," she mumbles as I literally pull her to the middle of the living room.

I love this song. I feel like I lost my soul, or maybe I never had one. All I know is right now, Emily and I are dancing seductively with each other, or I am dancing on her. *Whatever.*

I don't know what has gotten into me, but I am swaying my hips, and moving up and down on her. My hands tangle into my hair pulling out the messy bun, and I shake my hair free.

Rebel is sitting on the barstool staring, like she can't believe her eyes. Brandt is watching on the recliner, in shock I'm sure. I have no clue where that couple from earlier ran off too. They're other people too, and they all just watch entertained.

Most have shocked faces at this change in my behavior. Normally, it would bother me. I would shy away from this, and hide. But nope, not tonight. Tonight, I don't feel like myself, and that is the whole damn point wasn't it? Yes, yes, that was. Success.

I am drunk.

Some guy is trying to give Rebel a lap dance, and she just keeps shooing him out of her eyesight before lighting up a cigarette. Emily waves her over to us.

Emily parts her lips slightly, and Rebel places the cigarette in her mouth for her to take a drag. She nods her head to me to do the same, and I do, not coughing nearly as much as earlier.

Emily looks a little surprised, but she eyes Brandt, and something flickers sinfully in her eyes. She pulls me closer and really starts to move with me, touching me even. Nope, pretty sure I am imagining that...*maybe.*

Rebel inhales the tobacco and backs away to her stool, where she watches.

Card table guy #2 drawls, "Damn, y'all should kiss." I raise my brows at Emily, she glances at Brandt, and then I turn my eyes to card table guy, as well.

He is divine. He has on a pair of faded jeans with natural rips in them from being well worn. He is wearing a black t-shirt and a dog collar around his neck. His dark black hair is tussled and standing on end, like he just pulled his hands through it roughly. His eyes are the smokiest grey and are covered in eyeliner, which would be odd if we were anywhere but at one of 'Brandt's parties'. Being here, he fits right in.

Those eyes are simmering hot as they are watching us dance together. His arms are enticing and quiet eccentric, covered in colorful tattoos, a rainbow of a playground. He screams...dangerous, and my drunken brain thinks that equals delicious.

"What's your name?" I ask. And I'm a little stunned at the rasp in my voice.

Whoa! His voice. "Lucas." He leisurely eyes me up and down appreciatively, I think.

"Lucas." I repeat, testing the word from my mouth.

"Hmm...I like it." I say, and turn back to Emily with a wicked smile.

She shakes her head no, and I shake my head yes. I'm thinking, 'hell yes' actually.

"Me too." he says after I turn away. "So, about that kiss. You gonna do it?" he challenges me.

Emily looks over my shoulder to Brandt seeking help. She seems to be stalling, but I don't give her a chance to question this. I have been challenged.

I shrug and mutter, "What the hell." I grab her behind the neck and pull her face to mine. I lick along her lips and she tenses. But when I bite her bottom lip, she moans. Perhaps her slight tipsy brain says she likes this.

The music is tantalizing. She parts her lips and I push my tongue into her mouth. We kiss slow and provocative, just like the music.

I am making out with Emily. *Holy hell.*

My mind is definitely more fucked up than I realized. I have zero interest or attraction to girls. So this is way out of the blue for me. Something in me wants to be reckless. Emily is a safer bet to be reckless with because of this. What we're doing isn't real. It's nothing at all.

Our hands are in each other's hair, on each other everywhere. When we pull apart, we are both out of breath and flustered—looking at each other in complete shock that we just did that.

"That was hot," Rebel breathes heavily. I look at her, noticing that she is flushed. Suddenly it dawns on me. She has a thing for girls. Whoa! How come I didn't notice that?

"Fucking yeah. It was." The card table guy named Lucas, groans and adjust himself in his jeans.

I grin. Why do I grin? Guys like him disgust me.

People clap; some even gasp a little. However, all I hear is…

SLAM!

I jolt at the sound of the door slamming shut, and my eyes are immediately locked with hazel eyes, which have clearly witnessed my make out session with Emily.

His eyes are smoldering hot, and yet ice cold as they narrow on me. "Having fun?" He yells, tilting his head to the side, like he is trying to figure me out. He is definitely not happy.

"Was!" I spit, and walk back to the barstools, where us girls are gathering again around the tequila bottle.

I hear Brandt and Josh talking, and Josh thanking Brandt for texting him. Shit! I should have known better. Figures.

I grab the shot glass and pour the clear liquid as Lucas joins our end of the party. He is standing very close to me, too close for my comfort level, but I don't shift. I let him play his cards.

"To soft lips," I cheer, and smirk at Emily before I drink yet another shot.

I pass the bottle and glass to Rebel, "To wet panties," she drinks her shot. I place my hand over my mouth in shock, and they laugh.

She passes the bottle and glass to Lucas. He whispers in my ear, "to fucking—*hard.*"

My jaw hits the floor, and he grins like the devil when I turn to look at him. I can't help but let my eyes fall south, he raises a brow, and Josh clears his throat from the doorway.

"No fair. I didn't hear your toast," Emily whines.

Lucas brushes his knuckle against the outside of my thigh, and I shiver involuntarily. He gives me a side-glance, "To new friends," he says out loud and takes his shot.

Brandt comes to stand next to Emily. It's her turn. He kisses her shoulder and she giggles. "To tongues that twirl," she says and winks at Brandt. Everyone except me gives her a puzzled look.

I just laugh. "Yeah, bitch." I sputter. Like I would know what a twirly tongue feels like. I wonder if card table guy named Lucas has a twirly tongue.

I eye the group of shot takers with me, "she likes her kisses down low, makes her arch her back." I sing like Kelly Rowland.

Emily actually sputters her tequila and begins choking. "Hooolllllyyyy shit," she says.

Rebel dies laughing. "Ohhhh fuck. I looove 'drunk Riley'. She's funny."

"Real funny." Josh mumbles under his breath, clearly not amused by my behavior. Who the hell cares what he thinks? You do, my heart tells me. My head tells my heart to shut the hell up. Black. Dead. Remember?

Josh is radiating heat. I can feel the holes he is drilling into me. His hands are fisted at his side, and he looks murderous right now. I want to attack him in the dirtiest way. I am beginning to think tequila is not the best idea for my sexually deprived body.

CHAPTER 21

I'm angry, I'm turned on, I'm scared as fuck, and all these emotions include her.
It's a dangerous heady cocktail.

When Brandt text me that Riley was well on her way to being plastered, I got nervous.

When Brandt text me the second time saying '*he* was nervous,' I knew I should hurry and get there.

I had no idea what I would be walking into. Kissing Emily was definitely not what I imagined at all.

I have to admit. It was hotter than hell, the way she was kissing her, and moving with her when she danced. I have never seen her dance like that. But it fucking pissed me off when I saw the way that dick on the couch was looking at her, as though it were his own personal show.

As I stand here watching him gently touch her and whisper to her, my blood is roaring in my ears.

Riley is well beyond drunk. She starts singing about oral sex, and I am inches from losing my shit. I want to throw her over my shoulder and take her out of here before she does something she will regret.

I need to tread carefully with her. I've only seen Riley like this one other time, and that was after our parent's accident. She spent the entire night after that crying about how she never wanted to be like him, and yet she feared she was. She wasn't.

"Where are Beau and Kristen?" I ask Brandt after he walks over to me.

"Not coming, dude. They were supposed to be driving in for the weekend, but Kristen got sick or something. So, they aren't coming. Guess it's a good thing too. Since our girl here is out of her mind," he says gesturing to Riley.

"Dude, what the fuck happened?" he asks.

"Fucktons. And I don't even know what to do about it," I admit.

Oh hell, no. She leans into that dude's body, and I am fuming.

CHAPTER 22

Inhibitions out the door. Let's see who hurts who now?

I am feeling a little too brave. Inhibitions are practically non-existent. I turn angry eyes on my very hot and handsome best friend, or ex-best friend. Ex-boyfriend, almost boyfriend…what is he again?

Anyway, he chats it up with Brandt. I am sure discussing my misbehavior, and it pisses me off.

I wasn't sure in this state of mind if what I saw or felt was even reality or a hallucination. My balance felt a little off, and I didn't do it on purpose, but the effect it has on Josh makes me smile wickedly when I leaned into Lucas' side for support.

"Riley, let's go talk." He says reaching for my hand. I don't grab it. Actually, I look at it like it's poison and watch it falls back to his side.

That's right I don't need you this time. My inner bitch is lying to herself—again.

"What are you even doing here, Josh?" I grit through hostility.

His jaw is locked, and he looks like he might blow at any moment. I hope he does. Maybe then, I can lash out.

"I'm on friend duty." He doesn't sound happy about this *duty* and neither am I. And friend? Really? We are back to that?

I laugh, and it's not a laugh of amusement. It's a cold-haughtily-laugh that says, 'bullshit'.

When I'm done laughing like a bitch, I walk right up to him, and make a scene of looking around the room at all the faces.

"You sure about that, Josh? I am not so sure I see your *friend* anywhere around here." I back up right into Lucas' hard chest, again on accident.

Josh's eyes are on fire, and for a brief second I think I have pushed it too far. He is fuming, and it's sexy as hell.

Brandt steps in between us, "She's drunk man. Just calm down."

He doesn't listen.

Emily looks nervous. She is fidgeting with her fingers. Rebel looks amused. I can't see Lucas, so I have no idea what his feelings are, and the other viewers of this 'nightmare on Riley Street' look entertained.

Lucas wraps his hand around my hip. I almost jerk from his touch, but I realize he is taunting Josh and it's working, so I refrain from my instinct to pull away.

Josh steps down to where he is nose to nose with me. I swallow down the nerves and also the desire to grab him and take him on the card table.

His voice is so menacingly low that it sends chills up my spine. "Perhaps, I *was* mistaken, Riley." He stands and towers over me looking me up and down with a disgusted look on his face. "I *don't* see *my friend* anywhere."

"Stop, guys. Just stop. You don't know what you're saying." Emily's eyes dart between the two of us "Riley, tell him you're sorry. Josh she is drunk and hurt. She doesn't mean it."

She looks at Lucas, "And you, stop touching her." She pulls me out of his grip. He just smirks but releases me.

Josh and I don't move. We don't speak. We just stare for what seems like forever, but is more likely just a minute.

He turns and walks out of the living room with his hands in his hair, and his head to the ceiling on a growl.

I follow a few steps before stopping when the make out couple from earlier tonight walks into the living room from down the hall looking very well sated.

"Ah hell, no! Where did you two just come from?" Rebel gripes. They look guilty.

I watch Josh for a moment. My heart wants to go to him, but my mind isn't agreeing. My mind wins.

I don't pay attention. I'm too busy feeling bad. I don't want to feel bad. I don't want to feel anything at all. Wasn't that the point of coming to this party?

I'm so pissed. I'm so confused. I want to hurt him. I want to go hug him and keep him forever. I'm such an awful person. I don't know what I want, but I know he has killed my buzz. So I grab the tequila—*again*.

"Riley, I think you have had enough. You're ruining everything. Go fix this." Emily yells at me and snatches the bottle out of my hand, placing it back down, and pointing toward Josh's back in the living room.

"Fuck off, Em." I grab the shot Rebel was just about to take.

"Hhheeeyyy," she says when I steal it.

It burns. I am completely aware that I am, in fact, ruining everything. I am going to regret this tomorrow. Something is definitely wrong with me because right now, I just don't care. I can't stop now.

Brandt starts shuffling people out of his house, but for whatever reason this Lucas guy is left sitting on his sofa. I am thankful.

Lucas pulls me to the sofa to sit, and I stumble my way over. I sit on his side with my feet across his lap. I look at him...and I mean really look at him.

He isn't Josh. He doesn't have the same scent that I have grown to associate only to Josh. He doesn't feel as good as Josh does next to me, either. When I snuggle into Josh's side, it feels right, feels like where I belong, like I was made to be there with him. Like home. With Lucas, it's forced and mechanical. Just like it was with Dean. Fucking Dean.

I am proving a point. Josh who? Dean who? Yeah, who fucking cares?

"You are sexy when you're mad?" Lucas interrupts my thoughts with a line.

"Yeah?" My voice is dripping in sarcasm. He is so full of shit. And I'm sure he thinks he is getting 'some,' but it's not going to happen. Just you and your hand tonight, buddy. I might be drunk, but I most definitely am not going to just give it away to anyone on a whim.

"Hell yeah, you are. So, is that Josh guy your boyfriend?" he nods toward Josh, who is now facing us and staring seemingly phlegmatic.

He is completely unreadable and in control now. I can't tell if he is angry, curious or just being protective. I want him neither of those. I want him to feel in need.

I meet Josh's eyes, and my insides fill with longing, with pain.

I look back at Lucas to answer, "No. He's not."

A tear slides down my cheek, and I wipe it away quickly before either guy see's it fall. He's not my boyfriend. He was and then he wasn't, and it's in this very moment that I realize that is the problem. I want him to be, but I don't know how to express that. I don't know if I can. I also think Josh is playing mind games with me, and I can't figure out why. He *is* with Preslee. I believe that to be the truth.

I don't know why I do it. I think I'm fucking crazy. I think of all the times I saw Josh with some other girl. All the times I wanted it to be me, and he never saw it. I think about it, and I hate that I am thinking about it.

It's not fair. I know he watched me with Dean for two years, but right now in my state of mind...I'm selfish. All I think about is the pain *I* feel.

So I decide that if he cares at all about me, then if he sees me with someone else, maybe it will hurt him the same way. It makes sense in my fizzled brain. So, I lift myself to straddle Lucas's lap and place my hands in his hair. I hear a growl from across the room.

Lucas flicks his eyes briefly away from me and to Josh. But then he leans back, and his now hooded eyes lock with mine.

"Why do I feel like you're using me, sweetheart?" he asks in that voice.

"Because, I am." I answer honestly. I lower my face to his and bat my lashes sweetly. "Now kiss me," I demand. So, he does.

Josh immediately has me picked up and thrown over his shoulder, "Enough fun for you. I'm taking your ass home," he grunts.

Let's understand something. In my seventeen years of life, I have only kissed three people. Josh, because *I* had to, Dean, because *he* had to, and now...this Lucas guy—because he let me, and I am stupid.

Lucas is smiling. Why is he smiling? God, guys are the most peculiar species.

"Put me down, Josh. We can't just leave. I rode with Emily." I hit him on the back, and kick my feet trying to wiggle out of his grasp, but he is much stronger than I.

He smacks my ass HARD! "Ow," I squeal. Josh just squeezes me harder.

"Stop fighting me. Brandt already took her home. You were too wrapped up in revenge to notice." I slump.

"What? She just left me here. How was I going to get home?" I might be drunk, but I'm not stupid. Well, that is questionable too, I guess.

I sigh. I am pretty sure my 'Ginger' knew how I would get home. She did seem to be all, 'Team Josh,' today.

We get to his truck outside, and when Josh puts me down, my stomach suddenly turns. I know I am going to be sick.

"Oh, shit!" I rush to the grass. He holds my hair and rubs my back. I wretch until I dry heave. I feel like hell has swallowed me whole. I have just been a complete bitch to this boy, and he is standing here taking care of me. God, I feel beyond awful.

When there is nothing left, I stand. Josh pulls his shirt off and wipes my mouth, and tosses his shirt in the back of his truck.

"You okay?" he asks softly.

"No," I answer honestly.

"I didn't think so."

He takes my hand and pulls me into his chest. I hold him and breathe in his scent, the scent that I love. His skin is smooth and warm. Instantly, I know I have screwed up, but he is still *my Josh*.

I want him to always be just that. MINE!

CHAPTER 23

Even drunk, even angry...she still needs me. That say's something right?

I was patient for as long as I could be. Brandt told me he was taking Emily home because she wasn't okay to drive, and she was upset because it was her idea to bring Riley to the party. Thankfully, Brandt didn't drink tonight, filling in the older brother role as always.

Emily made me promise to bring Riley home, and if she refused she made me promise to stay here until morning when she picked up her car. She assumed Riley would pass out soon, but wasn't comfortable leaving her alone with Lucas.

Yeah, like I would let that happen anyway.

Brandt sent everyone home. Everyone but this prick on the couch with my girl. Evidently, the douche is staying on this damn couch for a while. He didn't elaborate with me, just said that he couldn't kick him out and asked me to not kill him. I laughed and made no promises.

When Riley straddles his lap, like she had me not too long ago, and begins kissing him, I feel a sudden bolt of rage flood my system, and a fucking need to protect her and keep her safe. It was my job. She was hurting herself, and it was my fault.

All these years it was Dean's fault but this... what she was doing tonight? This was my fault. Well, it technically was still Dean's fault, because it was Preslee's fault, but all in all—yep, it fell on me.

When I get her outside, she loses it, and I mean literally. Actually, even though it's gross, I am grateful. She has a helluva lot of tequila in her system, and I am glad she has emptied some of that.

As soon as we are in the truck, she lays her head on the center console and groans. I bet she feels like shit. If she doesn't now, she most definitely will in the morning.

I buckle her up and she doesn't move. I run my fingers through her hair and kiss the top of her head like I always do. I fear she has passed out, but then she sighs as though my touch hurts her.

"Riley, you are the most frustrating girl I know. Ya know that?" I say.

"M'hmm," she mumbles in approval.

"Thank you." she garbles, and I look down at her in confusion.

"For what exactly?" My tone is soft, and I can't stop looking at her face. I want to take her pain away. I want her to trust me, to never feel this way. But she just keeps trying to push me away.

"For... you... come... me... frust... ing... and... I... you...my... friend best...I'm sorry," she stutters.

I bit my lip to not laugh at her, because she is cute right now, and none of that made any sense whatsoever. "You're drunk, baby girl, and I have no idea what you just said, but I accept your apology. I think that's what that was anyway," I say.

She nods a little. I sigh and say, "I just wish you didn't hate me right now."

She attempts to lift her head but fails. She ends up turning her head a little, gazing at me with her beautiful eyes looking the prettiest shade of blue in the dim light. Her hair is in her face, and I tuck it away behind her ears.

She whispers, "I could never hate you, Josh. I love you too much. But...I hate me sometimes."

What does she mean by that? Why does she hate herself so much?

I don't get to ask her, because when I open my mouth to respond, her eyes are shut and her breathing has become shallow.

CHAPTER 24

Looking back, all the signs were there. My fear helped me ignore them and think I was safe. Even if I didn't give away my heart completely, he held enough of it to hurt me. He wasn't even supposed to have that much power. However, here I am feeling rejected and confused. It's all a blur of pain

I don't wake up until I am dropped into my bed through my window, and Josh is climbing in after me. I'm confused. Why didn't he just use the front door?

"I don't want you to get in trouble," he shrugs answering my unasked question.

I fall back onto my pillow on a groan. He is eyeing me all over, and I am eyeing him. "Be right back," he says and peeks out into the hall before walking out of my room. I shut my eyes.

Once he returns, he nudges me, and I reluctantly open my eyes. I'm so sleepy.

"Here, open." He says, handing me my toothbrush with the toothpaste already on it. I do as I'm told and attempt to brush my teeth.

"Spit," he places a cup before me, and again I do as I'm told.

He places a white pill into my palm and hands me a glass of water. "You will need this." I gratefully swallow the pill and drink the entire glass in one gulp. My mouth is parched.

He takes off my shoes and then pulls the covers away and tucks me in. He lowers himself to kiss my forehead, "Now sleep."

It is such a sweet gesture that I am falling in love with him all over again. He still has his shirt off, and I want to feel him, to hold him. I want his skin to warm mine.

I pout and hold out my arms "Stay with me," I whine and reach for his neck. "Pleeeaasssee?" I beg and pout some more.

He studies my face and sighs. He walks to lock my door, and when he turns around, I see the struggle in his eyes.

He uses his feet to take off his shoes, and when he unbuttons his jeans and takes them off, all I see is my Josh standing before me with nothing on but his boxers. I have forgotten completely about how sleepy I was, or that I was angry with him. I suddenly feel hungry—for him.

He climbs in and pulls my back to his chest to spoon, but that's not what I want, so I turn over. I wrap my leg around his hip and pull him close. I snuggle in tightly under his chin, breathing in his smell.

He tenses, and I can feel his heart beat on my cheek. Thump! Thump! Our music is going crazy inside of his chest.

I am engulfed in his scent and his warmth, and I am still a little drunk. And I am in need, but he doesn't move to touch me. Not yet.

I hear a little jingle from under my bed, and for a second, I'm confused as to what that sound is, but then I remember.

"What's that sound?" he asks me.

"That's my Tink. And her bell, it's on her collar. You get it? Tinker Bell?" I start laughing at myself, and I'm pretty sure it wasn't funny, but for whatever reason I think it is.

"M'kay," Josh says chuckling and snuggles me closer to him.

He brushes the hair away from my face and places a contented kiss on my forehead as he always does. He wraps his arm around my waist and hugs me tightly against him, resting his chin on my head. There is no space left between us. My leg is around his hip, my chest is pressed up against his, it feels—perfect.

Just for a moment, I let myself forget everything else. I need this moment of respite. I pull back just enough that our faces are inches apart now. His nose is almost touching my nose.

I watch his eyes study mine. I see it. Sadness. Regret. Remorse. Longing...even love. It hurts to see it, and I want to forget it's there, and that all of those emotions are sitting inside of me, too.

He moves his hand from around my waist and runs his fingertips down my leg over my hip and back up until his palm is cupping my ass.

An involuntary shiver runs up my spine, and delicious tingles are following his fingers path. I press my hip into him involuntarily. Now, we are perfectly lined up.

His eyes are boring into mine, penetrating every barrier. Everything I've tried to hide from him, I feel peeling away, and I'm scared shitless. I am open to him like this, and I can feel him in my most tender spot. His thumb is caressing the side of my shorts now and I want him to touch me. God, help me. I want him.

I shut my eyes and inhale deeply. I can feel his breath on my lips. He is so close, and I have a moment of trepidation. My body is covered in goose bumps, and now I have this coiling feeling in my stomach. He gently kisses each of my eyelids, my lips part as I exhale slowly. I feel him pull back slightly, and when I open my eyes dazedly, I find him studying my face. His eyes are clouded. He is fighting something. I can sense his inner battle.

"Josh?" I ask breathlessly.

He moves his hand away from my hip and skirts it up my side, brushing the side of my breast before he cups my cheeks with both hands. He's going to kiss me.

"Shhh," he whispers and then it happens. The Earth turns on its axis, my world stops. He so softly pecks my lips, gently licks along my bottom lip, parting my mouth, seeking permission to enter. A soft moan escapes me. My lips begin to quiver. His tongue enters my mouth and dances seductively with my own. The kiss is slow, sensual and damn near unravels me. It's over much too fast. He doesn't deepen it, even when I reach up and pull at his shoulders before tangling my fingers into his hair—begging him to do so. He keeps the kiss completely sweet and a breath away from innocent.

I am fully aware that this is blurring the lines of our relationship further. When he pulls back I am panting, I am shaking, I am beyond in need. He smiles the sexiest smile and taps his index finger to my nose.

"You need to sleep." He pecks my mouth one last time and rolls to his back, leaving me a quivering hot mess.

After a few minutes of silence and the sound of his breathing trying and failing to lull me to slumber, I take a peek and see his eyes are wide open and staring at my ceiling. Awake.

"Josh?" I breathe

"Hmm."

"Can I ask you something?"

"Go for it," he says without moving or looking at me.

"Why did you get me a white kitten? I mean...I think she is beautiful, don't get me wrong. But she is white as snow and had to be hard to find. I just wondered, why you chose her over others that are easier to find." I don't know why I choose this question now, but I've been wondering it.

She is a ragdoll kitten. And I know other kittens like calicos could be found free and anywhere.

He rolls onto his side propping up on his elbow. He gives me a look like he didn't expect to have to answer this question. "I chose her because white reminds me of purity...of innocence. It's how I see you, and her breed is known to be loyal to their owners, like a puppy would be. Everything about her seemed perfect and beautiful...like you."

Wow.

I watch his face closely. "You think I'm pure and innocent?" I state it like a question.

He frowns, "I see you that way. If you are or aren't doesn't matter to me."

Doesn't matter? It matters to me.

I sit up needing him to understand it. "Well, you're right you know?"

He reaches his hand up and smoothes my frown line. "Right about what?" his voice is soft and alluring.

This shouldn't make me sad, but it does, because I feel like I saved myself and in the end it was pointless.

"About my innocence. I um, I never, I mean...I am a—, Well, it doesn't matter, because, in the end...I'm not the kind of girl anyone wants anyway." I shake my head and look away from him.

"Ooookay" he says slowly. "Why do you say you're not wanted?"

Is he crazy? Because my boyfriend of two years dumped me after I wouldn't have sex with him. Because even Josh, who is lying here in my bed looking edible, would choose a girl like Preslee over a girl like me.

Sex. Sex. Sex. That is all they want.

"Because Josh. All you guys want is a girl that's easy. Y'all don't see it as something special to share with someone you love or care about. It doesn't matter that it's a big deal, a huge decision to make yourself that vulnerable." I whisper.

He sits up and turns my face to meet his. "Not all guys, Riley."

I want to believe him, but Preslee was at his house for a while *alone*. Like really? Am I supposed to believe they were just talking?

"Did I ever tell you why Dean broke up with me?" I ask.

He recoils slightly from hearing Dean's name and shakes his head.

"Well, it was simple actually. Have sex with him, or he was going to break up with me and find someone who would. I told him over and over again that I wasn't ready, to please not pressure me, but he was relentless. He tried to make me feel guilty, and it worked. I did feel guilty. Not for not doing it, but because I knew the reason I wasn't giving him what he wanted wasn't because I wasn't ready. It was because...I didn't want it to happen with *him*. He wasn't the one I wanted to share that with." I know I've just declared something huge to him—and to myself.

He clears his throat and shifts the comforter on his lap. It had fallen away from his bare chest when he sat up. His muscles, his tattoo, his chest all stir a desire in me. I study every inch while he looks at my face knowing I am doing so.

"Who did you want...ya know...um, to share that with?" He asks nervously, cautiously, even though he already knows the answer.

I don't hesitate in my answer, and I make sure my eyes are locked with his when I do. "You. I wanted you. I still want you." I say softly. I'm making myself vulnerable, but he should know, right? Right.

His chest is heaving, his eyes don't waiver away from mine. I'm very careful, very confident in what I am about to do.

I climb onto his lap slowly. He doesn't stop me. He just watches me with hooded eyes.

I touch his lips and then cup his cheek before moving to run my fingers through his hair. I feel his arousal, and my body is humming, aching for his touch.

"I'm just curious of something, Josh." I say, my voice sounding surprisingly seductive.

"What's that?" He says, refusing to touch me. No, his hands are placed carefully at his sides, although he is gripping the blanket as though he is fighting the instinct to touch me. I like it.

I reach for the hem of my shirt and pull it over my head. I'm wearing a black lace bra. He swallows hard, and his eyes are naturally drawn to where I want them. "What are you doing?" he asks me, his own voice sounding dark and needy.

"Testing a theory." I say as I glide one of my hands down my stomach to the buttons of my shorts, while I push his chest back to lying down with my other.

I have him positioned right where I want him, and I know he is completely affected by me by the dilation of his eyes and the groan he makes deep in his throat. I really like that sound.

I lean up onto my knees that are on both sides of his hips. I unclasp and unzip my shorts. I open them enough that my tattoo is visible, and he can see my nice black lace bra has a matching friend of black lace panties.

"Dean wanted someone who would be *open* with him, kinda like I am right now, I would assume. I wasn't that way for him, and he left me. I know the kind of girl Preslee is. I'm thinking maybe you like— no, let me rephrase that. Maybe you *want* the same kind of girl. I'm just curious, if I let you touch me here," I reach up and cup my breast with my left hand "or here?" I reach between my legs onto my panties to cup myself with my right hand. "Would you want me, would you choose me instead of her?" I breathe heavy and look down at him, waiting for his reply.

He grabs me by the waist, flips me onto my back leaving me breathless. "You're fucking killing me, Riley. You don't know what you're saying." He breathes holding his weight on his arms.

I run my hands down his arms, tracing the outline of *my* rose. "I know exactly what I'm saying, Josh. I want you, and I want you to want me to. No, I don't just want it, Josh. I need it. You told me 'anything I need' remember? I need you." I say shameless pushing my hips up to him.

"Fuuuuck." He drawls on a growl and rolls off of me onto his back, grabbing his hair and rubbing his hands across his face.

Immediately embarrassment and rejection fills me, and I begin to shake my head and cry. "You don't want me do you?"

"What?" He sounds shocked. "Riley, does this feel like someone who doesn't want you?" He places my hand on top of his boxers, and I can feel him throbbing and hard.

I try to grab him, to pull on him, but he grabs my wrist to stop me. He pins my wrist above my head and rolls back on top of me. My legs open to let him rest in between them. He pushes his arousal onto me, and I gasp at the feeling of it. "Oh God, Josh. Please?"

"That's what you do to me, Riley. I want you so damn bad it hurts sometimes, and what hurts more than that is you have no fucking clue. But you're drunk right now, and you d*on't* know what you're saying." He is looking directly in my eyes with a serious face.

I wrap my legs around his waist and try to grind my hips against him. My head falls back. Even that feels so good. I whimper and he grunts. I feel out of control. "Riley, stop!" He holds me still.

"Please, Josh. I want you to fuck me. I will let you, just like she does. I need you." I beg, and he curses again.

He releases me and jumps from the bed like I've burned him. He is looking down at me with such heat that I feel myself coming undone. "I can't," he whispers.

I sit up and pull the covers over my body. "Can't or won't?" I ask feeling the pit in my stomach grow wide.

"Both," he starts pulling on his jeans, and I know he is going to leave. He is telling me no. He is turning me down, and I am devastated. He doesn't want me. He isn't choosing me. Not even like this.

I roll onto my stomach to hide my eyes, hide my tears, but I know I am shaking, and he can hear me. I feel so stupid. Well, that is that. Not even nearly naked does Josh want me.

I feel the bed indent as he smoothes his hands along my back. "Riley, I'm leaving, because I don't trust myself right now with you. Not because I don't want you. Please, know that. When we do this, when we have this conversation again, and *we will* have this conversation again, just when you're sober. I want you to know what you are asking for. I want you to know it's what you want…I want you to *remember* it. You are drunk, and you're most definitely not yourself right now. Everything about tonight is not you, Riley. As far as fucking you…" He leans down to whisper in my ear, and I shiver from his warm breath. "I don't want to do that. I want to love you, baby. Nice and slow. I want to make love to you. I want to cherish you because believe it or not, Riley. I've been waiting to share it with you, too. There is no one better for me than you. *You* are what I want. You, Riley—just the way you are." He kisses the top of my head and leaves out my bedroom window.

I heard him but I barely heard him at all. All I know is Josh rejected me. He told me he can't and won't love me. I never should have said anything. I feel drained and completely exhausted. I hope I remember this tomorrow, or maybe I hope I don't. I'm not so sure of what I hope for anymore.

CHAPTER 25

Note to self: tequila makes Riley a damn good temptress, one I really didn't want to deny. If I had taken advantage of her like that though, I would have regretted that decision. Too bad every word she said tells me that what she believes to be reality is so far from the fucking truth that she was willing to do—that. FML

It's been one week, three days, six hours and 32 minutes since that beautiful day with Riley turned into a nightmare, one I can't seem to escape from.

She won't answer my calls. She won't reply to my text. She won't let me come over, and she avoids me in the halls at school. She flat out ignores me like I don't exist.

I hate every fucking minute and every damn second of it.

Every day I have slipped a yellow/red rose bud in her locker and watched from afar as she smelled the scent, touched it's delicate pedals, frowned and placed them in the trash in the hall. She doesn't look at me. She doesn't look at anyone.

In fact, Riley has been walking around in a shell of her old self, her head cast down, and her shoulders slumped as though she is carrying the weight of the world—in a complete zombie like state.

I miss her smile. I miss her laugh. I miss the way her blue/green eyes used to sparkle. Now...it's just all—absent. Missing. Not there.

The only person she seems to speak to is Emily, and unfortunately, Emily isn't speaking much to me either. So, I'm not in the know as to what is going on in Riley's head these days. Never in our entire life, have I not known what was going on. Never. This is a new territory, and I don't like it.

I couldn't take it any longer. I found a notepad at the store with Tinker Bell on it. I began leaving her little notes that I thought would break the ice.

"I miss you."

"I'm so sorry."

"Please, forgive me."

"I miss your voice."

"I need to talk to you."

"Call me."

Anything and everything and nothing from her.

It doesn't help that Preslee is becoming a constant thorn in my side. She was always trying to talk to me, popping up unwanted in places, which never fails to be somewhere Riley just happens to be around to see it—making yet another wrong assumption.

I headed to Collin's for a distraction. It wasn't supposed to be a party—just us guys hanging out. But being as though my luck has been shit lately, it shouldn't have surprised me that Preslee and Laiken walked in like they owned the place.

Of course, Collin is happy, he will be getting laid. Dean not so much, which makes me wonder if Preslee has finally told him about the baby.

She doesn't seem to care at all that he is blowing her off. In fact, she is back to being the giggling chick on my side, and I wish she would just leave.me.alone.

It's been days, hours, and countless minutes since I have talked to Riley.

When my phone rings and I see it's her name, my heart leaps out of my chest. Preslee sees the name too and grabs the phone out of my hand answering it for me. I have never wanted to hit a girl. Ever. But in that moment, I wanted to throw her as far away from me as I could. She was fucking up my life.

CHAPTER 26

It's crazy how things change with every breath you take. One minute you have both your parents, and the next minute one is gone and has taken the life of another. One minute you have a non-perfect relationship with a boyfriend, to not having one at all. One minute you finally get the courage to let yourself love your best friend, to then find yourself rejected. One minute you think you know everything about someone, and then you find out they have held a secret of their own from you. One minute you think it can't get any worse, and then it does, and your world is flipped upside down.

So much has happened since that wonderful day with Josh became one of the worst in my life. It's just gone downhill ever since.

The day after Josh rejected me and chose Preslee, I was a mass of confusion, and the shocking realization set in—humiliating me.

"Tatum, have you seen my keys? I can't find my keys, and I have a 10:00 appointment." I heard my mom shouting outside my bedroom door.

"Mmmm," I grunted as I ever so slowly tried to open my heavy lids. My head was pounding. What was I thinking getting trashed like that? I *hadn't been* thinking, and that was the goal. Gah, I tried to will my body to move. I was hurting. The room was spinning.

I must have been dreaming about Josh, because I swore I could smell him all over my pillows and sheets. It was a heady mix.

I dragged myself up when my mom started banging on my door.

"Have you seen my keys?" she asked me. *Please, don't yell.*

"No, sorry." I told her.

"Found em. Bye, girls. Be back later."

I walked into the hall and literally bumped right into Tatum mid-step and fell into the wall. "Oh, sorry." I grumbled, and she stepped back to help me.

"You ok? Oh wow, Riley. You look like hell. Forget your p.j.'s?" she giggled a little. "What time did you get home? I didn't hear you come in." she asked me and then sniffed me before I could even answer. "Ewww, you stink. Did Emily not roll the window down in the car or something" she scrunches her nose.

"Oh God, stop talking. Please. "My head is killing me. I don't know the answer to any of that, sorry." I said.

I sidestepped her to get in the bathroom. She just shook her head at me "Ok. Well, whatever..." and walks into her room.

I used the bathroom and hopped in the shower, praying my head would quit throbbing. I let the warm water trickle all over me. I washed my hair and then washed it a second time for good measure. I knew it smelled like smoke. I leaned against the wall and tried to sort out my head.

I couldn't remember how I got home, but I felt as though Josh had taken me. I hoped Emily made it home okay. "Oh God, Emily?" I shouted to no one. I'd kissed Emily, not just kissed, like I full on made out with her. Oh no!

Josh saw me kiss Emily. Oh and he was mad. I yelled at him. I yelled at Emily. Why would I do that? I think I even kissed that card table guy. What the hell was his name? Lucas, yes Lucas. Who was he anyway? Oh goodness, I kissed Lucas. And Josh saw that too.

My head was spinning, and I felt beyond nauseous right then. I let the water pour over my face and tried my hardest to remember the rest.

Josh had carried me to his truck. I'd thrown up. That is so embarrassing, I thought. But I just couldn't remember anything else. I was definitely in his truck. I thought I said 'sorry' or maybe he said 'sorry'. I'm not positive. He brought me home, though. I am certain of that now, but everything else was still a blur.

I wrapped myself in a towel and went to brush my teeth. "Where the hell is my tooth brush?" I said out loud to no one again. I moved some things around on the counter, but I couldn't find it anywhere.

"That's weird. Hey, Tater? Have you seen my toothbrush?" I shouted out the door.

"Nope, sorry" she replied.

Ugh! I thought. This was going to be a craptastic kinda day. I brushed my teeth with my finger and swished mouthwash until I couldn't take the burn any longer.

I headed back to my room to get dressed. I felt so yuck. I decided comfort was the way to go. I had no desire to get cute. So, I threw on my black, cotton shorts and a grey aero t-shirt. I quickly brushed through my tangles and pulled my hair up into a topknot. I stared at myself in the dresser mirror, and even I frightened myself by my own reflection.

I wasn't big on makeup, but that day I needed some. After I swept some powder and blush over my face, I leaned into the mirror to do my eyes. In the reflection, I noticed my bedside table. I didn't know why I even glanced there, but something seemed out of place. There were two cups and, "Hey there's my toothbrush?" I said out loud again. Apparently, that was my thing that day. Talking to myself. What's that doing there, I wondered?

In a matter of breaths, images flicker into my mind. I immediately turn my body around to face my bed, the table and the window. I rub my fingers along my temples and try to think. It was still fuzzy...but there.

I was in my bed. Josh was there. Based on my toothbrush being there, I'd brushed my teeth in there, but that didn't make sense. Why would I do that? Wait! Josh gave it to me. Another image flickered in, and I gasped. I covered my mouth with my hand and crouched down onto the floor. This was bad. Tatum had laughed at me in the hall, and she'd asked me if I forgot my p.j.'s. I wasn't wearing them. Where were they? And it slammed into me like a punch in the gut. "Oh, oh, oh my god. I…Oh!" I pulled my knees up and rested my head on them.

Tatum came into my room just as I remembered the most humiliating, the most devastating part of that night. "Why are you on the floor? You're really pale, Riley. Are you okay this morning?" she asked and knelt down to feel my forehead. Why couldn't she stick with one question? She asked one and jumped to another, and I couldn't keep up. "I uh, I think I'm gonna be sick" I bolted for the door.

I barely made it to the toilet when I proceeded to dry heave. I was a fucking mess. I was almost positive I had done something completely stupid. I heaved again hugging the toilet. "Oh shit, Riley," Tatum said from behind me. "I'm ok." I lied and face planted down onto the cool tiles of the floor.

They felt like heaven on my cheeks, and I just wanted to stay there. I didn't want to face what I thought was to be the truth. I'd offered myself to Josh, and he'd rejected me. He'd said some stuff and I couldn't remember what, but I knew he'd said no. He didn't want me. And feeling rejected hurt like a bitch.

I was so ashamed of myself. I couldn't believe I'd acted that way. That wasn't me at all. Although, lately...I was not even sure who the real me was anymore. I wished I had someone to talk to about that stuff. I really felt like I was falling apart. I was making one bad decision after the other. Fucking it up and then fucking it up again because of the prior fuck up. Yep, that was me—FUCKED!

I spent the rest of that day in bed listening to music and writing in my notebook the darkest of dark poetry. I bet Rebel would be so happy. However those words would probably make the fans of her band think they needed psychiatric help.

I was thinking I did as well. I texted Emily to see if she was okay, and she was. She wanted to come over, but I told her that I was hungover, and I would see her at school. I wasn't ready just yet to tell her what I had done. Josh had sent me a text asking me if I was okay. Apparently, we were all worried about each other. I replied with a simple 'yes'. He tried to call me, but I didn't answer, and when Tatum told me he was at the front door for me, I told her to tell him I was sleeping.

He knew I wasn't.

I couldn't go there. I didn't want to. I didn't have it in me.

I had been doing my best to ignore Josh, avoid him completely. An entire week went by and it was hard, really, *really* hard to not speak to him and act like I didn't see him.

We went to the same school, he lived next door and we were intertwined. It didn't help that he left me roses, and not just any rose but *my rose*—a color that represented what he and I shared. Then he started leaving me little notes on Tinker Bell stationary. It was torture.

I thought my shock would wear off, but instead, it was just buried underneath another shock to my system. A shock from yet another best friend in my life was about to shake me to the core with a truth I had no idea was coming my way.

"I did something a looooong time ago. I never told you, Riley. I didn't want you to hate me. And it was just a few times. I…I …" She sobs. Emily had been crying since she came over. It was Saturday night, and she was supposed to be keeping me company, something about, 'me becoming the walking dead' or some shit.

"Ooooookay," I say slowly. "Just tell me, Em. I could never hate you. Ever" I attempt to reassure her.

She takes a deep breath, she can't even look me in the eye as she speaks. "Dean and I…well, we kind of had a thing freshman year. But it didn't go anywhere. Remember? He liked you, and you and I weren't real friends then. I didn't care about your feelings like I do now. You never really seemed to like him. You kept pushing him away."

She clears her throat, "I was so jealous of you when he asked you to the freshman dance and not me. I started watching you, and you were always watching Josh. I knew then that you didn't really like Dean. He just seemed oblivious, but I saw it." She said every word super-fast. It was hard to keep up. It was like she had to hurry and say it before she changed her mind, like she had been holding it in and wanted to say it ages ago.

I go to speak to clarify. Well, not even to clarify, because she was spot on about my feelings for Josh and lack thereof for Dean.

She holds up her hand to stop me. "I need to finish. You need to know the truth, even if you never speak to me again." She frowns, and I have a sudden realization that whatever she is going to say is going to change our friendship, otherwise she wouldn't have warned me like that. I nod for her to continue and find myself holding my breath. I don't want to lose her too. I can't.

She swallows and puffs out a breath, "Sophomore year came around, and his crush on you only escalated. And well, mine on him did as well. I was surprised when the year began that y'all weren't together. Dean said you wouldn't make it official and…Just know…I never thought in a million years that you and I would end up being best friends, Riley. We did, though. Had I known you would end up meaning so much to me, I never would have…I never would've—,"

"Never would've what, Em? Just fucking, tell me! Rip the Band-Aid off. Do it!" I yell, growing exasperated. I had no patience for this shit anymore.

"I slept with him. I was Dean's first, he was mine. We hooked up several times sophomore year, but it didn't matter. I thought if I gave him something you weren't that he would choose me, but he didn't. He still kept pursuing you, and basically used me and tossed me aside."

Holy shit! Well, didn't that sound familiar? Except Dean took what Emily offered and still didn't choose her. At least, Josh had rejected me when I put the offer of my naked-drunk-self on his table.

"Oh my God!" is all that comes out my mouth. I have no words. I have nothing. I don't know what to say. I didn't see that coming. She was his first? But wait he had told me…he said he was a virgin.

"That doesn't make sense, Em. He told me he was a virgin. He broke up with me because I wouldn't sleep with him. He said I wasn't meeting his needs, and that he couldn't wait anymore, because he was ready and I wasn't. But…you're telling me he had already done *it* with you? He's been lying to me for two years? I mean…he's been lying to me for two years." It's no longer a question. He has! I'm sooooo stupid.

"You are a virgin?" she asked like it surprised her.

"Yes, that's not the point here. What a bastard."

She sighs and wipes the tears that have been falling freely since she walked into my room. Weird, I can't even bring myself to cry. I'm fucking pissed.

"Em, if he has been lying to me about that. Who's to say he hasn't been screwing around the entire time we have been together?"

And then I think, "Who was he with at that party with, when y'all all went bat shit crazy on me?" I ask her.

She frowns and shrugs, "I didn't see her. I don't know."

"But he was *with* someone? And I don't mean hanging out in the kitchen refilling their red solo cups. He was *with* someone?" I ask already knowing the answer.

"Yes, Collin said he was upstairs. He didn't say with who, and I never asked. I went outside to smoke, and when he came outside he was alone. There were several skanky girls there, Riley. It could have been any of them," she tells me honestly.

I nod and feel fury overtook me. The feeling to numb my pain is so strong. I want comfort. I want peace. I want to be in the arms of the one I love, but he doesn't want me. He wants girls the way Dean wants girls. Girls apparently like Emily. Well, kinda like Emily. She wasn't really a slut.

I'm shocked at myself for being so stupid. I'm disappointed in myself. I'd pushed away the one guy that I knew I loved, still love, in fear that I didn't deserve to be with him. Fear, because he held so much of my heart, to lose him would kill me. I'd convinced myself that Dean was safe, that our relationship was so innocent that being with him couldn't hurt me, but here I am. Hurt. Broken. Feeling lost. Alone. All this loss could have been prevented had I just chosen correctly the first time.

"Riley?"

I have so much pent up energy at the moment. My blood is boiling. I want to scream, I want to cry, and I want to throw things. Instead, I pace my floor. "I just need some time, Em. This is a lot to take in. Ya know? I just didn't realize the past two years was all a lie. None of it was real. I'm just so fucking angry right now. I wanted Josh. I still want, Josh. You were right. But then my dad died. My dad killed his mom and—shit! I just couldn't...I couldn't go there. And Dean, he never stopped pushing me, he was so sweet to me around that time. Josh had pulled away from me. I just figured he needed space from me. Dean slithered in at the perfect time. He knew just how to create those little doubts in my head. I attached myself to him. I don't know why I did. He felt safe, and he wasn't. It's just not fair. I was supposed to be with Josh. I'm supposed to be with Josh. Everything that has happened…Oh God!"

I felt the bile rising, burning my throat.

"It's not too late to fix this, Riley. Even if you hate me, it's not too late. Josh is still Josh, and you are still you. I know he cares about you. Hell, he might even love you if you let him." She says.

Love? What the hell was that anyway? Love wasn't real. Love broke hearts, betrayed trust, and left you alone in pieces.

"Love isn't real, Emily." I say. Silly girl.

She just looks at me like she doesn't understand, or doesn't agree. "Yes, it is Riley. Love can be beautiful. You've only been shone the ugly in it, but I've seen it, Riley. Love is beautiful, and you and Josh…you have a chance to let it be beautiful."

I wish that were true. I do, but I just don't believe in it. Not anymore.

I tell Emily about my drunken behavior with Josh, and how he left me in my bed—rejected me and told me he didn't want me. She is shocked most that I did what I did, but she is disappointed to hear that Josh was choosing Preslee over me. She doesn't believe it, but after everything else that has happened, her 'half glass full' speech from earlier is becoming more of a 'half glass empty' one.

The tears come unbidden. I love Emily. Regardless of all of it, I love her. I couldn't be completely alone. In my mind she is just as much a victim in this game as I am. She just chose to take her path a little earlier than me.

I hug her like my life depends on it. "Thanks, Emily."

"You don't hate me?" she asks my hair.

I shake my head and sniffle. "No way. You're my bitch. I need you."

She giggles and sniffles too. "You're my bitch, too. Always."

"Always."

After Emily leaves, I decide that I need to quit avoiding the inevitable. I need to talk to Josh. I miss his voice, and I just want things to go back to the way they were. Even if I couldn't have him the way my heart longed for him, I knew I needed to have him in my life anyway I could—even as only my friend. I pick up my phone and finally hit the call button, after my fingers hovered over his contact for minutes.

After two rings the calming voice I was missing was not the voice I heard.

"Hello" a female says. Not his sister's voice. I didn't speak at first.

"Heeeeello" she says a little slower and more antagonistic. I knew she knew who I was if she answered his phone. My name was stored in his phone. *That bitch!*

"Um, hi, is Josh there?" I ask, regret immediately washing over me. I should have never picked up my phone.

"Yeah, he is. But he's *busy*," she says laughing. I can hear Josh in the background. "Fuck, Preslee! Give me the damn phone."

OH MY GOD! I'm sitting here in tears, my life in complete shambles, missing him, and he's fucking with her. Who was I kidding to ever think I mattered to him the way he did to me?

"It's some girl, Joshie." Her voice sounded muffled like she was speaking away from the phone. *Some girl?* Back the truck up. Some girl? I am *his* girl. Oh, that's right. I'm not. Am I?

"Hey, where are you going?" she says, sounding further in the distance. I hear him say with his voice in the phone, "You can be a real bitch, Preslee." A door slams and then...quiet.

"Riley, baby?" He sounds nervous, anxious even.

My heart is in pieces. "Yeah, it's me" I sound breathless.

"God, I've been so worried about you. Are you okay?" Am I okay? I had no words. Really, his way of being worried about me sucked.

"Riley, you there?"

"Yeah, I'm still here. Look, I shouldn't have called you. I'm sorry. I know you're busy. I'll let you go." *I have to let you go.*

"Dammit! I'm not busy, Riley. Please, don't hang up."

"I um...I have to go, Josh. I just needed to hear your voice. But um, I don't need to so much anymore. Tell Preslee I said hi." I say with all the anger I am feeling.

"FUCK!" he yells "Fucking hell. Please. Don't hang up, Riley. Talk to me," he begs

I can't stop the tears from falling. I try to choke back the sobs I feel coming but it is useless. I am crying in the phone, and I know he can hear me.

"It's not what you think. Baby? Please, talk to me!" he pleads again, and my heart breaks further.

"I can't. I have to go. Goodbye, Josh" I hang up and drop it like it burned me to hold it.

Josh was going on with his life like nothing happened, and I was stuck. I was like a record spinning in circles stuck on the same lyric—on repeat. HE IS MINE! He was supposed to be mine. The thought strangled me, but never stealing enough air to let me find peace.

My phone immediately starts ringing. Josh calls over and over and over again, before I finally shut my phone off. It's over. I can't love him. He doesn't love me. Love doesn't exist in my world. It never has.

CHAPTER 27

Loneliness is a crippling son of a bitch. Ya know who else is a bitch? Preslee. I don't know what game she is playing, but it's costing me EVERYTHING!

Riley no longer meets me at our tree for lunch. I go to the lake to walk, just hoping one of these times I will run into her at our spot. I don't. My emotions keep filtering between angry, sad, confused, pissed off to now worried.

That's right, I am completely freaked out and worried about her.

She looks like she is losing weight. She looks a mess, and my heart is tattered watching her be so broken.

It's like watching a train wreck happen, and I can't stop it.

Yesterday, I finally had enough. I was going to make her talk to me. I went to meet her in the hall during lunch break where I saw her standing with Emily. They had just come out of the bathroom.

My stomach twisted into knots when I noticed she looked as pale as a ghost. I called her name, and when she looked at me, I was shocked by the expression she was wearing on her face. Emily shouted at me that 'now was not a good time.'

I ignored her and tried to make sure Riley was okay, but then Dean came out of nowhere and started rambling shit off to her that I couldn't hear. Not that I physically couldn't hear him, I just didn't hear him. I was too focused on the emotion I saw on Riley's face.

She looked sick, scared, and sad. I didn't understand it. Out of the bathroom across from us walked up Preslee, and in an instant fear prickled in my soul. "Ugh…is she like sick or something." Preslee said. Emily responded with "Or something."

Riley began to struggle to breathe. She was making wheezing sounds, was hunched over like she couldn't grab enough air. Within a minute, she passed out right there in the hall. I've never been so scared.

Something was definitely wrong. Preslee freaking shrugged and walked off. Like I said, what a bitch.

Nurse Carmichael took Riley away, and she didn't come to school today. After school, I plan on going to her house and making sure she is okay.

CHAPTER 28

Shockwaves like a tsunami kept knocking me over, pushing me further back but never drowning me. Eventually, I would swallow enough, be without oxygen long enough that I would drown. Would no longer have a heartbeat, maybe then I would feel peace.

I am laying on the couch in the living room on my mom's lap. She is worried about me. What mother wouldn't be when the school nurse calls to tell you that your daughter passed out at school?

"Mom, do you think it's possible to know someone your entire life and not really know them at all?" I ask her.

"I'm not sure how to answer that, sweetie. Why don't you tell me what happened yesterday, Riley?" she spoke softly playing with my hair.

"Okay. Well, Dean and I broke up. Not yesterday but we broke up."

"I see, that explains some things." She says.

"Well, I decided to take your advice. I told Josh how I felt about him. He um…he told me he felt the same way, but he lied to me. He has a girlfriend, or well…another girl, at least. He told me otherwise, but it wasn't true."

"Oh, Riley. I'm sorry, baby girl." She consoles me sympathetically.

"That's not the worst part, Mom." I can't get Preslee's words out of my head.

When Emily and I walked to the bathroom during lunch break, we came to a silent dead stop as Preslee and Laiken were in one of the stalls talking to each other.

"What are you going to do Preslee? I can't believe this is happening to you." Laiken said.

"I know right. Like I don't know really, but I feel like so much better about it after I talked to Josh." Preslee told Laiken.

"But a baby, Preslee? You're only seventeen. Your Dad is going to lose his shit."

I didn't hear the rest. I literally grabbed Emily's hand like a lifeline and stumbled out of the bathroom. A baby? She talked to Josh? All I heard was she was going to have a baby with Josh. A baby.

"What's the worst part, Riley?" My mom asks breaking into my reverie.

"He's gonna have a baby. With her." I say quietly as tears well up in my eyes and trickle down my cheek. I've lost Josh.

"Oh, God. Oh sweetheart. I'm so sorry." What else could she say? It's like déjà vu for her, except I'm not the one pregnant.

Rain is pitter patting against my window, and the rumble of thunder and a strike of lightening make me jump. Eventually, the trickle of rain and the sound on the roof lulls me to sleep. I doze off on the couch and the best dream turned into the worst nightmare in a matter of deep breaths.

Josh and I were baking brownies in my kitchen, and he told me he loved me, only me. There was no Dean, no Preslee. We were in this bubble of just us. He said he was going to stay with me after graduation. We got married in this beautiful church surrounded by our families. My dad was still alive, and he and my mom were holding hands with smiles on their faces, completely in bliss. Josh's parents were together too and very much in love. Tatum, Joey and Emily were my bridesmaids. Brandt, Collin and Beau were Josh's groomsman. It was perfect until it wasn't. When the wedding was over, we walked outside where various colors of rose pedals were thrown at us. Symbolic. The sky turned black and dark, thundered rolled, and it frightened me. I looked down at all the rose pedals—no longer full of color—they were all now black. They swirled in the wind as the scene changed, and we were at the reception. Josh and I were dancing slowly and ever so sweetly, but he was distracted. His eyes weren't on mine. His eyes were across the room, and when I tracked his line of sight…I saw her—Preslee—at our wedding. I guided his face back to mine where I kissed him, and he embraced me. Then fear shook me, he vanished with my arms suspended in mid-air, my lips puckered to a ghost. I searched frantically, looking left and right. Everyone laughed at me sinfully. I couldn't find him. My dad walked to me, his arms around some woman I didn't recognize. His voice when he spoke to me was full of resentment toward me, "It will never work, Riley. Some choices are mistakes. You were my mistake. Because of you, I spent years with the wrong person," he said full of hatred and bitterness. My mom was at a nearby table crying with Tatum. I still couldn't find Josh. I ran from the church as fast as I could, until I was back in my room at home. It was there when I saw him through my window, through his window, naked and having sex with Preslee. I screamed, and he looked at me smirking wickedly, before taking her again. I watched with horror as they moved together, the erotic sounds of pleasure filling my ears painfully. He wasn't looking at me anymore, but his voice was right there whispering in my ear as though he were standing right next to me. I got a chill as I felt his breath, but he wasn't by me, he was by her, he was on her, he was inside her. "There is no one better for me than you," he said. I remembered hearing that before, but I couldn't figure out from where. I turned my eyes away from what I was witnessing and slowly toward the voice, and there he was standing beautifully in his tux. He placed his hand to cup my cheek, and I leaned into his touch. He lowered down to kiss my lips. He was a breath apart from my mouth, but he didn't touch me. No, he just laughed and guided my head back to the window and pointed, "Except for her," he said. And then he was gone, just as a bolt of lightning struck the ground, and I jolted awake.

It takes me minutes to catch my breath, to calm myself. I can't help but sob, my body shaking in fear. My insecurities and my doubts are contaminating all of my thoughts, now even my dreams.

After school, Emily stops by. We are sitting in my room eating sweets (starbursts, skittles and chewy sweet tarts). A good sugar rush might make me feel better. She gives me all the pink and red starbursts because they are my favorite. However, I give her all the red skittles because those are her favorite, and I hate those.

I have Stone Sour playing *Through Glass* on my iHome. It means something to me. I feel each word all the way down to my soul.

I tell Emily all about my dream, and she hugs me sympathetically. "It's going to be okay, Riley. I promise." Promises can't be kept though can they? They always get broken somehow.

"Please, just tell her I want to talk to her." I hear Josh's voice loud and clear from the front of the house.

"Not now, Josh. Look, she isn't feeling well today, and Emily is over right now." My mom explains to him.

"At least, tell me she is okay? I'm worried about her." He says, and my heart splinters further.

"She will be, Josh. Just let it go for now. Okay? I will tell her you stopped by." She tells him, shutting the door.

Emily and I stare at each other the entire time. Screw sugar, screw music. I don't know what I need, but I'm tired of crying. I don't need this.

My sister walks into my room sheepishly and concerned. "Hey, Ri. Can I come in?"

I shrug, and Emily tells me she is going to the bathroom. Tatum sits down and goes to steal my pink starburst. I swat her hand away and give her an orange one. "What's up, Tator Tot?" I ask her teasingly. Of course, she frowns and sticks out her tongue. It makes me laugh which is a welcomed feeling.

"I just wanted to say that, I think you should talk to Josh. You should see him, Riley. He is all-kinds-of-pouty. Josh pouty is kind of cute by the way, but that's beside the point." She says with wide, pretty, blue eyes like our daddy's.

I immediately think that, of course, Josh is pouty, but I don't believe it has anything to do with me. I grab my sister's hand, tilt my head and smile. "Look, I know you want me and Josh together, but I just don't think it's going to happen." I clear my throat, "It was a stupid thing for me to do anyway, and I shouldn't have let it happen." I say.

"What was stupid?" she scrunches her face in confusion.

I sigh and in a small voice I whisper, "Falling in love with my best friend."

Tatum feels my forehead all dramatic like. "Are you crazy, Riley? It wasn't stupid, and it wasn't something you could've stopped from happening either. It was meant to be. He's your soul mate. Face it, you will never love anyone the way you love Josh."

"I agree with Tot." Emily interjects, coming back in my room.

Awesome. But she was right.

I will never love anyone the way I love Josh.

 Josh

CHAPTER 29

And like the snake he is, I see him slither in holding out that apple for her to taste, and vulnerable as she is…she does!

Days are blurring into each other. Before I know it, a month goes by and then another. Soon it will all come to an end, and I fear it will be without my best friend. I've lost her.

I walk out of the door of the school to a sight I wasn't expecting at all. Riley is sitting there on a bench and beside her is Dean? He is holding her hand, and her head is tilted on his shoulder. I guess I shouldn't be completely shocked. They do have a two-year history, and she isn't aware of the monster he is underneath that fake exterior.

I could tell her. I could blast it right now. But what would it matter? She doesn't believe anything I say. It's too late to go back and change that now. Her eyes meet mine as I walk past.

She lifts her head promptly and sighs when I look between them. I keep on walking without saying a word.

I'm sitting in my truck in the parking lot, just watching like a caged animal ready to strike. This is the worst kind of pain imaginable, but I can't look away.

I jump when someone taps on my window. I look over to the window and it's Emily.

"Watcha looking at, Josh?" she asks like she hasn't been ignoring me for weeks.

I nod my head in the direction of the love I lost, and watch as Riley hugs Dean. I'm coming undone.

"Oh!"

"I just don't get it. Why is she even talking to him? She won't speak to me but she will *him*?" I ask out loud, not really to Emily, but just out loud.

"Can I get in? It's kinda hot out here," she says.

I look at her confused, but I figure maybe she is ready to explain the pieces of this puzzle I must be missing.

I pop the lock, and she walks over, hopping into my truck. She doesn't say anything at first.

"I don't think it's what it looks like. Trust me. She can't stand Dean after the things I told her months ago." Emily explains.

"Is that so? I assume you told her he cheated then?" I ask her and she nods.

"Yeah, she feels betrayed, but that wasn't the biggest shocker for her." She admits, and I don't know how she found out, but I assume she has.

"So, she knows about the baby?" I ask. Emily makes a strange expression. Although, I'm starting to question that truth myself. Preslee isn't showing any signs of being pregnant.

Emily makes a sound in her throat, "Yeah, she does."

"Then...why the hell is she sitting there with him all cozy? Isn't she pissed that he lied to her?" Something just isn't adding up to me.

Emily looks confused, "Josh, what do you expect for her to do? Yeah, she is fucking pissed at him for lying, but I think she is more heartbroken at the fact that *you* lied to her."

I look at her shocked and confused, "I never lied to her. I have been telling her the truth over and over, but she won't listen to me. He is the liar." I point out the front windshield at the devil in disguise. What are these girls not understanding about this? My story has never changed, because it's not a damn story.

"Josh, c'mon? We heard Preslee tell Laiken about the baby."

"So?"

"Are you kidding me? What do you mean...so? You did lie to her, Josh. We know Preslee is pregnant with your baby."

Wait! What?

"What the fuck? What? Oh no, no! What are you talking about, Em?" Ah, hell no.

"Riley and I overheard Preslee tell Laiken about the baby. *Your* baby." She speaks cautiously and is looking nervously at me.

"FUCK!" I shout and hit the steering wheel. I look over at Emily as she has her hand on the door like she is ready to bolt. "I NEVER touched her." I shout. "I have tried and tried to get her to leave me alone, and she is just always there like a disease without a cure. That baby isn't mine, if there is even a baby. And if there is, it's Dean's. She told me herself…the night she came over and ruined everything. She told me she was pregnant with *Dean's* baby." I soften my voice because I can tell I am frightening her. I am frightening myself.

Emily's cogs are turning. I can see her dithering in what I've just said. "Dean's?" she says like it's a question but could be a possibility.

I bob my head up and down, "Yes. Dean knocked her up. I've never even fucked her." I say a little bit harsher than I intended.

I see it the minute she believes me. "Holy shit. Josh, Riley thinks that baby is yours." She yells and slaps her hand to the dashboard looking over at me.

When I look back out to where Dean and Riley were just standing together, I see nothing. They are gone. I had the sickest twisted knot in my stomach.

"I have to go," I tell Emily. She nods and apologizes, but then gets out.

I'm not taking no for an answer this time. Riley *will* speak to me.

"Please, Ms. Claudia. I need to talk to her. She is misunderstood about something. I need to explain to her before it's too late. I need to fix this." I beg.

"Josh, I don't know if that's a good idea." She says hesitant to let me in.

"Please, I'm begging you. Please, let me talk to her." Her eyes soften and she sighs.

"She's in the shower right now. You can wait in her room. Look, I need to run an errand and Tatum is at your house with Joey. Josh, I swear to God, if I come back and my daughter is more broken up than she is now—she pauses a long time— just don't make me regret this. Okay? She finally seems more peaceful. You know?"

I don't know. She is crawling back to Dean, nothing about that will be peaceful for her.

"I won't. I'm sorry. I just…thank you." I tell her.

I understand why she pushed me away, I just don't agree with her. Never one to walk away from a challenge, I made the decision for us both. She was mine, and I sure as hell belonged to her.

I sit in Riley's room on her bed—remembering that night, and remembering the nights before that. I'm in a state of silent reminiscent as memories of her flood my brain. Her coconut, almond, vanilla scent is all over this room and enticing me. Her dark poetry scattered around. I notice a page with words that rip me to shreds. This one was new.

AWAKENING

NO ONE LISTENS, NO ONE HEARS ME
I'M SPEAKING, I'M SCREAMING EMPTY WORDS
INVISIBLE BREATHS OF FRUSTRATION
CLOSED IN SAFE WITHIN MY OWN SKIN
INSIDE THESE SAME FOUR WALLS AGAIN
IN DESPERATE NEED OF AN ESCAPE
IN SEARCH OF SOMEWHERE TO HIDE
SOMEWHERE TO RECREATE
A LIFE I LOVE, A LIFE I HATE
WHY CAN'T YOU EVER HEAR ME?
I'M CRYING OUT
I DON'T WANT TO BE HERE ANYMORE
LOST IN THE CROWD
FEELING CLAUSTROPHOBIC AND SHUT AWAY
WHY DID YOU HAVE TO HURT ME THAT WAY?
YOU WERE SO WRONG
YET, OH SO RIGHT
YOU LEFT THERE ALONE THAT NIGHT
I OPENED UP, ONLY TO BE BETRAYED
THE COLORS ARE LONG GONE
I'M STUCK IN THE GREY
I POURED OUT MY SOUL TO YOU
ALL I WANTED WAS TO JUST BE WITH YOU
MY TEARS HAVE DRAINED ME INTO DEHYDRATION
NOTHING IS SIMPLE, HELD BACK BY COMPLICATIONS

I CLOSED MY EYES TO A DREAM
WHERE I WAS SUCH A FOOL
HOW US IT THAT I NEVER MATTERED TO YOU?
AWAKENING, ONLY TO BE BROKEN BY REALITY
OUR SONG IS DEAD, BLACK AND BLEEDING
I LOVE YOU!
EVEN BROKEN, I STILL DO
THOUGH, I WISH IT WERE A LIE
IT'S IMPOSSIBLE TO REMOVE YOU FROM MY MIND
IN TIME ALL OF THIS WILL DIE
AND I WILL NO LONGER HAVE TO TRY

CHAPTER 30

Waving the white flag doesn't mean I have forgotten, or even moved past it. It just means...I'm too weak to do anything else about it.

At school Dean approaches me sitting on the bench.

"You look so sad, Riley." He says.

I shrugged, "Well, I am." I reply truthfully.

He sighs—probably thinking vainly that it was all about him, his ego getting a boost from my evident pain.

"We have been friends for a long time, Riley…even before we became more. We were friends. Ya know? I miss you." He tells me as he sits down and grabs my hand.

I inwardly cringe and recoil away from him. However, outwardly—I do nothing. "I know," I say.

I don't miss him. I don't need him. In fact, I resent him. So why is it that I rest my head on his shoulder? I'm asking myself that same thing as I stand in my shower. Replaying that thought and the image I saw on Josh's face when he walked by—looking at us—as though something was there between us. There wasn't.

I miss you, Josh.

I decide after my shower to toil without respite. I wrap myself in a towel and walk across the hall to my bedroom. I have my head cast down, flipping through the playlist on my iPod settling on, *Wish you were here* by Incubus. I kick the door closed with my foot and walk into my closet.

"We need to talk," a voice says from my bed. I jump, dropping my iPod on the floor and nearly losing the towel covering me, as well. I step out of my closet, stand in the middle of my room, and narrow my eyes at my best friend. Ex-best friend? Preslee's baby daddy? Ugh!

"Damn it, Josh. You scared the crap out of me. What are you

doing here?" He drags his eyes lazily up and down my body before narrowing them on my face.

"I just told you. We need to talk. You won't answer your fucking phone, or return my calls, or talk to me at school. So, here I am," he says dryly.

"Um, if you haven't noticed, I'm kind of naked here. I, uh, can you like shut your eyes so I can put my clothes on? Then we can talk?" I ask him feigning exasperation, when actually I'm feeling flushed and nervous as hell. I've missed him, his nearness, his voice and those eyes.

The way he is looking at me—it's so intense. I can't help but feel affected.

He stands, and walks toward me. For every step he takes, I take one away, until my back is pressed to my shut bedroom door. He is standing so close to me that I can feel his breath whisper along my cheek. He puts his hands on opposite sides of my head on the door, caging me in. He is looking down at me with such heat in his eyes that I don't know what to make of any of this.

"I noticed," is all he says on a growl.

He trails his fingers along my cheek, down my throat, to my collarbone, where he pauses and looks up into my shocked eyes.

"Your pulse is racing, Riley. Am I making you uncomfortable?" He asks in a voice that is almost foreign.

I shake my head back and forth, "No, yes, no. I'm confused." I sigh and look down. He tilts my chin up with his index finger. I keep my eyes cast downward, not wanting to look into his eyes. If I look into those hazel eyes, I am afraid of what I will see—of what it will do to me.

"I see that, Riley. Look at me." His voice is soft, but demanding. I don't want to look at him, but I can't get my body to listen to my brain. I feel possessed. I meet his eyes just as a tear rolls down my cheek and then another and another. Damn it. I am so weak. I can't do this.

He watches my tears fall and drags the pad of his thumb under my eyes to wipe them away. I can't stop them from falling.

He seems just as lost as me in this moment, looking back and forth at each of my eyes. Studying me. Breaking me.

"I'm sorry, baby." He rests his forehead on mine, his dirty blond hair tickling my eyes.

I begin to shake uncontrollably. "I…I…I can't do this, Josh. You need to leave, please. Please, leave me alone." I stutter as I tremble.

"I can't. I can't leave you alone." His eyes flick to my mouth, and very slowly he places his left hand on the door and raises his right hand to my face. He slowly pads his thumb along my bottom lip that is quivering now.

I can't help but shut my eyes and let my head fall back to the door. I feel dizzy. My breaths are coming shallowly, and my heartbeat feels like a marching band has taken up residence inside my chest—thumping so loudly, that I know he has to hear it. I'm losing control. I want him to stop, to never stop. What is wrong with me?

He lowers his head to my shoulder. His breath is so hot on my neck.

"Riley?" He moves his hand away from my lips and is now tickling his fingers up and down my arm, leaving a tingling sensation and goose bumps in their path.

"Hmm?" I didn't know what to say anymore.

He slowly lifts his head, dragging his nose along my cheek until our lips are almost touching. His mouth is only a breath apart from my own. I see a million emotions shadow his eyes as he looks down at my face. His breath is minty and tantalizing me. He presses his chest into my own, causing me to gasp. I look into his eyes, locking into a silent debate of will. He wraps his hand around the nape of my neck, his other hand cups my cheek, and I am certain he is about to kiss me. I don't have the strength, or desire to stop him.

If I lean in, we would kiss. One last taste would put me in my coffin—be my poison. I'm addicted to his poison, though. I want it on my tongue, inside my mouth. *Kiss me.*

He doesn't kiss me, though. He steps back and stares at me for the longest time.

"I'm sorry. I can't think straight with you like that. I'll shut my eyes so you can put clothes on, and then we need to talk." He says, gesturing to my towel wrapped body and turns his back to me. It's not up for question. We are going to talk.

Okay then.

I dress quickly in white shorts and a teal camisole. My mind is reeling of airing all of this with him. What was he going to say? How would I respond in hearing it? What should I say?

I walk over to my bed where he is sitting with his elbows rested on his knees, his head in the palms of his hands. I place my hand on his shoulder, and he looks up at me with wary eyes. I place my body in between his legs looking down at him.

His eyes are indecisive and full of worry. I rub my index finger along his brow line to smooth it. "Do you remember when things used to be so easy between us? When we used to laugh together? When you would climb through that window just to annoy me?" I ask looking at the glass that holds so many good memories.

Tears are brimming in his eyes, "I remember every fucking minute I ever spent with you, Riley."

He interlaces our fingers, and he seems to be watching mesmerized as he does. I look at our intertwined hands and back to his face. I bite my lip nervously. His eyes look to my lips and then back to my eyes.

"Are you getting back together with Dean?" He asks abruptly.

My mouth falls open in shock. What's he smoking? For real? Seriously! Like, I would ever do that. Doesn't he realize any of this?

"Hell, no! What would make you think that?" I ask him incredulously.

He lifts a shoulder and tilts his head to the side. "You were with him today, holding his hand—hugging."

I imagine it did look like that from his perspective. "He was concerned about me, but nothing has changed between him and me." I swallow and hold his gaze, "Whereas *everything* has changed for us right?" I state forlornly.

He growls, "I'm *not* with Preslee, never have been. I know you think I lied to you, but I didn't."

"I'm beginning to think the definition of lying is different for guys and girls." I release his hand and back away to put some distance between us.

"I.am.not.lying," he grates through clenched teeth. "I know you think she is pregnant with my baby. I'm not the one who got her pregnant. In fact, I've never even had sex before, Riley. I'm sure that is a shock to you but it's true. I'm a virgin just like you."

Again my mouth falls open. "How do you know I am a virgin?" I ask him.

"You told me the night we were right here." He says, palming the mattress.

"Okay. But, seriously? You expect me to believe you have never had sex Josh?" I ask not believing this.

First, Dean tells me that bullshit to get in my panties. Now, Josh? Really? What motive is there to feed me this crap again? Do I have a sign on my head that says naïve freak or gullible broken mess?

"It's true. I told you this the night we were here." He explains.

"You mean the night you rejected me?" I cross my arms over my chest.

He sits there with his eyes on my face. "Riley, I didn't reject you. You must not remember everything that happened. I didn't have sex with you, I didn't stay with you, and you are right about that. But I didn't reject you. I told you why I was leaving. I didn't want your first time to be like that, or our first time together to be with you drunk." He sighs, "You have no idea how hard it was to not give in, Riley. God, I wanted to, I wanted you. I still want you. I'm not lying to you. I promise you. I'm not lying. It's always been you. It will always only be you. Please, believe me."

I study his face looking for the lie. I don't see it. I don't respond just yet. I don't have the words, but when I do, I'm more confused than before.

"Josh, I might not remember everything, but I do remember explaining to you why Dean broke up with me. Did you know he told me he was a virgin too? That having sex with me for the first time would make it special for him? Except, he wasn't a virgin, Josh. It was just a ploy to get me to do what he wanted." I say.

"I'm not Dean, Riley. I'm not trying to play with your emotions. I'm telling you the truth."

I don't know what to believe. "If you didn't get her pregnant, then who did?" I ask just as the doorbell to my house rings.

"Hold that thought." I say, and walk to the living room with Josh trailing behind me.

When I open the door I am floored yet again today. What the hell? Dean is standing there with his hands in his pockets. Why is he here?

"Dean, why are you here?" I ask what my mind is wondering.

His eyes aren't looking at me. They are looking over my shoulder. His jaw tightens, and his eyes narrow before meeting mine and softening.

"I came to talk to you. Ya know, as a friend." He says as Josh coughs bullshit.

I glance over my shoulder with a warning look. When I look back at Dean, I swear his chocolate eyes have darkened to almost black. His hands are balled into fists by his side, and his stance is that of a predator about to strike its prey.

"I'm good, Dean. Besides, now is not a good time." I say hoping he will leave, but I'm suddenly pushed aside by Josh further opening the door and gesturing for Dean to come inside.

"Nah, Riley. We need to air out some shit. Let him in. Maybe now you will understand who the lying player here really is." Josh tells me.

CHAPTER 31

Saved by the bell. When Dean shows up at Riley's, it's like fate is telling me to bury him and save myself. Let's just hope Riley can forgive me for hiding the truth from her.

Riley looks at me confused, and a little irritated as I invite Dean into her house. I can see the battle behind her eyes before she relents. "Okay?" She says, stepping aside for Dean to enter. "Come in. I guess."

Dean steps inside and shifts uncomfortably. "Alright, Parker. Let's air shit out as you said," he says a little too confident.

I grab Riley's hand and rub my thumb across her knuckles. She looks down at it but doesn't pull away or flinch. If anything I think she relaxes a little.

I swallow and try to find the right words figuring I have one shot at this. "Dean, I've been thinking about some stuff…thinking that I've sat in the background watching for far too long. If I want something, I'm gonna have to fight for it, and I want Riley."

Dean's eyes narrow and Riley gasps, "Is that so?" he says with smugness.

I nod and pull her hand to my lips kissing her knuckles. Her eyes widen, and she inhales a deep breath before puffing it out. I turn my eyes away from her and back to Dean. "It's so, but here is where I face a roadblock. See, you have spent the past two years filling her head with so many doubts and insecurities, that now she can't see when someone is telling her the truth."

"I'm not following you, Parker. How exactly have I done such a thing?" he asks clearly thinking he is in the clear here.

"Let's start with the fact that you are not a virgin, dude. You and I both know that you have been fucking girls that aren't Riley well before y'all broke up and leading her to think that she should feel guilty for waiting." I tell him, and in an instant, I realize my mistake.

Riley pulls her hand away, and I feel her heated gaze on my face. "What do you mean, you *both* know?" she asks with a shaky voice.

Dean has the nerve to laugh, and she shoves him in the chest. "You think this is funny, Dean? I knew you lied. Emily told me about you and her, but Josh makes it sound in the plural tense. Dean? Is it true? Have you been cheating on me the entire time we were together?" she asks him, and he actually shrugs like it's no big deal.

Emily? What is she talking about?

"And you knew?" she turns those blue/green eyes on me. I see a thousand questions there.

"I knew he wasn't who you thought he was, and that when you weren't around he acted like he was single. But I didn't know for a fact that he took it beyond that until that night at—,"

"At the party right?" she cuts me off, and I nod.

"With who?" she asks, her voice soft but then she looks at Dean and shouts, "Who the fuck was she?"

Dean just stares, offering her nothing—no peace, no denial and no answers.

I give her what she needs. "He fucked Preslee that night, Riley. He's been fucking Preslee for a while now. I'm not the one she's been with. He is. He's who—," I trail off. She knows.

She covers her mouth and looks like she is going to vomit soon. Dean looks concerned yet confused by my declaration. She still never told him? More and more I'm thinking Preslee has been lying this whole time but why?

"Oh, God. I…uh…I have to go." She says looking back and forth between us before running out the open front door.

I quickly debate kicking his ass or chasing after her—I choose the latter. He isn't worth any of my time, whereas she is *everything* to me

CHAPTER 32

Out of breath, out of mind, out of control—I just need to escape it. All of it. The doubts, the fear and the loss of everything I want. It was in my hands, and I let it slip through my fingers because I couldn't see past the shit in my head.

Tears are streaming down my face. In protecting my heart from Josh, I let Dean have a little piece, and he burned it to a crisp. Josh knew, and held a hidden piece of crucial information from me, and I feel betrayed. They both broke my heart, broke my trust.

I take off running as fast as I can. Who cares that I have no idea where I am going, or that I might die of a heat stroke in the process? Or that I'm barely dressed and barefoot.

I can hear them calling my name and then yelling at each other, and even that fades the further away I run. I shut out the noise.

Life is full of many moments that make up time and memories. Some moments are small and easily forgotten. Other moments are monumental and life changing, making forgetting them impossible. Then they're those moments that almost happen and become nonexistent, blowing away in the wind.

The second I chose friendship over love years ago, a special moment became lost in the wind. An almost moment, that was stolen from us, yet not really stolen at all, because I never allowed it to happen in the first place. I stole it from myself. I betrayed my own heart, time and time again.

All these years, it should have been Josh, but it was Dean instead. My heart isn't safe anywhere. I run away from my house, leaving something behind, something we wouldn't get back. I've blamed Josh and pushed him away. There is no way he will forgive me now.

Running is pure agony. My mind is racing with a thousand thoughts, a million more questions at the same speed my feet step on the pavement. Left. Right. Breathe in. Breathe out. Dean cheated. Josh knew. I hate him. I love him. FUCK!

I can't slow my cogs enough to gather my own thoughts. The blood is roaring in my ears. Images that were probably not that of reality are filling my mind. Dean having sex, various faces flickering in and out as he betrays me—Josh choosing one friend over the other—not choosing me, just like I hadn't chose him.

It's pouring down rain, in a matter of seconds. I still don't stop. I take the sting and let it hurt me. I deserve it.

I don't hear it—don't even hear him yelling my name. Everything happens so fast yet in complete slow motion. It wasn't until I am yanked into mid-air and falling to the pavement behind me on a hard thud that I stop. My breath is knocked from my lungs.

"Jesus Christ, Riley. Are you okay?" Josh asks concerned and eyeing me all over the place. I don't understand why.

"What?" I choke, as I try to get the air back into my lungs.

"I didn't even see her. She just ran out in the road. Is she okay? I almost hit her." A voice muffled says stepping toward me lying back on the pavement struggling to still gather air.

"She's okay. I think. I grabbed her before she...Riley, baby? Can you sit up?" Josh asks me.

It's only now that I see I'm at the edge of the road, with a car parked to the side. A young woman is kneeling down in front of me, getting wet from the rain. She almost hit me? How? I'm on the sidewalk.

I sit up and shake my head, "I'm okay. What happened?" I whisper.

Josh pulls me into his lap, squeezing me tightly. "Holy shit, Riley. I was screaming your name, and you just kept running. You ran right into the road in front of her. I'm sorry, I yanked you back and down so hard, but she almost hit you. You didn't hear the horn honking?" He is still looking me over, searching for wounds. My wounds can't be seen with his eyes.

I shake my head and feel my body shaking. I hadn't heard it. I hadn't heard him. It was all muffled jumbled noise inside my head. I wasn't paying attention. All I'd felt was the welcomed sting of raindrops and the blood roaring behind my ears.

I rest my head into the crook of his neck, "I'm sorry. I'm so sorry." I mutter as tears fall from my cheeks.

He cradles my head, and runs his fingers through my hair calming me. "I'm the one that is sorry, Riley. Shhhh…I've got you."

The lady gets back in her car and drives away leaving us sitting on the sidewalk in a heap of misery and regret.

I am lost in the scent of Josh as his arms envelope me. He feels like home to me. My world feels flipped upside down, but I have him here with me. I don't know why he kept the truth from me, but I know I can't lose him. I just can't. I love him—desperately love him.

I hear the roar of Dean's motorcycle pull to the side, "Is she okay?" he speaks loudly to Josh.

"She's good, man. Just go. Okay? You need to have a talk with Preslee and tell her to leave me out of it from now on." Josh tells Dean.

I don't look up at him. I keep my head buried where it is, my tiny hand gripping his shirt.

"Oookay will do. Listen, Riley. I am sorry, and I meant what I said about us being friends. Maybe one day?" he says wistfully but I don't reply, and he rides away without closure.

The rain is cold, and I'm shivering. I'm holding onto Josh like he is what will keep me breathing. In this moment, I think he is. I think my sanity depends on him. Without him, I don't know who I am.

I finally feel my breathing become normal, and everything slows and settles. Josh brushes the wet hair clinging to my skin out of my face. "God, you're so beautiful. Please, don't do that again," he says.

"Do what?" I ask him.

"Run from me."

I look down, "I won't, and I'm done running, Josh. I'm sorry I didn't believe you." I say ashamed.

"I should have told you, Riley. I'm sorry I didn't. Fuck! I should have done so many things differently." He tells me with one hand gripping me around the waist as his other hand holds my face. "I've missed you so much."

My tears begin to fall because I understand. I should have done so many things different. God, I could have prevented all of this if I had just saw the beauty behind the ugly and just let it be, like my mom had said. I didn't understand what she meant, at the time, but I think I do now. Sometimes, the beauty of what can be is hidden underneath a bad situation or an ugly emotion like doubt.

"I've missed you, too." I say, gripping his shirt in my hands.

I lock eyes with the hazel ones I love. His hair is drenched and sexy. This moment is familiar. Feelings of déjà vu of the night by my window where I wanted him to kiss me, where he admitted to wanting to kiss me, urge me to not let this moment slip through my fingers, return to my mind.

I'm so close to the edge of the cliff that I know one more breath, one more inch, I could fall. For the first time ever, I escape the fear and believe that Josh will catch me.

I take a deep breath, and like the floodgates have been opened, the words rush from my heart. "I've spent the past two years fearing the worst and believing that I chose safe arms to hold me, when his arms weren't the arms I longed to be in, nor were they really safe. I thought it's what I deserved. I thought I couldn't belong in the arms I wanted to really hold me." I confess.

His eyes glass over and he swallows, "Whose arms did you want to hold you, Riley?" He knew the answer, he always knew.

My eyes are cast down full of shame that I let myself doubt where I belonged for so long. "It wasn't a want Josh. It was a need…an ache so deep I couldn't escape it. I tried so hard to fight it, but it consumes me."

My eyes slowly meet his, and he asks me again, his own voice cracking from the emotions. I notice a tear fall down his cheek, and I have an urge to kiss it away. "Whose arms, Riley?"

I swallowed down the lump in my throat and fall from the edge of the cliff. "Yours. I belong in your arms, unless it's too late. Tell me it's not too late. Please?" I beg. My tears trickle down my cheeks mixing with the rain falling on my skin.

He looks down and in that moment I feared it was. *Too late.* In my attempt to escape ever being heartbroken again, it was me that did the most damage to the organ.

The rain continues to pour, the sky is just as sad as I am.

I need him to understand, to hear me. It can't be too late. He isn't saying anything. He just looks down and is breathing heavy.

"Josh, it can't be too late. I know I did it all wrong. I know I pushed you away, and I believed the fears in my head instead of you, but that never made my feelings for you change. Even when we were kids and you shared your pudding cup with me, or how you made me play hot wheels when I wanted to play Barbie's...I still wanted you, and the way you would play your little guitar for me, and I would make up words to *our* music...I still think about those things. I knew, even then, that there was nothing I would never do for or with you. I loved you even then. It's changed, shifted into different kinds of love, but it's always been you. You are my first best friend, my first crush, my first kiss, my first dance partner and my first love. Josh, please don't be my first heartbreak. I want you to be my first everything. Please, don't let it be too late. Please? Let me love you, because I don't think I can stop even if you tell me to. I'm sorry. I'm sooo sorry I doubted you." I confess through sobs, and my body is trembling, but now it's all out there.

I'm about to hit the bottom, and I'm scared he isn't going to catch me. I'm scared he is going to let me hit the bottom and there will be nothing left of me without him. When he takes a few deep breaths and still doesn't meet my eyes or speak, I panic. I feel lost, and I hate myself. I hate myself for not allowing just a sliver of happiness to be mine. With a huge sense of regret and a heavy heart, I pull myself up to stand and begin to walk away. I make it two steps before Josh seizes me by my elbow. I stop, but I can't turn around to face him. I'm splintering right here. I slowly turn around, but I keep my head down. I can't look at him. It hurts too much.

He squats down to look into my face. He cups my chin and guides me to look up at him. I do, but I keep my eyes shut.

"Riley, look at me." He says in a soft gentle voice.

My eyes slowly meet his and tears are streaming down his cheeks. His bottom lip is quivering. It might be raindrops falling down his face and not actual tears, although his eyes are glassy. I've never seen him this way. It breaks me, melts me. He is looking down at me with such intensity that I'm not sure what he is about to say.

"I'm yours, Riley. I don't think a time in my life existed that I haven't belonged to you. I knew even when we were kids that you were going to be special to me. I've always been yours. It's never too late. I've been waiting for you, baby." He breathes the words to me, "I love you, Riley Shaw." He is grinning now, and he wipes away my tears as they mix with the rain.

I hug him tightly. I'm aware we are on the sidewalk, and the world can see, but I don't care. I love him. He loves me. There is no doubt. No fear. I feel the relief ripple away, leaving in its place a renewed sense of hope.

He pulls away from me, "Say you want me to kiss you. Say I'm not crazy, that you think of me, that you feel this. Say that when I touch you that you want more, that you want it all. Say it, Riley. I need to hear it. Say this is real. That *you* are real." He demands and pleads and then pulls me back tight to him like if he lets go I might vanish or change my mind. *I won't.*

I back away, and my eyes are locked with his as my hands hold his cheeks. The sound of rain is diminished by the sound of my breathing and my dancing heartbeat. "All the time, Josh! I want your mouth on mine, all the time. I can't stop thinking about you ever. I try, but you are always there. The smallest touch has me coming undone, has me in need of more. I want it. You're not crazy, and I want you. It's real. I want it all…with you, only you."

I press my lips to his, tasting the mix of salty tears, raindrops and everything that is Josh. His arms snake around my back and pull my body closer to him as though he needs to be closer. I can't get close enough. Our breathing is fast and years of yearning is being unleashed right here on this sidewalk. He pulls me up, and I wrap my legs around his waist never breaking contact.

When we are out of breath and someone honking distracts us, he pulls away. "Come with me," he says pulling our mouths apart as I whimper in protest.

"Okay." There is no longer a question. I will go anywhere with him.

CHAPTER 33

Nervous energy is running through my system. The way Riley feels in my arms, the way she looks drenched in the rain, the taste of her lips, the whimper she makes when she doesn't want me to stop and the words that come from her mouth. I can't wait to be alone with her.

"Where are we going?" she asks as I carry her back to her house.

"First, we are going to get you out of these wet clothes." I feel her tense, and I realize that didn't sound right. I laugh. "And into dry ones, Riley."

She visibly relaxes in my arms. "Okay. Then what?" she asks clearing her throat.

I chance a quick look at her face. She is nibbling on that bottom lip, and something tells me she is thinking about us without clothes.

"I have a surprise for you, but I can't tell you about it. I have to show it to you." I tell her, making her smile. I love when she smiles. I missed it badly.

When we get to her house, her mom is getting out of the car with grocery bags. I put Riley down and help her carry the bags in. She looks between Riley and me in our drenched clothes with a puzzled expression. "Do I even want to know why you both look like wet dogs?" she asks clearly amused.

Riley answers, "No. But I was wrong about what I said, Mom. It was a misunderstanding. I will fill you in later if that's okay? Josh wants to show me something."

Oh no. She actually told her mom about me—and *everything*. Well, that explains why she wouldn't let me come around.

We get in the house and her mom gives me a once over, and then looks at Riley with a soft smile, "It's like I told you before, baby girl. Sometimes, the truth is hard to believe because the lies before overshadow them. Find the beauty behind the ugly, Riley and just let it be its own kind of beautiful." She squeezes her hand and shoos us away.

I tell Riley to change and to meet me outside in twenty minutes. Thankfully, the rain has stopped. The sky has become the prettiest shades of pink and orange, like it's completely happy, the tears were shed, and now all is right in the world.

Let it be beautiful…that's what her mom said. I think we can do that.

CHAPTER 34

Josh looks like a little kid on Christmas, overly excited and fidgety. I don't know where we are going, but his happiness in showing me his surprise makes me share in his mood. It's contagious.

Within minutes, that happiness becomes nervous energy. I see the trepidation in his eyes when he glances at me—the way his back straightens and his grip tightens on the steering wheel. It makes me question his nervousness. However, before I do, I realize why, when I see where he has taken me.

"Why are we here, Josh?" I ask him as he parks the car in the cemetery where his mom and my dad have both been buried. This place does not give me serenity. It gives me the creeps and reminds me of what happened three years ago when everything in our lives changed.

He shifts in his seat and takes my hands into his. I can't look at him. My eyes are on the graveyard filled with death. The rain earlier and the temperature outside have caused a dewy fog to rise from the ground. It is…unnerving, makes me shiver and causes the hairs on my neck to rise.

He sighs heavily watching my reaction. "Riley, it's okay. Listen, I know this is not where you want to be, and trust me, this is not my surprise. That comes after here. I brought you here because I want you to see that this is okay." I finally meet his eyes.

"Okay?"

"I brought you here actually for two reasons. One, because I want you to see that I can be here holding your hand, seeing our future, and there isn't a question in my mind that it's where I belong. I know you blame yourself—as twisted as that is—for what your dad did that night. But it was a mistake, Riley. It was a bad decision that spiraled out of control. My mom was in the wrong place at the wrong time, and she died in the accident. I was angry with your dad for a while just as you were. I was even angry with your mom after you explained to me what happened. But, Riley...NEVER, was I angry with you. I never saw it that way."

I blew out the breath I was holding. "Josh, when you look at me every day for the rest of your life you're going to remember my dad killed your mom, and one day, Josh—"

He interrupts me before I can even finish. "I'm stopping you there, because you are already wrong, Riley. Every day for the rest of my life—if I'm lucky enough to keep you that long—I will *not* see that accident. I will see a beautiful girl who is lost in a sea of uncertainty but wants so badly to dive in, but thinks she can't. But you can, and I will hold your hand when you do. I will see my best friend and the girl that I am desperately in love with. I will see you, Riley. Just you."

I swallow down my impulse to argue him and nod. He is so adorably sweet.

"The second reason I brought you is a little harder to explain. See the night of Collin's party, the night everything became...obvious. I had two choices, well, three if you consider telling you the truth about your asshole ex-boyfriend. But two were what I focused on. The one I settled on was coming here to talk to my mom. It was one of many times that I just needed her to explain to me how the female mind ticks and if I was doing any of this right, because I just felt that I wasn't."

He squeezes my hand and looks out the front windshield to the earth that holds our past. When he turns his eyes back to me, I feel the tears brim in my eyes. I don't want to cry but some wounds just don't heal. Some scab over and just one little thing can open the wound as the pain bleeds out unbidden.

I blink my eyes a few times, holding the tears at bay. "Did she help you?" I ask not quiet understanding if it's possible. Every time I talked to my dad, I never felt better.

He nods, "She loved you, Riley. Before the accident, when everything was just normal, she used to tell me all the time that the cute little brunette next door would be her daughter-in-law one day." He laughs like the memory is right there for him to grab. "I thought she was crazy. Hell, we were fourteen but when I look at it now. The me that I am now, knows that, without a doubt, my mom was a smart woman, and she knew what she was talking about." He smiles at the memory.

I can't help but smile back. I knew she loved me. His mom was the nicest woman I had ever met. She meant a lot to me, and I know without doubt as well that she would have been an amazing mother-in-law. "That was sweet of her." I say softly as a tear escapes. I wipe it away and sniffle.

Josh frowns, "I don't want you to cry, Riley. It kills me inside when I see the pain you carry behind your beautiful eyes. A lot of things have happened that have kept us apart…decisions of others, mistakes made, our own fears, lack of trust. We don't have to be a cliffhanger novel, Riley. We don't have to wait for the rest to happen to us or for it not to. We can have the happily ever after…write our own story. I want all of it with you, the good, the bad, the ugly, the beautiful, the tears and the smiles. All of it. I want to hold you when you're scared and make sure you know it will be okay and that I'm here with you. And I know it's not going to be perfect. I know there will be times you are going to try and push me away again. But know this Riley, I'm done letting you. I need you. You need me. I'm giving you all I have to give, and I hope you take it." His voice is full of emotion and desire.

"God, I love you." I confess.

"Say it again," he whispers.

I crawl onto his lap accidentally honking the horn in the process. He laughs. I don't. I'm wound too tight. "I love you."

I tangle my hand in his hair. I love his hair. The dirty blond mess of unruliness is hot. His hazel eyes sparkle with his own love for me. I love him. I love him so much it hurts sometimes.

I kiss his forehead, "I love how you get me like no one else, how kind and caring you are."

I noozle his nose and kiss each of his eyes. "I love your eyes, the color, the way you look at me and how it makes me feel."

I nuzzle into his neck and inhale before placing a kiss there too. "I love the way you smell, how it comforts me, gives me peace and how it also ignites me and makes my heart race.

I place my palm on his heart and smile. "I love this most of all, because it's mine now, and it's special to me. I promise to not push you away. I can't promise it will always be rainbows and sunshine because that's not reality, but I will take this piece and cherish it, and I hope you do the same with my own."

I touch his lips softly and lean down placing a feather light kiss to his mouth. "I love this mouth, too. The things it says, the way it touches me. How it's perfectly soft when I need it to be, and how it's more when I need more. The taste is addicting too, by the way." I smile crookedly at him.

I interlace my fingers in his hand and kiss his knuckles. "And I love these hands. How they touch me just the way I need them to, how they hold me and hug me and keep me safe." I lean into his ear to whisper the rest. "How they never push me for more until I'm ready. And Josh?" I lick his ear and he groans.

"Hmm?" he says groaning. That sound he does in his throat that makes me hot.

"When the time comes, I'll be ready with you…only with you, my first and my last will only be with you."

When I pull back to look at him, his eyes are dark and clouded with lust. The wind howls outside, and I pretend it's our parents giving us they're blessing, although I'm sure the 'I'm ready' part is being frowned upon.

Josh pulls me in for a kiss. When we are done, we are both out of breath. I climb off of him and sigh, because it's getting harder and harder to not fulfill these needs by going further. I want too. It's still too soon, though.

"We should go. I have a surprise for you, remember?" he says grinning at me and shifting in his seat, which makes me grin.

"Right, the surprise. So, are you going to tell me where we are going now?" I say with the biggest smile on my face.

He grins and taps my nose. "Nah, if I told you then it wouldn't be a surprise now would it?"

I shake my head and continue smiling. It's a weird feeling being happy and content.

When we pull up to the theatre at the mall next to a cheesecake bistro, I'm puzzled. Getting food or watching a movie? Not what I was expecting but okay.

"Josh?"

He smiles sheepishly, "Well, I decided on the fly that you owe me a scary movie, and I owe you a brownie. Um, is cheesecake okay, though?" He tilts his head and lifts one of his shoulders with a crooked grin gracing his face. It's so cute and I literally swoon at how adorable he looks right now and also how completely sweet he is.

I smile, lean over the console and kiss his cheek. "It's perfect. Thank you."

Scary movie…bring it on.

Embracing this new journey with Josh is scary enough, but I have his hand to hold while doing it. I'm not sure what the future holds, and I'm okay with that for the first time ever. I am letting go of my doubts, because I have him—my soul mate, my best friend, the one and only true love of my life. I am ready for this new adventure as long as it is with him.

To be continued...

Please, show your support to the author by leaving a review. Thank you.

End of Us

Don't talk, don't kiss me, and don't tell anyone we did this—those were the rules for them. The rules for me weren't as simple. Pretend the chick below me is someone else entirely. Forget the guilt because it's just sex—sex with the wrong girl. Don't feel too much, because it isn't real, and she (whoever she may be) isn't Riley.

"Riley, c'mon we have been together two years. What are you waiting for?" I ask her for the trillionth time it seems. She stops us from going further...again! I'm so frustrated. We've been doing this same song and dance for months—for me...years. I just want to be inside her, to possess her, to claim her *finally*. So, she will see me, feel me—say my name.

She pushes on my bare chest, and I roll off her, loving and hating that she is breathing fast and that her body is trembling. In my mind, she is panting because she is turned on, and she is trembling because my touch is fucking making her shiver. But then, she opens her damn mouth and everything I want crashes and burns. "I'm just not ready. You promised to not push me, Dean, and yet, every time we make out, we end up in this same position."

She is exasperated, I can hear it in her tone, but my head doesn't care. I'm stuck on Riley and me in various positions. Jesus, she would be like heaven if she would just let me try it. Missionary maybe? No, her on top—definitely her on top—riding me while I palm her breasts, or maybe, her bent over the bed with me behind her? But that would be more like fucking—more like what I do with Preslee. I don't want to fuck Riley. That's a lie, I so badly want to fuck her, but I want to love her too...

Nice. Slow. Sweet.

Until she begs me to be...

Rougher. Dirtier. Faster.

Damn.

I start kissing her neck, and nibbling on her ear. She always gets hot and bothered when I do this—I think it's her spot. Then she usually shivers and my shirt comes off, and we kiss like she is finally tasting me and not dreaming of other lips on hers. "I could think of some other positions we could try." Let me convince you baby, *please.* She isn't convinced. She never is.

She sits up completely pissed off and it's sexier than hell. "Dammit, Dean. Back off. I'm not ready. Stop pushing me."

This time I listen. Sexy or not, I'm over this shit. She is pissing me off. I'm not fucking stupid. I know she isn't opening her legs for me because she wants to open them for Josh. All the more reasons why I don't let the guilt of lying to her affect me, not entirely. She is lying to herself if she thinks being with me this long isn't lying to me—or herself. She has no intention of ever letting me in. Does she? Her eyes always drift to that fucking window. *He isn't going to come save you. He isn't your knight in shining armor. He's just a punk who let you go when you needed him the most. I was there for you. I was fucking there for you.*

I growl as I put my shirt back on, feeling all the rage inside of me build. I stare at her curled up on her bed, she just looks at me like some peculiar puzzle she can't figure out. The feeling is mutual. However, my puzzle is put together. I've mapped it out—the way she feels. I just hate it and want to mix it back up, to where her and I are the missing pieces connected. We're never those connected pieces. Ugh...Fuck it!

"How about I do us both a favor and back off completely, Riley?" I ask her. She doesn't want to be alone. She hates being alone. That is when the darkness seeps in, and she remembers things she doesn't like to remember. *Say no. Say you want me, that you need me like I need you.*

She doesn't. She shrugs, like she doesn't care one way or the other. She throws her hands in the air and says, "Whatever." *Whatever?* What the fuck ever? That is what she has to say?

Fine...I'm done.

Not just yet...

"I'm serious, Riley. I'm tired of going in this circle with you. You're hot then you're cold. You kiss me like you can't get enough, grab at my shirt like you can't wait to be undressed, and then you just pour the ice on it. I'm a guy, Riley. I have needs and you…well, you aren't meeting them." Damn it, my dick twitches just thinking about touching her.

She pulls her feet under her and is sitting up with narrowed eyes on me, focused on me, determination set in those gorgeous eyes. "So…what you're saying is, you are breaking up with me for good if I don't have sex with you?" She makes it sound so cold. I'm breaking up with her because she is in love with someone else, and she won't admit it. I'm breaking up with her because she never smiles for me. She's mechanical and forced——and because it breaks my heart that she doesn't know how much I wish it were me she was truly with. I'm breaking up with her because it hurts too much.

I shrug and tell her the truth (well most of it), "Not to sound like a dick or anything, but yeah, pretty much. Riley. We've been friends our entire life. I've been a patient guy for two years, but you just don't seem to know what you want." She knows—she just doesn't say it. She tells me she cares for me. She doesn't care for me. I'm just her distraction. I keep her mind off of him—off of the life she saw for herself and lost. I'm nothing to her.

Her mouth falls open, evidently shocked. Oh well. She says, "I know what I want. I want you to stop pushing me to do something I keep telling you I'm not ready for. If you cared about me at all, you would understand my feelings, and stop making me feel guilty." If I cared about her? I fucking love her, I'd do anything for her, go anywhere with her. I'm not trying to make her feel anything but something other than numb with me. Just stop feeling nothing and feel something—for me.

I sit on her bed, and place my hands on top of her legs—smooth skin beneath my palms. I just want to glide my hands up her thighs and in between them. Focus, Dean…focus. "I do care about you, Riley. I'm not trying to make you feel anything, but I *am* ready. I have been ready for a very long time. I want my first to be with you, baby. It's only special when it's with you. But I don't want to wait anymore, so unless you are willing to move forward *with* me, I need to move on *without* you."

Okay, maybe I am a dick for lying. She won't be my first. But my first was forgettable, my own distraction from what I couldn't have. And the rest...never meant a damn thing to me. Laiken has a great mouth, and Preslee knows the game well. She follows the rules. She lets me pretend, and that's why I will be calling her when I leave here—this time probably leaving for good. Fuck!

I meet Riley's eyes and let her study mine, and just for a second, I think there might be hope. She seems to be weighing her options but then she sighs and leans into kiss my cheek. "I'm sorry, Dean. But maybe, we should just break up."

I can't help but frown, that's not what I want. I want her. I nod because what else am I going to do? She doesn't love me, she doesn't want me, and this is done. "I'm sorry too." I peck her cheek and leave—phone in my hand—ready to send my text.

Me: BUSY? IF NOT, WANNA BE?

Her reply is quick as it usually is.

Preslee: BE THERE IN 20

Me: GOOD

Preslee is good. She lets me try all kinds of things. She is kind of crazy. Most the time I like it, it's opposite of Riley's sweet, and I let my mind pretend Riley wants me so much that she can't help but be wild in bed.

Tonight though, I want sweet. I want to pretend that Riley didn't tell me 'whatever' like I didn't matter, like she didn't shrug as though she were relieved to have ended us. I want to pretend that she had my shirt off, and her hands gripped my shoulders tightly as I touched her in between her legs for the first time. I want to pretend that she moaned and whimpered and said my name as she let me slip inside her with precise precision—knowing we fit perfectly together. I want to pretend that I made love to her, and she let me, and that when she came she felt love for me and I for her—just us. And now...I'm ready to pretend literally not just mentally. But I have to wait for Preslee to get here so I have someone to pretend with.

The doorbell rings, and being as though my dad is always at a bar or somewhere that isn't here—I get the house to myself, which is convenient. When I open the door, Preslee is standing there looking appetizing, but all wrong for my taste. I try not to let that thought linger, and instead, I open the door to invite her in.

She studies my eyes a moment longer than usual. I'm sure she senses something is different about tonight, or maybe I am different.

"You okay? You seem...I don't know?" She says slightly hesitant to come in—she still does though.

"I'm good. No more talking. Let's go." I grab her hand and we go to my bedroom.

Let the pretending begin.

Once we're in my room, I shut the lights off. "Why do you always want it so dark, Dean? Just once, can we do it with the lights on?" She asks.

"No, we can't." *Because then I would see you. I would know I'm inside you. I don't want to know or see that. I'm pretending, and in the dark, I can do that better.* "You know my rules. If you don't want to play anymore just say so."

She is quiet for a little bit, and I think she may just leave, but then she reaches for my zipper and all is good.

"I'll play, and I'll be anyone you want, Dean, but I need to add my own rule." She is negotiating with her hand around my dick. How am I supposed to say no to something she asks when that feels...so...good?

"What's that?" I ask through a groan.

She comes up close to me, I tense when I feel her mouth near mine. I can feel her breath as it mixes with the air from my own lips.

"I want to kiss you. I need to kiss during sex. I won't talk. I won't say anything at all—just moan like you like. But I want to be kissed when we move together."

I don't kiss her—ever. It's too personal. I know that sounds crazy, like sex isn't personal. But to me—what we do together isn't personal. It's just an escape to where I need to be in my head. To kiss her would mean to feel something more than my escape. I don't want to feel anything—for her.

She is stroking me at a perfect pace, then she licks my lips and my head spins. *I don't want to kiss her. I don't want to kiss her. I don't want to kiss her*. My mantra disagrees with my head, or perhaps it's my other head that told the mantra to fuck off. I grab her cheeks and press my mouth to hers, she gasps like it was unexpected. She moans, and it's the best damn sound ever. I lick into her mouth and tangle my tongue with hers. She tastes fruity like she just ate a candy. It's sweet. Sweet—just like Riley. I'm kissing Riley. It's okay.

I reach behind my neck to grip my shirt and pull it off. Her hands glide up my chest and around my neck as she pulls me closer. She needs to be closer to me. I let my hands trail down her neck and her rib cage to her stomach. I remove her shirt, as well. I undo the clips of her bra and let it fall away, and then I feel her up. Perky, full, and slightly bigger than Riley—NO! Shit—just like Riley—she is just like Riley.

She tugs my jeans down and lowers herself to her knees. I stop her. "No, not your mouth. Not tonight." I step out of my jeans and rid myself of the rest of my clothes.

I unzip her skirt and let it pool at her feet, and then I hook my fingers in her panties and pull those down. "Open," I say as I reach my hand in between her legs to make sure she is ready. She is. "Wet. You're always wet for me. Just me. Right, Riley?"

She just moans and reaches her hands around my neck as she lifts one leg around my waist, letting me touch her. She tightens around my fingers and whimpers when I withdraw them. I lift her up, and she wraps both her legs around my waist completely. She grabs my face to kiss me, and again I let her. *Why am I letting her?* I don't know why this time is different.

I lower us to the bed, and we touch each other everywhere. I lean back and lick my way down to where I know she loves to be kissed. I lick and suck, loving having her legs wrapped around my head, and how she writhes into my mouth with her hands in my hair. She tastes so good. I can always get her to come this way. Not tonight, though. Tonight, I want to bring her to the edge and make her beg for me. The way I beg for Riley. Maybe tell her no, the way she tells me no.

Every time I feel her shiver and jerk, I stop. Her whimpers get closer together, until she is pulling on my hair hard and pushing my head into her. I pull back, "If you want it, ask for it. Tonight only, beg baby." I lick straight up her center and press my tongue onto her clit. She arches her back without speaking a word. She plays the game so well. But tonight, I need her words. I'm so far gone to recognize her voice as any other voice than the one I want to hear. I lift up off of her giving her nothing more. She growls at me. I almost laugh. Get frustrated—like you frustrate me.

I'm hovered above her, ready and waiting. Ask for it. Want me. She is still playing the game—not close enough yet. I reach down in between her legs, and she is riding my hand and obviously thinking I will let her get off that way. I won't. I hold still as she tries to grind faster on me, moaning loudly. I remove my hand and sit back on my heels as she sighs heavily in her chest.

"What the fuck, Dean?" Preslee hollers at me and flips on the lamp next to my bed. NO, no, no! This isn't the way this works.

"What the fuck, Preslee? Turn the light off." I snap at her.

She sits up, glaring at me as she climbs under my blankets to cover herself. "No. Why are you being such an asshole tonight? What's going on? You never want me to talk, and now you want me to beg? What the hell? It's like your torturing me. We do this and we move on until the next time. Means to an end, remember? You're not yourself right now. What th—,"

"Be quiet. Stop talking. I...I...FUCK!" I climb off the bed and put my boxers back on. I run my hand through my hair and growl at my ceiling. What the hell is wrong with me? I walk out of my bedroom and slam the door. I head to the kitchen in search of something, of nothing. I pull a beer out of the fridge and down several swigs. I'm seriously fucked up in the head.

I have my head down and my hands gripping the edge of the kitchen counter when I hear Preslee's footsteps round the corner. I turn my head to see her standing there in nothing but my track t-shirt. I let my eyes look at her. She has long legs, beautiful blonde hair, and gorgeous blue eyes like the sky on a summer day. She is pretty. She just has the wrong hair color, the wrong color eyes, because she isn't her. She isn't Riley.

"Wanna talk about it?" She asks with a soft whisper. Do I? Could I even explain it? None of it makes sense, not even to me.

I turn my body to face her, take another swig of my beer and place it down. Her eyes never leave mine. "Why do you do this with me?" I ask.

Her face is completely unreadable, and she isn't smiling or frowning, just staring. "Why do you?" She asks in a voice that is barely above a whisper.

"Answer me first."

She nods, "Well, same reason as you I presume." She walks over to me slowly, and I let my eyes trail down her legs as she moves. She reaches over and grabs my beer and slowly moves it to her lips to take a sip.

"And that would be?" I ask, taking another beer out of the fridge since she is obviously taking mine.

She hops up on the counter and crosses her legs. "Are we going to keep answering questions with questions?" She asks.

I take a second to really look at her. She is here—with me. Do her reasons matter? Do mine? Tonight for whatever reason they do. "I'm just curious. So why, Preslee? I'm not exactly nice to you, and we don't like each other at all."

She smiles, "No, you're not and that is true. We're not that different, though, so I don't hold it against you. I do this because it helps me not think about what I can't have. For just a little bit I let myself think that he—," she trails off like she almost said too much.

"It's okay. You can say it. You pretend it's not me, right?" I ask.

She nods, "Something like that." She downs the rest of her beer and clears her throat. "Can I ask you something?"

I shrug, "Since tonight seems to be all about questions—shoot."

She leans forward uncrossing her legs just a little. "You're with Riley. Like y'all have dated for two years. Why am I pretending to be her?"

I'm not with her anymore. Was she ever really *with me*? "We broke up. Besides, she is in love with someone else, always has been. She doesn't...I mean...we don't have sex."

"Ah...it sucks when all you want is for them to notice you, but their eyes are always trained on someone else," she says looking lost in a thought.

"Exactly," I say. That is exactly the way it's always been for Riley and I.

"I get it," she says with a slight frown marring her features.

For about a minute, we just stare at each other, not speaking. I'm tired of feeling unwanted. I'm tired of thinking about Riley while she is thinking about him. I'm just tired. Preslee speaks, and it's the best suggestion I've heard all night. "Wanna forget it all for a night? No pretending. Just us, helping the other forget for a while?"

I move to stand in front of her, and she opens her legs for me to stand in between them. I let my hands glide up her legs, under her shirt and around her waist. At the same time, she is touching my face with a look of wonder. It's intimate, and tonight, I just let it happen as us. She runs her hands through my hair, looking back and forth at my eyes.

"I'm going to kiss you now." She tells me but I was already leaning into her—ready to the do the same.

It's been two days, two fucking days since I've talked to Riley. I miss her voice, and I hate that I do. She never misses mine. I'm sure I haven't even crossed her mind, even though she never seems to leave mine.

It's the anniversary of her dad's death, and unbeknownst to her, I followed her to the cemetery. I've been sitting under this tree—out of sight—wondering what she is thinking, wondering if I should go to her—if she would embrace me or push me away.

She has traced the letters of her dads name over and over again. The pain on her face is evident, and it pains me to see it. I just want to hug her and make it not be there anymore. I'm close to doing just that but then I hear a vehicle pull up, and my heart plummets to my stomach. Josh.

He walks to sit down next to her, interlaces their hands and speaks. "I thought I would find you here. You okay? You look far away," he asks caringly.

She nods, swiping a few lost tears, and my insides coil, as he is the one that will comfort her this time. "I was just remembering that day. Their angry words thunder so loudly in my head. It's been three years today, and it still hurts." She says as she rubs a spot on her chest.

He pulls her to his side, kisses her forehead the way I've seen him do a thousand times before, and it never feels good to see it.

He says, "I don't think the hurt of losing someone goes away. Some days are better than others. But missing them—that feeling—I think, it's always there, lying dormant. Something as simple as a song on the radio, or the smell of their perfume on someone else, triggers all those memories. And in one moment, you're trapped in the past." I'm an asshole because I hate him right now. He is comforting her for her loss when he has his own to deal with. I hate him because this connection to the pain they share is just one more connection they have together that I don't.

She looks at him with those sad beautiful eyes, the guilt she carries on her shoulder evidently so heavy to carry. It breaks my heart. "I'm sorry, Josh." She whispers. God dammit, she is sorry? I've known the guilt she carries, I've even known the feelings for Josh that she thinks she keeps secret. But in this moment, it slaps me in the face—she is sorry. I finally get it—she doesn't let herself act on her feelings for him because she thinks she can't, she shouldn't. How fucking twisted is that? What am I at all to her? A distraction? Time filler till the pain heals? Second choice—that is what I am.

He cups her chin, tilting her face to his and tells her, "Riley, we do this every year, and every year you apologize to me. It's not your fault that your dad got in the car that night, or that my mom was a victim of his drunk driving." He's right. It's not.

She argues him on it, "It's my dad's fault and my mom's fault. Therefore, I am guilty by association. He never should have been on the road. I'm sorry we came into your lives. Because of that, you don't have your mom. It's not fair." *Why isn't it fair? Because it happened or because it changed her future with Josh?* Life isn't fair. Life is shit to be honest. Life gives you drunken dads that use fist instead of words. I hate to say it, but how come it wasn't my dad on the road that night. His drunken stupor always leads him down the wrong roads. Riley's dad was a good man who obviously had a bad night.

Josh abruptly stands, pulls her to her feet and places his hands on her shoulders. "Riley, stop blaming yourself, because I sure as hell don't. Yes, it hurts. God, it hurts some days to not have her here, but never, and *I mean never*, have I wished for even a second that you not be in my life. You mean the world to me, Riley Shaw." And there it is...the untold truth. He wants her. He always has.

They just stare at each other. She doesn't reply but she nods. They are doing that thing where they are exchanging thoughts without words. They do this, and it's another thing I hate about them both.

He grabs her hand and places a soft kiss on her palm. I want to punch him in the throat.

They begin to walk back to his truck when she stops suddenly and turns around with determination set in those blue eyes. "You mean the world to me too, Joshua Parker. I lov...I care about you so much," she admits. FUCK! FUCK! FUCK! Never, in two years, has she said, 'Dean, you mean the world to me,' or almost let the L word slip from her tongue—NEVER! I'm so pissed. I want to jump out there and lay into them both. Doesn't she know that I care? Doesn't she get it at all?

He stares at her for the longest time—he caught that almost slip, because he eventually smiles and interlaces their fingers. His world has just been shone a glimmer of hope while mine crashes and burns. "C'mon, your mom is worried sick about you. If I don't get you home soon, she is going to send out a search party." He laughs and they walk hand in hand back to his truck.

He has the window down and I can hear him ask her, "Why is Dean not here with you, Riley?"

I AM, BABY! I am.

I went to Collin's with one thing in mind, to get wasted and crash on his couch. I was a fucking mess. The girl I loved, loved someone else, she always had. I'd never had a chance in hell with her. Even after two years together, it wasn't going to be me that she let down her walls for.

I was watching Josh shoot pool with Preslee hanging on his arms and batting her lashes at him. He never even paid a lick of attention to her. I finally saw it—Preslee wanted him—and he wanted Riley. I understood her a little better then. We weren't that much different, after all. I was *her Josh* and she was *my Riley* when we fucked. Well, except for two nights ago...that was just us helping each other—as Dean and Preslee.

Josh kept looking at Preslee clearly annoyed, and she would just smile and continue to flirt—epically failing at it. It had been going on like this for at least thirty minutes. I must have been a little tipsy because I thought she looked hot. I actually looked at her and thought that fool was crazy to not see such a great piece of ass offering herself up to him on a silver platter. I most definitely thought I wanted that piece of ass to be mine tonight. Distract me. Help me escape. Make me forget—whatever...just be mine—and not his.

Her blue eyes met mine as I stare at her, not even hiding the fact that I was checking her out. She has a peculiar face as she looks back at me, but then she releases Josh's arm and stares back at me. She grabs her cup and downs whatever is in it. When she reaches me, she stares a bit longer but then she grabs my face and we kiss. Whatever was in that cup lingers on her tongue, cranberry maybe. It tastes good.

When we pull apart, I whisper in her ear my request to go upstairs, and she nods. I glance at Josh, noticing him staring at us both with a look of hatred. The feeling is mutual, Parker. He doesn't call me on it, he never does. I've often wondered why he doesn't tell Riley I'm unfaithful. He doesn't, though.

We pass Collin and Laiken on the way up, trading spots. Collin and I have this arrangement down pact. Before my dad ruined everything by 'being himself' (a dick with a fist), we were family, and families share everything. Collin and I shared *a lot* together, for a second I debate sharing Preslee again with him just so I can watch. I don't, though.

Once we're upstairs, we move quickly, removing clothes, and preparing each other for the rest. I realize I don't have a condom, and in my tipsy state, I do something stupid. "It's okay. I'm on the pill." Preslee says. I shrug and we handle business without any barriers between us. For the second time, I fuck her—Preslee. This isn't pretending anymore. This is me, breaking my rules and letting myself enjoy someone else for a change.

I head downstairs before Preslee does, and all hell is unleashed on me. Emily is screaming at me because apparently Riley showed up and knows I was here with someone. My heart races, regret filling me instantly. She doesn't know what I was doing—or whom I was doing. I can still fix it. I will fix it. I was furious to find out Josh was the one to take her home. I was curious to know if he told her since he knew. But then, I was relieved when he showed back up informing us she didn't know the details.

A lot of words are thrown back and forth between Emily and me. Who is she to judge me? She is the one who sucked my dick and let me bang her under the bleachers sophomore year and never informed her so called best friend of this. I'm grateful she hasn't, but still—who is she to judge me? It wasn't just a one-time thing either.

I don't know why I'm pissed when I see Josh standing with Preslee at lunch, but I am. I can't figure out if it's jealousy, or just anger at the fact that she seems to be getting what she wants, which is Josh, and I get nothing. She told me last night that we're done, and that she doesn't want to have casual sex with me anymore. Evidently, now that her and Josh have become a thing, she doesn't need me to distract her any longer.

For a second, I feel pity for Riley when I see her watching them together. I feel fucking livid when he crooks his finger for her to walk to them and then kisses Preslee right in front of her face. I'm a dick, but I'm not a dick in her face like that. That was shitty. When I see Riley's face pale and Josh look back and forth between them like he is indecisive—I have to walk away before I lose my shit.

I decide I'm going to try again with Riley. Josh is with Preslee, and Riley is alone on Valentine's Day. I'm on my way out to pick up a gift when I get a text from Josh.

Josh: PRESLEE IS AT HER HOUSE WEARING PINK LACE...ENJOY!

What the fuck?

Me: ISN'T THAT YOUR PRESENT TO UNWRAP?

Josh: I HAVE MY OWN PRESENT TO DELIVER, AND IT ISN'T TO HER.

He's going to Riley. It's not a question in my mind that going to her is his intention. He played Preslee. Ah hell, no. I'm going to Riley. Forgoing the gift, since I feel the need to rush over now, I leave and walk to her house.

I freeze when I see her press her lips to his, stumbling back with her hand over her mouth. "I'm sorry I shouldn't have done that," she says.

"No, you shouldn't have," I snap. I continue walking up her driveway, and feel enraged when I see that he brought her a kitten. What the hell? A white fucking kitten.

"What are you doing here?" Josh asks me, his voice full of anger. *That's right bitch, I didn't play into your game.* "I thought you had plans?" He continues. *You thought wrong.*

I step up to the stairs, staring at that damn kitten in her hands, she snuggles it closer to her protectively. I then turn cold eyes onto Josh, "Don't go there, Parker," I growl.

Riley looks at me confused. "Why are you here, Dean?" Josh's eyes are daring me to say something, declare some reason why I am here and not there. He is setting me up.

I look between them both and attempt to still salvage my plan. "You won't return my calls or my text and you ignore me at school. It's Valentine's Day, and you're my girl. I needed to see you." *You could be my girl, if he didn't exist.*

Her mouth falls open and she says, "I am not your girl anymore, Dean."

"But you should be. I think we should get back together, Riley. I love you." I've never told her before.

"You love her?" Josh shouts and then begins laughing. "You have got to be fucking kidding me, right?" He snarls at me.

"Fuck off, Parker. This isn't your business." I snap at him. I'm not kidding. It might be twisted, but it's true nonetheless.

"Hell it isn't. You don't get to shit all over her and then tell her you love her, and think everything is just gonna be peachy again." He says. I'm thinking...this is it. He is going to tell her my secrets.

"Isn't that up to her? Pretty sure she can tell me what she wants. Right, baby?" I ask her sweetly.

She says, "Right." She takes a deep breath, about to say more. *That's right, baby. Tell him to leave and we can start over.* "I want you to leave, Dean. I'm not your baby, and I don't buy for a second that you love me. I smiled for the first time in a while just now, before you came up and took the smile from me. So...please, leave me alone. I just need some space, Dean."

No!

"You smiled because of him?" I ask and she nods.

I no longer feel a willingness to try. In fact, I'm feeling a whole lot of willingness to beat the shit out of Josh and hurt her. No, I don't want to hurt her. Yes, I do. He makes her smile? "Ya know, Riley? It seems like he makes you smile a lot, don't ya think?"

"He's my best friend. So...yes," she answers with a lie. He isn't just your best friend. Is he?

I look between them and realize something. I tilt my head to the side as I think it. Surely not, I have to be wrong, but what if I'm not? "No, it's more than that. Are you fucking him?"

I don't even get her reply before Josh's fist collides with my face. I'm taking that as a 'yes.'

"Stop, stop. Oh my God! Just stop." Riley yells and tries to pull us apart, I'm sure more worried about him.

We listen. I wipe the blood from my nose and lick the metallic taste off my lips. I'm not done. Not by a long shot.

She looks me right in the eyes. We are at eye level with her standing on her porch, "I think you should leave, Dean. Now!" She growls the words at me and then reaches for Josh's hand.

Fucking bitch. At this moment, I hate her—until I remember that I love her.

"Fine by me," I shout and leave the way I came. Leaving her behind and my heart completely shattered.

Bring on Plan B.

Where it all began for Riley
Empty Promises

I loved lazy days at the beach, picking up shells, digging for sand crabs, making my best friend Shannon a Mermaid while I buried her and built a tail around her legs. I loved the waves rippling at my feet, the warm sunshine on my cheeks—the way the waves ebbed and flowed almost knocking me over and how my feet would sink into the sand squishing between my toes. What I didn't love was the salt that burned my eyes. What I didn't love was that my daddy was not here to play with me. What I didn't love was seeing all the other families laughing *together* while mine stays *always* apart.

No true happiness boiled up inside me. I also didn't love that my mommy didn't play with me either. She just laid in a lounge chair sunbathing, sipping on a drink from one of the beach huts that she said was 'mommy's juice,' and wouldn't share with me, even though she refilled it multiple times. She talked more and more loudly with Shannon's mom as each cup of her juice disappeared. She always told me not to bother her, and I tried to be a good girl and listen.

Ms. Linda came to the beach with us, and she was a lot of fun. I liked her. Actually, she came with us everywhere because she stayed in our house most of the time. At night, she would read me stories and sometimes even let me watch the TV a few minutes past my bedtime while mommy and daddy went to work. She was pretty too.

She had long, dark blonde hair and pretty, blue eyes. I really liked when she let me play with her hair, or how when I colored pictures for her, she wouldn't tell me to not bother her. Instead, she would smile and tell me that my drawing was lovely. Sometimes, when my mommy didn't want to brush my hair, Ms. Linda would brush my hair for me, and she would braid it too if I asked. She made me pretty, like her.

Today, Ms. Linda put my hair in pigtails, and she painted my toenails pink, like hers. She was really nice, and I was so happy that she was my babysitter, because she was the bestest ever.

I was going to kindergarten soon, and I loved writing my name. Sometimes, even on the wall of my room with a crayon, but that got me in trouble, so I only did it like maybe twice before I stopped. I didn't like getting in trouble.

Shannon and I were playing in the sand. She made a smiley face, and I wrote my name in the sand with my finger. I wanted to show my mommy and was patting her on the shoulder. Mommy was talking and laughing with Shannon's mommy, not paying any attention to me. "Mommy, look I write my name in the sand. Look, see, look, I did it nice and neat." I pointed in vain to the sand near us.

My mom sighed, placed a finger in the air to Shannon's mommy halting their conversation, and then looked in my direction irritated. "Not now, Riley. Mommy is talking with Mrs. Grace about grown up stuff. It's rude to interrupt. Go show Ms. Linda and Shannon. Okay? I'm sure it's beautiful, but mommy is busy right now. Now, run along," she flipped her wrist and went back to her conversation laughing.

I came back to Shannon and Ms. Linda with tears brimming in my eyes and a pout on my face. Before I said anything, I stomped my feet in the sand, erasing my name and then plopped down on my bottom pulling my knees to my chest. I didn't cry, but I wanted too. "You ok, Riwey?" Shannon asked me. She never said my name right. It's Riley. Not, Riwey. I nodded, still pouting. I was used to mommy and daddy always being too busy, but I still wanted their attention.

Ms. Linda picked me up and placed me in her lap. "Why did you do that, Riley? Your name was very pretty." She spoke consolingly and rubbed my back. I shrugged and curled into Ms. Linda's chest. "Mommy doesn't like me." I said feeling blue.

"Oh, that's not true. Your mommy loves you. She just—," Ms. Linda was going to explain but mommy interrupted her.

"Liiinnnda….My mom voice sounded like a song. Do you have plans this weekend?"

"Not really. Do you need me to watch Riley?" she asked sweetly, while continuing to rub gentle circles along my back. My mommy didn't even notice I was upset. She never did.

Mrs. Grace picked up Shannon, and swung her in a circle making her giggle. It made me jealous of Shannon. "I am treating Claudia to a

New Orleans getaway this weekend for her twenty first birthday, since she didn't really get to celebrate it last week. You know? I can't believe you're only twenty-one. You are like a baby fish." Shannon's mom said laughing teasingly at my mommy. Mommy gave me a strange look I didn't understand.

"I asked Evan if he wanted to make a weekend of it together, but he couldn't this weekend…not a good time for him or whatever. He suggested leaving Riley with my mom but she can't keep her this weekend. So, I need you if you can." She frowned at Ms. Linda. "It's just gonna be a girls' weekend away instead."

My mommy chirped with a smile that didn't reach her eyes, like she isn't really happy about something. "I'd invite you to come along with us Linda…but well, you know." She explained. What did Ms. Linda know? She just nodded.

"Sounds fun. I'd love to stay over this weekend with Riley. We will have a girl's time ourselves too, right, Tinker Bell?" I nodded. "It's not a problem." She told my mom.

She laughed and as much as I loved her—I was sad. Ms. Linda normally had every other weekend off, and it wasn't my weekend to go to my Nana's or to have Ms. Linda. It was my weekend to have my mommy and daddy with me. We were supposed to go to the movies and get pizza, and daddy promised me an ice cream cone after. What is New Orleans anyway, and why is her birthday so important? It's over. My birthday is next month, and no one has mentioned it.

Someone tapped my shoulder and I jumped, startled. Daddy was downstairs playing cards with some friends of his, and I was watching from the stairs dressed in my favorite princess costume, Tinker Bell. I was lying on my belly holding on to the rails with my fingers and just watching. I wanted daddy to play a game with me that night, but he didn't.

Mommy said he wouldn't be home but he was, so why wasn't he playing with me?

"Riley, there you are. Let's get you back upstairs, Tinker Bell" Ms. Linda said whispering. She grabbed my hand to pull me back up to my room.

She handed me my pajamas and walked me to the bathroom. I was being directed to brush my teeth and change, and it isn't long before Ms. Linda was tucking me into bed and switching off my lights. "Ms. Linda, can I ask you something?" I stop her before she leaves my room.

She turned to me, seeming a little exasperated with me tonight, although I don't know why. I haven't misbehaved, really. She seemed upset, though. It confused me. "Sure, Riley. What is it?" she asked with a clipped tone.

I sat up a little in my bed, "Does it make you sad that you don't get to play with the grown-ups?" Ms. Linda was pretty and she was 'a big people.' I bet she got bored hanging out with me all the time.

She looked at me a beat before she spoke. She almost seemed nervous to answer me. "No, Riley. It doesn't make me sad. I enjoy my job watching after you. Besides, our pretend tea parties with Ken and Barbie work just fine for me." She said making me giggle. "Why do you ask such a thing?" she asked me.

I shrugged because I wasn't sure, I was just curious. "When I get big and I am a mommy, I don't want to play with the grown-ups." I confessed.

Ms. Linda came to sit with me, flipping on my lamp, which made my pink room glow pretty. "What do you mean, Riley?" she had her sweet voice again.

I may have only been four years old, but I knew the things that bothered me, and the things that made me happy. "Well, I think grown-ups need to play with little kids, that's all." I said as I yawned.

Ms. Linda nodded and sighed, "I see. Not all families are picture perfect, Riley. You have good parents. They may be a little preoccupied with grown-up stuff but they love you. Adults need time to be adults sometimes without little ones around, and if your dad didn't work as hard as he does, you wouldn't live in this beautiful place, or have me to watch you when your parents need me. But…your future family sounds like a delight too." She ruffled my hair, "Now get some sleep."

She flipped off my lamp and left me to dream. I don't know what she said, other than adults needed to be with adults and my house was pretty.

I don't know what it was that woke me up. I had a bad dream but I couldn't remember what it was and then I needed to potty. I went to the bathroom, and I decided that I wanted to go find my daddy and maybe have him tuck me back into bed.

I tip-toed to the hall and looked down the stairs, but it was dark. So, I went to his room. I opened the door and walked to his side of the bed, but it was empty. "Daddy?" I whispered. He didn't answer. My tummy felt funny, and I didn't want to go to my room by myself.

Ms. Linda was staying over tonight, and her room was down the hall from mine. I felt like I was going to cry, and I didn't know why really. I just wanted someone to hold me and help me go back to sleep. The light was on in Ms. Linda's room. I could tell from the light underneath the door. I knew she was awake because I could hear her talking, but then it got quiet. I didn't want to get in trouble, but Ms. Linda hardly ever fussed at me, so I thought it would be okay to see her. So I slowly opened the door but what I saw confused me.

"Daddy?" I said in a soft voice and he jumped away from Ms. Linda, who was sitting on her bed with her legs wrapped around his waist.

She said, "Oh my God," and tried quickly to button up her shirt where my daddy's hands were just on her. Ms. Linda covered her mouth and made a funny noise. My daddy didn't have his shirt on at all, and his pants were unzipped. I thought Ms. Linda painted his mouth and neck with makeup, but then I thought that was strange because boys didn't wear makeup, and Ms. Linda usually played dress up with me.

I started to cry, and my daddy put his shirt back on, fixed his pants and bent down in front of me. He was shaking. I think he had a bad dream, as well. I guess he needed Ms. Linda to hold him, too.

I didn't understand why daddy had his mouth on hers, though. I tried to kiss Kevin at Shannon's house once, and Mommy fussed at me. She told me 'only mommy and daddy's kiss each other, and of course, Daddy kisses your cheek because he loves you But, Riley, sweetie, you don't kiss your friends. You only hug them or hold their hand ok?' So, I didn't know why Daddy would kiss Ms. Linda, because they were friends, unless he loved her too.

Daddy looked at Ms. Linda, and she shook her head at him. Then daddy picked me up to carry me back to my room. "I'm sorry, Daddy. I had a bad dream, and I couldn't find you." I said.

He squeezed me extra tight and kissed my forehead. I loved kisses on my forehead. "It's okay, Tinker Bell. But this is our secret, okay?" What was our secret?

One time, I whispered something in Shannon's ear, and Mommy told me telling secrets wasn't nice, and I shouldn't do that. "Ok, Daddy. What's the secret?" I asked feeling confused.

He placed me down in my bed, and covered me up with my Tinker Bell blankets. He kissed my nose and said, "It's nothing, Tinker Bell. Just get some sleep and stay in here. Okay?"

I stayed in my bed but I had a hard time going to sleep. Daddy and Ms. Linda weren't being good friends. They were fighting, and Daddy made Ms. Linda cry. I didn't want to get in any more trouble, so I stayed put in my bed. I decided to draw Ms. Linda a pretty picture on my doodle to show her in the morning. That would make her smile. Daddy needed a time out.

I didn't see Ms. Linda the next day or the next or the next…

It was two weeks without Ms. Linda, in fact. When my mommy came home from whatever New Orleans was, daddy told her something that made her mad, and she took me to my Nana's house.

When we went back home, daddy was all smiles. He hugged me so tight, and he even gave my mommy flowers. She kissed his cheek and it was then that I heard the noise from upstairs.

Ms. Linda was packing up her room and sniffling when I made my way up there. I ran to my room to get my doodle and brought it to Ms. Linda's room. I grabbed her leg, and she made a sound in her throat.

"I drew you a picture, Ms. Linda. So you will be happy." I smiled at her. She looked at my doodle, and she looked even sadder after that, which made me sad. Maybe I didn't draw it pretty enough, I thought.

"Oh, Riley." She said and picked me up to hold me tightly. "It's beautiful," she told me as she wiped under her eyes.

"Then why you cry?" I asked in a small voice. I don't like Ms. Linda sad.

"Because, sweetie. I'm just a little sad right now, but it has nothing to do with you. Okay? Your picture is beautiful, and you are the greatest little Tink, ever." Her voice was shaky and cracked with each word. She began to cry even more, and I didn't know what to do. So, I just kissed her on her cheek, because Mommy said it's okay to do that if you love someone. I loved Ms. Linda. She put me down, and I watched her put more stuff into boxes. "Are you leaving, Ms. Linda?" I asked.

She nodded and wiped under her eyes. "I have a new job, Riley. I'm moving. So, I won't be your babysitter anymore, but I bet you get a new one that is super awesome." She was moving? A new baby sitter?

I ran to my room to grab my Tinker Bell Barbie doll and brought it back to her room. I placed it in one of her boxes. She looked at it and back to me, not understanding. "It's so you have another Tinker Bell with you, so you don't forget me." I said.

She smiled and hugged me sooooo tight. "I will never forget you, Tinker Bell."

I went back downstairs to Mommy and Daddy, and they were in the kitchen talking in a serious tone. "Evan, it's not just that. My mom wouldn't even watch Riley for me to go to college. Why would she care to watch her so I can go wait tables at Hooters? Having Linda was perfect. She has been there for me through everything. I can't believe she would just walk away without any explanation." My mom had her hand on her hips and was pacing back and forth around the island.

My daddy took a sip of coffee and leaned back against the counter with his ankles crossed over the other. "It's going to be fine. I wanted to talk to you about something anyway… something big. I think we should move to Grandbury. They have a nice little subdivision near the lake called Willowbend. It's beautiful. I found the perfect house and they have great schools for Riley, and you can do whatever your heart desires. We won't need anyone to sit for her anymore once she is in kindergarten. I can get a job in the city or start my own business, and we can live in a small town. It will be great." He said smiling.

"As in us moving? My mom is here," she asked him

He nodded, "It could be good for us. Starting over. Just you and me and our little Tinker Bell, it was always supposed to be that way. It's only a few hours away. " He put his cup down and walked over to give my mom a hug and a kiss.

"Okay?" he asked whispering.

"Okay." she replied.

The next month, Mommy didn't go to work anymore. She stayed home with me all day and all night. At night, she wasn't happy with me, though. She made me stay in my room. During the day, she used to take me places, but now she takes naps, and I watch cartoons. Mommy would get sick a lot. Her tummy was upset, and she would throw up in the potty. Daddy said it would go away in a few months. Mommy said Daddy was to never touch her again. I don't know what either of them was talking about.

Today, Mommy and Daddy took me to the park. I was so excited because it was Wednesday, and Mommy and Daddy never take me places together during the week. Daddy pushed me on the swings, and Mommy was busy watching another mommy push a baby in the bucket swing next to me. Mommy frowned and Daddy sighed.

After the park, they took me to Target to pick out a new baby doll. We took my new baby doll to the boardwalk and rode on the merry-go-round, and I even got Cotton Candy. All of that attention was new, and I was happy. I liked it.

"Does daddy's 'Lil' Tinker Bell like her new baby doll?" he asked me later back at the home as I sat in mommy's lap.

I nodded, "Yes. She has a pretty green dress on. I like green."

Mommy sniffled, "Would our 'Lil' Tinker Bell be happy to have a real baby, not just a doll?" she asked me.

I shrugged and put my baby dolls bottle to her mouth. "Shannon says babies are stinky and they cry a lot." I told them.

Mommy sniffled again and daddy sighed again. "Well, yes. Babies do stink sometimes with dirty diapers, and they do cry a lot, actually. But you were a baby once, Riley, and look at how awesome you are now," Daddy said.

"Do you want a baby, Daddy?" I asked him. He smiled nodding yes.

Mommy grabbed my hand and put it on her tummy. "We are having a baby, Riley. It's right here sleeping." She said softly frowning at daddy. She didn't look happy with Daddy right now.

"Oh, wow!" It was all I said, before I took my baby doll with me to play on the carpet.

I was sitting on the grass pulling pieces of it out. I had my new baby doll with me, and I was dressed in my favorite Tinker Bell costume like always. Daddy was unloading the truck with boxes into our new house. Mommy was talking to our new next-door neighbor.

Her name was Mrs. Jessica, and she was having a baby, too. Mommy had a new friend. I was sad because the ice cream truck was at the curb down the road, and Mommy wouldn't take me to get an ice cream.

I wanted some ice cream, "It's no fair, Mommy. I want some ice cream," I whined.

"Not now, Riley." She said exasperated with me.

"I can share mine," a little boy said coming up to stand next to Mrs. Jessica. He had an ice cream sandwich in his hand that was melting all over the grass as he walked. He tore it in half and was about to hand me the piece, when he stepped on his untied shoelace, tripped and fell, dropping both pieces of ice cream in the grass.

"Uh-oh" he said, his voice like a singsong.

I stood up worried that he hurt himself and walked over to him. His Mommy wasn't paying attention either so she didn't see him fall. "Are you okay?" I asked him.

He nodded and stood up. He looked down at the ice cream in the grass and on his shirt. "Sorry, I gonna be right back," he told me, and ran into his house. I shrugged and went back to my baby doll and pulling up grass, pouting. No ice cream for me.

"Wow, Claudia. We will be having our babies at the same time. My son Joshua is so excited to have a baby brother or sister. Is your daughter excited?" Mrs. Jessica said with a huge smile. She was pretty.

Mommy looked down at me and back to Mrs. Jessica. "Not yet. She might get more excited once the baby is here, just not right now." She admitted.

It's true, I am not happy about a new baby. Mommy and Daddy already don't spend a lot of time with me. If a new baby comes, I will have to share, and I don't want to share. No babies.

"Here," the little boy said, giving me a chocolate pudding cup and a spoon as he sat down next to me.

"Thank you," I said, taking it from him.

My dad came back outside and walked over to us, in the middle of the two yards. "Well isn't that cute. Now, Jessica I am going to have to keep an eye on that little boy of yours, aren't I?" he laughed jokingly. They all laughed actually. 'That little boy' and me just ate our pudding, oblivious to the world.

"I'm Riley, I'm four," I told him.

He smiled at me. "I'm Josh, I'm five now" he said.

I frowned. I want to be five now.

"Daddy, when will I be five like Josh?" I asked him.

Daddy bent down and tapped his index finger on my nose. "Next week, Tinker Bell. Maybe your new friend here can come over for cake and ice cream. We'd love to have your whole family actually, Jessica." He told Josh's mommy.

"Can I go? Mommy, please?" Josh asked his mommy.

"Sure, sweetie. I will let y'all get back to unpacking. If you want, Riley can come over and play with Joshua for a little bit, so she isn't in your way. Would that be alright?" she asked my parents.

"Can I go Mommy, Daddy, please?" I begged then.

They both agreed, and Josh held my hand the whole way to his house, which is next door to my new house now.

On my birthday, my new friend Josh and his parents came over to eat cake and ice cream with us. I like Josh. He's fun to play with. He doesn't make fun of me for wearing my Tinker Bell costume all the time like Shannon used to do. He would say I'm cute and he called me Tink. It's a little strange being best friends with a boy now. He doesn't play dress up with me, and he wants me to play boy stuff with him, but I like him. So, I do what he wants. Plus, he has this little guitar, and he strums it for me, and I like to sing, so I make up songs for him. We call it our music. Josh is the best.

"Mommy let me pick out your present, Tink," he told me smiling.

His mommy laughed and ruffled his hair. "Yes, I did. But I also picked out a present for you that I think you will like." She said sweetly. Josh's mommy was nice.

I opened both. Josh bought me a lime green hot wheel car. "It's the color of that dress you like, the one you wear all the time." He said. I smile. I don't want a hot wheel car, but Josh got it for me, so I will keep it forever and always. Mrs. Jessica bought me a Barbie doll dressed in a Tinker Bell costume like me. It made me smile real big.

I had a Barbie doll like this one in my old house, but I gave it to Ms. Linda when she moved out, when I told her she could have another Tinker Bell to watch. She told me she was crying happy tears. I hadn't thought about Ms. Linda that much lately. I missed her, though.

"Look, daddy. It's like my Barbie I gave Ms. Linda." I told my daddy, his face fell. "Wow, Tinker Bell. That's so great."

"Who is Ms. Linda?" Josh asked me.

I smiled big. "She's daddy's friend, but she didn't want to stay with us anymore. Daddy made her cry." I said, and Mommy dropped her glass on the floor spilling punch everywhere.

"Oh dear, I made a mess. Evan grab the paper towels. NOW!" Mommy snapped at Daddy.

"Why did he make her cry?" Josh asked me.

I was going to tell him but his mommy scooped him up nervously. "Joshua, it's time to go home now. Right, honey?" she said, giving Josh's daddy a certain look.

"Right, right. Thank you so much for having us over guys. We'll see you later." He said and they left in a hurry. I wondered why?

After Mommy cleaned up the punch, she came to sit by me at the table.

"Honey, she is only four. Why are you getting so upset?" he asked with a crack in his voice.

"I'm not four, Daddy. I am five now." I said holding up five fingers.

"Yes, you are sweetie." My mommy said, "Now, tell me...how did Daddy make Ms. Linda cry?" she asked and my daddy said..."Shit!"

"Daddy that's a bad word." I corrected.

"You are right, sorry." He apologized.

"Riley, did something happen with Daddy and Ms. Linda that mommy needs to know about? You're not in trouble, okay?" she picked me up in her lap.

Daddy was facing the counter, his hands grabbed the edge, and his head was down. "I don't know. I think it's my fault." I said.

Mommy and Daddy both said, "What?"

"Well, I had a bad dream, and Daddy and Ms. Linda were playing dress up. But Ms. Linda didn't do it right, it was messy."

Daddy looked confused and Mommy asked, "Do what right?"

"The lipstick. It goes on your mouth like this," I moved my finger along my lips. "Daddy had it everywhere, and that's messy, but he's a boy, and boys don't wear makeup. Right, Mommy?" I said.

Mommy gave my daddy and angry face, but looked back at me smiling. "Did Daddy do anything else *not right*, Riley?"

I nodded, "Yes. You said friends don't kiss each other. Only mommies and daddies can kiss each other."

My mom cleared her throat and my dad made a loud banging sound on the counter that made me jump. "But it's a secret Mommy. You can't tell, cuz telling secrets isn't nice. You told me that. I don't want to be in trouble." I said.

"Oh.my.God!" My mommy said in a low voice that scared me a little. She stood with me on her hip and looked directly at my daddy. His face was grim.

"Riley, you are not in trouble, but Mommy is going to put you to bed a little early tonight. Okay? I promise, if you stay there like a good girl, I will take you somewhere special tomorrow. Now tell Daddy, goodnight." She said and put me down.

I ran over to my daddy and he looked down at me with sad eyes. He picked me up and squeezed me tight.

"I love you, Daddy." I said after I kissed his cheek.

"I love you, Riley" he kissed my forehead and put me down.

He didn't call me his little, Tinker Bell.

Why didn't he call me his little, Tinker Bell?

The next day Mommy and Daddy didn't talk to each other much. Mommy kept rubbing her belly and crying, and Daddy left the house with a suitcase. He told me he loved me and that he had to go on a trip for work, but he would bring me back something shiny and pretty.

Daddy's trip for work was a long one. It had been twelve days to be exact. My Nana came to stay with us. She said some 'not nice' things about my daddy, and she bugged me. Today, she kept trying to get me to put on this big poufy yellow dress with flowers on it, and I didn't want too. I liked my Tinker Bell dress.

"Riley, bless your princess heart. You are not going to be able to wear that costume of yours to school, dear. Why don't you go try on the dress Nana bought you from Dillard's? She asked for like the third time that day.

I twirled in a circle in the living room, "No, thank you, Nana. Maybe, tomorrow."

She blew out a puff of air from her mouth, stood from the couch and placed her manicured hands on her hips. "Claudia, you are going to have to break her from that dress eventually. She can't wear that to school. You know that."

My mommy sighed, "Yes, Mother I know. But right now, things are bad enough, and I don't need to do it at this very moment. Just let it go...for now, please." She snapped.

"Riley, Mrs. Jessica invited you to go to the park with her and Joshua. Would you like to do that?" she asked me.

"Yes. Yay!" I jumped up and down clapping.

"Okay. Well, let's not wear your costume to the park. It will get dirty. Can you put on your romper, please?" My mommy gave Nana a knowing look.

"Or your pretty yellow dress?" Nana asked.

"Oh my God. Mother, drop it. She doesn't want to wear the damn yellow dress. Leave.her.alone." she yelled, and my Nana's mouth opened wide like a circle.

"Go change, Riley." Mommy told me.

I nodded. "Yes, ma'am." And I ran to my room to change into my romper, not the giant yellow dress. I liked fairies, not Big Bird.

At the park, Josh held my hand as we played and ran around. Shannon used to tell me, 'boys are yucky, and they have germs'. I didn't think so. Josh wasn't yucky, and he was my bestest friend. If he had germs, then I liked them.

The park was by the lake. They have a swing by this big tree. It was my favorite spot. I'd claimed it as mine. There was also a pier to the lack that you could walk out to. That was Josh's favorite. He liked to scare the ducks and I liked to feed them bread.

"Hey, Tink. You want to race?" he asked me.

I nodded and he smiled at him. "Okay, on your mark, get set, go…" I said, and we run as fast as we could.

I was laughing until I tripped on my flip-flop and fell down, scraping my knee. "Owee, Josh it hurts." I cried.

"Oh no, let me see." Mrs. Jessica said sweetly, checking my scraped knee.

It was stinging, and it had a small trickle of red that made me cry worse when I saw it.

"I'm sorry, Tink. Mommy, let me take care of her. She is my best friend." Josh said kneeling down by me.

"Ok son, I'm gonna go in the bathroom right there and wet a paper towel to clean your knee. Ok?" She ruffled his hair and stepped away from us briefly.

"It hurts, Josh." I sniffled.

He leaned down and kissed my boo-boo softly. "There. I kissed it better. Does it hurt still?" he wiped my tears away with the bottom of his shirt.

I shook my head. Kisses always made things better. "Not anymore. Thank you, Josh. You're my bestest friend. I love you." I kissed his cheek.

He grinned with a dimple and kissed my forehead. "I love you too, Tink." I loved kisses on the forehead.

Kindergarten was so much fun. Josh was in my class, which our mommy's said was probably not the best idea. I got lucky, though. I think it's great. Mrs. Mathis was our teacher. She was really nice, and we had a pet fish in our class. I don't know if she was a boy or a girl. She was a beta fish with pretty colors, and every day the line leader was allowed to feed her. Her name was Guppy. Or his name? I didn't know.

My mommy and Josh's mommy walked us to and from school every day. Josh always held my hand. My mommy said he's my little boyfriend. Mrs. Jessica said that was fine by her, because I'm sweet. He was my boyfriend. Whatever, that means.

Today at recess, this mean boy named Dean pulled my hair and pushed me down. "Ouch. That's, mean Dean. I don't like you." I yelled.

He laughed, "Well, you're mean, and I don't like you either."

I stuck my tongue out at him.

"She is not mean, and you don't do that ever again." Josh said pushing Dean.

"Okay, okay. Now break it up." Mrs. Mathis said standing next to us.

"Now, Dean. Why did you just do that to Riley? That wasn't very nice." She scolded him.

He pouted, "cuz, she doesn't like me. She only likes Joshua." He folded his hands across his chest.

Mrs. Mathis nodded her head at his response, grinned and looked toward me. "Riley, sometimes boys don't know how to talk about how they feel. So you see, when boys like you they sometimes pick on you, or do mean things." She looked at Dean disapprovingly when she said, 'mean' and he frowned.

"Well, do you like Riley, Dean?" she asked him.

He nodded and then shook his head back and forth. "Not really, she smells like strawberries."

"I do not!" I shouted.

"Do to!" he shouted.

"Enough!" Mrs. Mathis frowned. Josh grabbed my hand, interlacing our fingers as always. He was giving Dean some pretty mean looks.

"I like strawberries." Dean said in a little voice.

"I am not a strawberry." I frowned at him.

"So what? You smell like one. Joshua says so, too. Hmpf." He crossed his arms and turned around.

"Josh, did you say that about me?" I whine looking at my best friend.

"Well, yes. But I like it. You smell good, Tink. It's like a strawberry." He smiled. If Josh liked it, then I liked it.

"See, Riley Shaw. You smell like a strawberry, and you look like one too." Dean was so mean. I didn't like him, not one bit.

"Now, Dean. Stop picking on Riley," she told him.

Then she turned to me, "Riley, I think that maybe Dean wants to be your friend. Maybe you three can go play on the slide together. What do you think?" Mrs. Mathis was so nice, but why would I want to play with Dean?

I looked at Josh and he shrugged. "It's okay with me." He encouraged me to make a new friend.

I huffed, because Josh was the only friend I wanted, but whatever. "Fine, let's go play."

Dean smiled really big. "Thanks, Riley. You're the best."

When we walked away, Josh whispered in my ear, "I don't like Dean, Tink."

I smiled at him and lifted my shoulder, "Me neither." I mouthed and went to play with him anyway.

By the end of the week though, I had two boyfriends—Dean and Josh. I'd rather just one. Josh.

Twenty days later, my Nana went back home, and I never, ever, ever put on that big yellow dress. Daddy came home too, but he never did give me my something shiny and pretty.

My baby sister was born. She was pretty icky when I first saw her. But, she was just pretty now. Josh had a baby sister too the next month. They named her, Joey. It was short for a long name I couldn't say right.

Now that Daddy was back, things were back to normal. Except, Mommy and Daddy don't say nice things to each other anymore, and just like I thought, the baby steals all their attention. Thankfully, I had Josh to play with, because he said the same thing happened in his house.

Daddy didn't call me 'his Tinker Bell' anymore, now he called Tatum his 'Tater Tot.' *I was just, Riley.*

I didn't know why, but I thought Daddy was mad at me.

"Oh my God, Riley. Why did you do that?" Mommy asked me, after I cut up my Tinker Bell costume with scissors.

"I hate Tinker Bell. She's stupid." I pouted.

"Since when do you hate Tinker Bell?" Daddy asked, walking into the playroom holding his 'Tator Tot.'

She is stupid, too.

I shrugged, "I don't know. You hate her too." I said, stomped my feet as I stormed around them going to my room.

Daddy came to meet me in my bedroom without the baby. *Stupid baby.*

"I don't hate Tinker Bell, Riley. Why do you say that?" he asked softly.

"Because, you don't call me your little Tinker Bell anymore, and you left me for a long time?" I began to cry.

My daddy pulled me into a giant hug, hushing my whimpers. "You will *always* be my little Tinker Bell, Riley. I'm sorry I hurt your feelings. Daddy didn't mean to ever do any of this." He kissed my forehead.

He reached into his pocket and pulled out a tiny silver charm bracelet, and on it was a Tinker Bell dangly charm, a heart engraved with 'Daddy's little princess.' It was my something shiny.

I cried and hugged him so tight. I will always be his little girl, his little princess, his Tinker Bell.

Always.

Embrace the Moment

Torn apart by a tragedy, pushed together by fate. Nothing is coincidence.

Riley and Josh have been through it all together, first as best friends and now as a couple.

Faced with a decision that will test their relationship, these two learn to fight harder than ever before to keep their hearts intact. Once the decision is made, there is no going back. With the past creeping into their present, and miles between them, they learn nothing is easy. Every moment matters.

Can Riley and Josh survive the first year of college apart? Will their love remain strong enough to embrace every moment that belongs to them? Or will someone from the past interfere, take what he wants and ruin them forever?

"For each star in the sky, I have a reason why I love you. When you look up at night, never forget this truth." –Josh Parker

Recommended for 17+ due to underage drinking, sexual content and adult language.

www.ingramcontent.com/pod-product-compliance
Lightning Source LLC
Chambersburg PA
CBHW051427170626
46809CB00006B/2357